THE ROSE AND THE WAND

A Magic Collectors Novel

E.J. KITCHENS

To my family, with love

There is the great lesson of "Beauty and the Beast"; that a thing must be loved before it is lovable.

—G.K. Chesterton, *Orthodoxy*

AUTHOR'S NOTES

Undoubtedly, the most familiar version of the classic French tale *La Belle et la Bête* is Walt Disney's animated classic *Beauty and the Beast*. It was my introduction to the story, and out of its prologue was born the idea for this book. Who was the enchantress who cast the spell on the prince? Was she some do-gooder wandering around, looking for someone to enchant? What if she were under a curse herself? She's barely mentioned, yet without her there would be no story.

While *The Rose and the Wand* is the enchantress's story, it necessarily includes Beast and Beauty's story. I thoroughly enjoyed reading and watching different versions of their tale as inspiration for my own. I was particularly intrigued by Jeanne-Marie LePrince de Beaumont's *La Belle et la Bête*, which is probably the most well known of the early French versions. It was originally published in Beaumont's *The Young Misses Magazine, Containing Dialogues Between a Governess and Several Young Ladies of Quality, Her Scholars*, and was designed to teach that virtue is more important than superficial attributes. (This is also one of the lessons of Jane Austen's *Pride and Prejudice,* one of my favorite stories.) For those unfamiliar with Beaumont's *La Belle et la Bête,* I have included a brief summary at the end of this introduction.

But back to the enchantress. Her identity was not the only question to have plagued me concerning *Beauty and the Beast.* What would be the consequences of a prince suddenly disappearing from society? Did he have family or connections who would notice his sudden seclusion? How did the villagers not know there was a castle nearby, especially if their prince lived there? Or was he their prince? How did he support himself during this time?

Different versions of the story have different answers, and to follow suit, I have my own. I hope you enjoy them, as well as my imagining of the enchantress who turned the proud prince into the hideous beast we, like Beauty, came to love.

❦

A brief summary of Jeanne-Marie LePrince de Beaumont's *La Belle et la Bête* (1756)

Beauty is the youngest and most beautiful daughter of a wealthy merchant. While her siblings are arrogant and selfish, Beauty is kind and loving. When her father loses his fortune, the family is forced to move to a small house in the country. There, Beauty willingly takes on the task of caring for her family, doing the duties their servants had done previously, while her sisters look on in scorn. Only her father loves and values her.

On his return from a business trip, her father gets lost in a snowstorm and takes shelter in a seemingly abandoned castle. Invisible servants take care of his needs and send him on his way the next morning. Passing through a garden on his way out, he picks a bouquet of roses for Beauty—no roses grow near their home. A beast suddenly appears and demands his life in payment for stealing the roses, which are the thing the beast values most in the universe. When the merchant begs forgiveness, citing a desire to please his daughter as the reason for taking the roses, Beast says he will forgive him if he brings one of his daughters to live at the castle. Otherwise, he must return in three months' time.

The merchant hurries home, planning to say goodbye to his family, but upon telling his tale, Beauty insists on going to the castle. Brokenhearted but unable to prevent her, the merchant takes Beauty to the castle.

Beast treats Beauty very well, and each night he asks her to marry him. Beauty soon grows accustomed to Beast's appearance and comes to see great kindness in him and to enjoy his simple, but honest, conversation. He gives her a mirror that allows her to see her father.

After three months, he allows Beauty to visit her heartsick father on the promise that she return in a week. She need only lay her ring on a table before going to bed to travel to her father or to return to Beast.

Her father is overjoyed at her return, but her two unhappily married sisters—one married to a handsome but selfish, vain man and the other to a witty man who uses his gifts to demean others, including his wife—conspire to make her overstay her week's visit. Envious of the gowns and gifts Beast has given Beauty and resentful of the contrast she provides to their selfishness, they hope Beast will eat Beauty for not returning at the designated time. Beauty at last realizes her sisters' wickedness and the depth of her affection for Beast and returns to the castle.

Beast is dying from a broken heart because he thinks Beauty will not return. She begs him not to die and declares her love for him, vowing to marry him. He transforms into a handsome prince, and then a beautiful woman appears and commends Beauty for her choice and turns Beauty's sisters into statues.

"Beauty," said this lady, "come and receive the reward of your judicious choice; you have preferred virtue before either wit or beauty, and deserve to find a person in whom all these qualifications are united." (Jeanne-Marie LePrince de Beaumont's *La Belle et la Bête*, 1756)

CHAPTER 1

BEAUTIFUL, FLAWLESS, GRACEFUL, poised, exquisite. These were the epithets bestowed on our family. People said it was as if the most skilled sculptor in the world carved us out of purest marble, draped the night sky upon our heads for hair, stole the changing colors of the sea for our eyes, and crushed the silky rose petals to tint our lips.

A few of the servants believed this was true, especially with regard to us being carved of marble. Doubtless, the idea addressed more than our perfectly formed figures and unblemished skin.

Beautiful were our persons and beautiful were our tastes. We cared for nothing that was not lovely and approaching perfection, be it person, painting, animal, or dress. It was our greatest fault, though we knew it not.

We soon learned.

An enchantress's wand was light, though sturdy, yet holding it out for an extended length of time proved unpleasant for the arms.

"How is the sketch coming, Gabriella?"

My sister glanced from her sketchbook to the brightly colored bird suspended over the forest path between us, held in place for as long as my wand-arm held steady.

My horse shifted under me, shying to the right, away from the other forest creature I held in place. Caught charging between two fir trees, the snarling wolf eyed the horses hungrily even in its frozen state. Alas, my training had not taught me how to cast a lasting spell of this sort.

The wrinkles of concentration disappeared from Gabriella's face and were replaced by the glow of enthusiasm. "Wonderfully. This species has such rich colors and is so rarely seen in this part of Sonser, especially in the winter. Papa will be delighted to have it included in his book."

Her enjoyment, and the prospect of my father's upon receiving the hand-illustrated book of birds as his birthday gift, eased the burning in my arms. But not much.

"I meant, how much longer?"

My sister glanced between the bird, the wolf, and my outstretched arms, a mischievous smile curving her lips. "You could try singing to them. You do have a lovely voice, Alexandria. You could charm them into friendship with you."

I squeezed my eyes shut as my arms sent a fresh reminder of their discomfort. "I am not a princess in distress, or one in need of help cleaning. Although, I must admit I would gladly burst into song if the forest creatures would support my arms as readily as they do a princess's broom."

Gabriella chuckled, her pencil moving in quick, short strokes. "I'm almost done."

As she worked, I studied the wolf. It was taller than I expected. With its mix of black and light gray fur and its sleek build, it must be quite a stunning sight racing through the forest in the dark of night with moonlight shining on its coat.

But its bared, bright red gums and sharp teeth painted a different picture of it. The unique yellowish-green of its eyes slipped from exotic to eerie, and I shivered.

If only I could leave it there for our gamekeeper to take care of, but the wolfhounds would have to find it again.

Although wolves were typically more of a danger to livestock than humans, Papa's guests would have to be warned, though few ventured off the well-worn path to the river. My father, like his father before him, was a widely respected statesman and much sought-after lecturer. It was customary for many of the notables of Sonser and the neighboring kingdoms to spend a few weeks with us for his birthday celebration. Our house was always full of guests during this time, and this year was no exception. My sisters, Eva and Gabriella, and I mingled occasionally with the visitors, but my father usually kept them well occupied. I didn't mind. I preferred it that way. I had more than once sought the solitude and beauty of the fields and woods of our estate during their stay.

A single strand of hair loosened in the breeze and tickled my nose. I bent my head back to shake it away. "It's a pity the sun is not out. Your bird's coloration would surely be brilliant in the sunlight."

"Yes, I know, but I'll make do. It will only be another minute or two. I appreciate your patience, Alexandria."

"I can last a few more minutes." With a diversion. I studied the horizon.

Thick, low clouds trailed across the sky above like the train of a gray robe. Winter was king, and his touch left the sky dull and the air chill. His was a silent kingdom. Even the forest had little to say. The soft crunch of a light, late snowfall under the horses' hooves, the whip of wind through the bare branches above, were but gentle whispers in the peaceful wood. Even the rush of the river, high with melted snow from a short thaw, was muted from its passage through the trees.

I marveled at the transformation the forest went through every year, at the harshness of winter bringing beauty in spring.

"Lady Gabriella. Lady Alexandria. May we be of assistance?"

I jerked at the Duke of Lofton's voice, but not in displeasure. Tall and pale with silver hair and a distinguished air, Jonathon Lofton was one of the few truly acceptable guests staying with us this year. He also had the distinction of being a prominent enchanter and an old friend of my father's.

Alas, the crunch of snow accompanied not one, but two gentlemen as they walked down the snow-lined path.

"Good heavens!" The other—tall, thin Lord Ellsworth—stopped so quickly he nearly tipped over. He pointed a shaky finger beyond me to the stationary wolf.

"That's a wolf." Lord Ellsworth swung around to face Gabriella. "Why haven't you fled? That's a wolf, not some overgrown box, I mean fox. It … it could easily take down your horse and you with it."

"Really, Lord Ellsworth." I stopped the young man's impertinent lecture with a glare since Gabriella didn't seem inclined to do anything but gape at him. "I have the situation under control. You might have noticed that the animal hasn't moved."

He swallowed his next words and obediently followed my gaze to study the wolf. He brushed his shaggy hair, a peculiar shade of red, from his eyes. "No, it hasn't, but—"

The Duke of Lofton's chuckles drew everyone's attention to him as he walked to the wolf, his wand in his hand. "Neither have you, Lady Alexandria. Have you not been trained to leave a lasting spell? Release the wolf. I will take care of it."

My arm ached to obey, but I stiffened it. "But, Your Grace, you're so close."

"It will have no time to recover from the shock of your spell, I assure you." The confident smile he gave with his sideways glance eased my concern, and I scolded myself for ever having doubted him.

I made a flinging motion with my fingers and gladly drew my burning arm to my chest, just as the wolf appeared to melt and reform into a fluffy, white sheep.

In my shock, my wand-arm went slack, and the bird's chirp, long captive in its throat, escaped. Then it went silent again, frozen in place once more.

While the rest of us stared slack-jawed, the duke, snickering like a little boy at play, slipped his wand back into its place. He rubbed his hands together before straightening his jacket and meeting my eye. He shrugged, a grin making him look much younger than he was, and gestured to the sheep. "I couldn't resist. The spells will last for an hour, and then the animals shall return to normal."

"Everything I have heard of your skill is true then."

He shrugged again and brushed a soothing hand over my horse's muzzle. "That depends on what you've heard. I have had more time for learning and more occasion for using magic than most." His focus, seemingly far away for a moment, snapped back to the present, to me. "I commend you for being able to do what you did. Few bother to learn more than the basics now. I would gladly teach you and your sisters more advanced spells. You're more than capable."

My aching arms were proof enough of how little training I had compared to the duke, and among my peers I was not reckoned to be lacking. Although I doubted I would ever need to know how to transform one beast into another, a Floraison never turned down an opportunity to improve, especially not from such an instructor. A thrill of anticipation and gratefulness swept through me.

"It would be an honor to learn from you, Your Grace." I looked to Gabriella, anticipating her excitement at his offer, but she was handing her sketchbook and pencils to Lord Ellsworth, telling him of following the bird until I caught it in a spell and then the wolf sneaking up on us.

Quiet laughter passed between them, and she smiled down at him. At the plain, awkward Marcel Ellsworth, who tripped over his words and feet with equal frequency.

And that was more alarming than the wolf that would soon return to life.

⁂

"She actually called him by his Christian name." I stared down the arrow's narrow shaft to the gold center of the target seventy yards away, near the end of the lawn dedicated to archery, and then released it. In quick succession, I nocked and shot another arrow, and then another, hitting each of the three targets dead center.

"You're joking." My sister Eva, drawing and shooting at a leisurely pace, put four arrows around each of mine, each along the rim of the gold center.

"I thought I had misheard, but it happened twice." It was simply unfathomable. What could she mean by it? At nineteen, she was two years too young for suitors, and such informality as calling a man by his Christian name might be considered encouragement. Not that she could ever wish to encourage the likes of Lord Ellsworth. Only someone equal in talents, beauty, wit, and rank was suitable for a Floraison.

Using the remaining arrows in my quiver, I outlined one-half of the gold center of each target with arrows. Eva completed the outline as the clip-clop of hooves announced Gabriella and Sterling, her giant of a horse.

I took a few of Eva's arrows and nocked one, preparing to do a tighter circle around the dead-center arrow of the nearest target. I paused as the wind whipped across the lawn, swaying the dangling branches of the weeping willows scattered along the walk from the pleasure gardens behind us to the river some ways down the walk to our right.

"Don't be afraid of the wind, Alexandria." Gabriella, bow in hand and quiver dangling from her belt, laughed at me from her perch on Sterling.

"Who's afraid of it?" The chill breeze continued to lash my face and my neck, but I shifted my stance, took aim, and let the arrow fly.

Slightly up and to the right of dead center instead of directly above it. I *tsked* and quickly nocked another arrow and let it fly. *Perfect.* I settled for an incomplete circle and sent Gabriella to fetch the arrows.

On her return, she galloped past the targets, sending an arrow into the golden heart of each.

Clapping and a few cheers drew our attention to a group of Papa's guests strolling down the path to the river. Marcel Ellsworth was among them. His gaze fastened on Gabriella, and he stopped and tipped his hat at us, his pause nearly tripping up the man walking behind him. He and the other gentleman laughed and clapped one another on the back. With another glance at Gabriella, whose own smile indicated amusement—one could almost say fond amusement—he continued on with the rest of the guests.

"That Lord Marcel Ellsworth," Eva, seventeen and the youngest of us, added with a smirk at the hat-tipper and a quizzical glance at Gabriella, "makes me glad I am too young for suitors."

"I've never seen anyone so gangly in my life." I nocked another arrow and pulled back the bowstring. Had I truly seen fondness in her smile? Surely not. "The man looks rather like a stork, and is about as intelligible. He stutters and stammers so that one cannot get a full sentence out of him."

"Who would want to talk with him anyway?" Eva ran a gloved hand along the arc of her bow. "*He* would never do as a subject for one of my portraits. His face has no symmetry. His ears are too big for his head, and there's a gap between his front teeth," she said matter-of-factly.

"Marcel—Lord Ellsworth, I mean"—Gabriella's horse snorted and pranced under her as she spoke—"may not match the Floraison standard of beauty and poise, yet I find him an agreeable companion." She frowned as she leaned forward to rub the horse's neck, the frown making her look much like Mama when she was about to scold us. The displeasure in her voice was reminiscent of Mama's as well. "You might like him, too, if you would speak to him kindly and get to know him." She glared at me. "Give him a chance, Alexandria. You too, Eva."

I huffed as I refilled my quiver with the arrows Gabriella had brought back. "An artistic critique is the only notice Lord Ellsworth deserves to receive from the daughters of the Duke of Henly, Gabriella."

Gabriella's lips pressed together in a thin line.

"You always did have an odd attraction to the runts of the wolfhound's litters. You don't extend those feelings to gentle-men, do you?"

"Certainly not!" Gabriella's rosy cheeks turned a deeper hue, and she cantered off for another set of shots.

So I had hit a mark. But from where did this indignation spring? The implication that she favored Marcel? Or the comparison of Marcel to the runt of a litter of puppies? Surely, she understood he did not possess the qualities necessary to fit into the Floraison family. Indeed, few were eligible for admission.

It may have been cruel of me to press the issue, but as the eldest daughter, I felt it my duty to protect my sisters from foolish fancies, from heartbreak over men the family would never approve of.

"Imagine Lord Ellsworth's portrait," I began as Gabriella returned to us, bringing all the shot arrows with her, "hanging in the family gallery next to the one of Grandfather, who was considered the epitome of manly beauty. Or next to Papa's, for he's almost the exact image of Grandfather and is known far and wide for his skill as an orator and statesman." I gestured toward a willow gracing the lawn's edge as if it were the offending likeness.

Gabriella and I both gasped as an image of Marcel appeared in a shimmering gilded frame over the table holding the archery equipment.

Eva, the culprit, giggled as she flicked her wand, tweaking Marcel's ears and nose into a ridiculous caricature of himself.

A blue blur streaked past me through the illusion, and Marcel's face melted into streams of color that flowed to the table and disappeared with a poof.

Gabriella lowered her bow. "Yes, I get it. He's no Adonis. And though he's not nearly so unattractive in appearance as you make him out to be, he would look plain next to Papa or Grandfather. But have you nothing better to accuse him of?"

Well, yes, actually. He was clumsy, he stuttered, and his rank, though I hadn't delved into his family history, was inferior to our own—just for starters.

But I held my tongue. Gabriella's tastes, I sometimes noted, were not as refined as the rest of the family's, but I doubted even she would develop a serious affection for a mudpuppy like Marcel.

But she held my gaze as if expecting a reply. A frustrated sigh escaped her as she finally turned away. "Sterling and I are going for a ride. I'll see you later," she muttered as she left.

Eva scoffed and picked up her bow. "Let's back up a few more paces, shall we?"

Several shots later, she squealed as her arrow thudded into the grassy mound beyond the target. I barely bit back a laugh of surprise. She'd not missed the inner rings and gold center of the target since she was seven, and the target itself since, well, ever. "Whatever happ—"

"Really, Alexandria!" Her eyes flashed as she spun to face me. "You could have warned me you were going to practice some of the tricks the Duke of Lofton has been teaching you this past week."

I looked at her quizzically, then took my shot. "I don't know what you're talking about—Eek." My own arrow, my perfectly shot arrow, plunged into the grass next to Eva's.

There was only one explanation: someone had bewitched the arrows.

"Father." Eva punched her hands to her hips and glared at Papa and the Duke of Lofton as they emerged, grinning, from behind the nearest willow.

"My, my. *Father*, is it?" Papa tucked his wand away in his navy blue jacket. "I must have committed an egregious offense to have earned that stiff title. I had no idea it was such a serious competition. What were you shooting for? Not for one of the single guests, I hope."

"Gracious no." I set my bow aside and hugged Papa before curtsying to the Duke of Lofton. "Good morning, Your Grace."

"Good morning, Lady Alexandria. Lady Eva." The Duke of Lofton returned my greeting with a graceful bow. A man like him, only much younger, would be perfect for Gabriella.

Papa wrapped my arm around his, and I was surprised how nice his warmth felt. "I was about to show Lofton our collection of enchanted mirrors. Won't you two join us? We seldom make use of them, or enjoy them."

I stepped closer to Papa as another breeze whipped my skirts about my legs. "You've piqued my curiosity. I will gladly accompany you." And the library always had a cheerful fire burning in the hearth.

Eva left us for a history lesson with Mama, and the duke, Papa, and I retreated to the warmth of the library.

Papa unlocked and opened one of the drawers forming the base of a section of shelves in the corner of the room.

"This is an interesting one. You'll never guess what it does, Lofton." A boyish expression, one like pride in a sandcastle, softened his face. He held up the Fête mirror, its square back and handle a dull off-white, an exact match to the linen tablecloth used at dinner.

With an inquiring arch of his eyebrow, the Duke of Lofton accepted the mirror from Papa. A crimson blotch appeared on the mirror's back as it touched his hand.

I smothered a smile, stepped up to Papa and took his arm.

Papa smirked at his friend. "Did you perchance spill a drop of the red wine served with dinner last night?"

"Yes, but how did you know?"

Papa turned the mirror over in his hand and pointed to the spot. "The Fête mirror, better known as the 'What's for dinner?' mirror, shows the kitchen and dining room of our house as well as those of our neighbors and the villagers. It also tends to mimic tablecloth designs … and stains."

Turning the mirror back over, the duke snorted. "What toys we enchanters have. What of the other mirrors?" He glanced over the many drawers and shelves holding our collection of rare books and treasures.

A frown gave Papa wrinkles he didn't usually have. "They're not toys. Though this one seems childish enough, I believe it is nothing more than an apprentice's exercise, a stepping stone."

"A stepping stone to what? A mirror that lets you smell dinner?" The Duke of Lofton's eyes twinkled. "That would be tantalizing."

Papa tapped his friend's arm. "A stepping stone to something you'd be hard-pressed to equal, even in all the spells and enchanted objects mentioned in your closely guarded *Enchanter's List*."

The duke arched a white eyebrow. An arched eyebrow, as Papa always said, was the voice of skepticism. And challenge.

Papa cocked his head to look at me. "What say you, Alexandria? Shall we take him to the pinnacle of magic mirrors straightaway or one step at a time?"

The steps being the Fête mirror, the Rappelez-vous mirror, and the Demandez à Voir mirror, I presumed. The latter was certainly unique and dangerous in the wrong hands, but I wasn't sure I'd call it the "pinnacle of magic mirrors." Papa did know it better than I, however. "By all means, let us build the suspense for our guest. The saying 'save the best for last' may be hackneyed, but the idea is just as true."

"I quite agree, my dear." Papa took the Fête mirror from the duke and laid it on the small end table separating the shelves and a comfortable reading chair.

The duke smiled, as if humoring us.

Papa pulled a ring with three small keys from his waistcoat pocket and unlocked the two drawers below the one that housed the Fête mirror. He opened the middle drawer. An ornately carved ebony mirror rested in it.

Papa picked it up. "The Rappelez-vous mirror reveals

memories." He paused at a rap on the door and then bade the servant enter.

James stared but a moment at the mirror before remembering himself. "Excuse me, Your Grace, but you requested I find you a half hour before your next session was to begin." He cleared his throat. "It's a half hour before, Your Grace, and you have two requests for private meetings, a Lord Gibbon and a Lord Vandross."

The Duke of Lofton chuckled at Papa's crestfallen look. "A mentor's work is never done."

Shaking his head, Papa laid the mirror beside the other on the table. "Won't you come? I believe your knowledge would benefit Lord Gibbon in particular. We can finish this later."

The duke shrugged. "I don't recall the name, but I have a better memory for faces than names. I will come with you."

Papa cupped his hand over my elbow. "Would you put these away for me?"

"Of course."

He pointed to the bottom drawer, unlocked but unopened. "But remember—"

I held up my hand. "We are not to allow the Demandez à Voir mirror to tempt us to become Peeping Toms or international spies." I finished his teasing warning.

Smiling, he gently squeezed my arm and followed the duke out of the room.

As the door closed behind them, I pulled out my own set of keys—a gift and responsibility given to each family member, and only family members, on his or her twelfth birthday.

Bending over, I found the key to lock the bottom drawer. The duke hadn't even caught a glimpse of the famed Demandez à Voir mirror. Neither had I for several years. I let the key fall back against the others and opened the drawer.

Silver with roses twined about its handle and back, the

Demandez à Voir mirror lay off-center in the drawer. An oval ruffling of the velvet lining opposite it was the only trace of its lost mate.

The most fascinating, and, according to my father the most dangerous, this mirror could conjure an image of whomever or whatever was requested. No person was too distant or place too obscure. It was a gateway to the rest of the world and to the secrets of its inmates. Though Papa hinted that wasn't the limit of its abilities, he never gave any indication of what else it was capable of doing.

Light glinted invitingly off its rose-wreathed handle. What mysteries would its silver face illuminate? I reached out, but my fingers never touched it. It was an understood rule that the mirrors, and this mirror in particular, were not to be used lightly.

With the soft scrape of little-used tracks, I shut the drawer and locked it.

After putting the Fête mirror back in its proper place, I reached for the Rappelez-vous mirror. I touched it and drew back. An unnatural warmth seeped from its handle. A silver line raced the contours of a rose on the back of the ebony mirror. I blinked, and it was solid black again.

I poked it with my finger. It was still warm. *Well, it is an enchanted mirror, after all, and wands grew warm at an enchanter's touch. Why not a mirror?* Scoffing at my nonsense, at my rapidly beating heart, I got a firm grip on the mirror and held it before my face.

"Mirror of memory, of things forgotten and things remembered, a memory I ask of thee, a memory of ..." Which would I like to see? One I couldn't recall on my own would, of course, be the only thing worth viewing. "My father's mother, my namesake, who died before my first birthday."

Its face, a dull bronze in the tradition of ancient mirrors, slowly filled with spots of white as bright as the sun until I was forced to turn away.

When the light dimmed, I opened my eyes.

In the mirror's face was the image of a woman, lovely and young, yet not so young as I, seated at a writing desk. She resembled my grandmother in her wedding portrait.

What memory was this?

The woman sifted through palm-sized slips of newspaper.

"What are you doing, Mama?"

I cocked my head at the child's voice coming from the one whose memory I was viewing. A young boy's?

Perhaps the mirror had prepared this memory for Papa as he held it in his hand. In which case it was also a memory I'd asked for—one of my grandmother, Alexandria.

The woman looked down at the boy, the mirror, me. She smiled in the loving way of mothers. "Alfred, where did you come from? I didn't hear you come in." She extended her arm, curving it just enough to fit a young boy's shoulders.

My vision shifted to see my grandmother's side and then a spread of clippings on a table.

"What are the pieces of paper?"

"Clippings from the newspaper. Whenever I come across a story or article that interests me, I clip it and put it in this box." She waved her clippings-filled hand over a worn hatbox. "I've been doing this since I was a little older than you." She laid her handful on the table.

"Are you going to read them all again?"

She chuckled. "No, I was looking for two specific articles. I felt when I clipped them as a girl that there was some connection between them, that they were important somehow, to someone."

"To you?"

Her forehead wrinkled. "No, not to me, or to you. Not

directly, at least." Her face relaxed and she smiled. "I wanted to find them again to figure it out. Won't you help me?"

Grandmamma's face moved up and down, presumably as my father nodded.

He watched as she sorted through the papers until, with an exclamation of joy, she laid two pieces on the table in front of them. I listened as she read the articles to him, pointing out the words as she did.

The Enchanter's Journal, "A Mystery in Sonser"
October 20, 1756

The Duke of Henly recently announced that one of the Demandez à Voir mirrors has <u>vanished</u> from his estate near Florenburg. The fact only one item was taken makes it doubtful the Magic Collectors were behind this latest theft of an enchanted object. The mate of the <u>missing</u> mirror refuses to show the image of its lost twin, or of anything else, but such is the way with these enchanted mirrors. "The <u>disappearance</u> of the Demandez à Voir mirror is a complete mystery to me," declared the Duke of Henly. He is offering a reward for information leading to its return.

The Gilden Times, Society Column
November 2, 1756

Silk and satin abounded at the funeral of the Princess Simone. As beautiful and cold in death as in life, the princess was laid to rest in a cream-colored dress of exquisite lace. Conspicuous by his <u>absence</u> was the lady's only living relative— her nephew, Prince Gérard Bête. He appears to have retreated to his castle at Silvestris, undoubtedly to escape his inferiors. Yet, who isn't beneath a handsome and wealthy man with the hereditary title of prince? Princess Simone battled pneumonia for a month before her passing. Her elegance and beauty will be greatly <u>missed</u>.

Squiggly pen strokes underlined several related words. I glanced at the date of the earlier article. 1756. My grandmother would have been eleven. Was the connection one of vocabulary?

Yet, Grandmamma was said to have had a special sense about things, about the future. After all, she had a clipping concerning the disappearance of the Floraison's Demandez à Voir mirror ten years before she married into the family.

The yellowed papers faded back into the green bronze of a reflectionless mirror.

Wondering if Grandmamma ever discovered the connection, I locked the mirror back in its drawer and left the library to prepare for dinner.

❧

The next morning, I sat reading in the morning room until I had too much of the fire's warmth and then headed upstairs to fetch my cloak and handbag for a walk. The bang of the main door as it swung open and the masculine shouts that blew in caught my attention as I descended the stairs.

Terrible grammar.

It could only mean one thing—a peasant was seriously ill or injured.

Gabriella rushed across the foyer, her cloak flying behind her and her cheeks red from the bite of the cold wind blowing in with her. "Alexandria, do you know where Papa is? A wild boar gored one of the villagers as he was hunting."

My stomach twisted. "He left earlier with his guests. I'm not sure where they went. Have you sent for the surgeon?" I glanced at the family crest and motto emblazoned over the door.

Mercy, Justice, Charity.

The latter of the family motto tended to bring us a lot of unpleasantness.

"He's on his way." Gabriella turned down a corridor, and I followed, barely making out her reply over the clip of our heels on the marble floor. She glanced over her shoulder. "I wish Mama wasn't visiting Lady Tannon today."

So did I.

A glimpse of white apron pulled us to a stop outside of the breakfast room. Wide-eyed, the maid stared at us as we rushed in.

"Mary, there's been an accident. Send for Papa—the surgeon may want him to assist. And tell Johns to open the surgery."

"At once, my lady." She curtsied and dashed out the door and down the passageway.

Gabriella and I raced back to the main entrance and out the door. Four men neared the stairs, each gripping one corner of a coarse blanket on which moaned a walrus of a man. A crimson line marked their path.

My breath caught.

Without Mama and Papa there, it fell to me to be hostess for this unfortunate guest. I shuddered and then squared my shoulders.

The villager who'd come ahead and warned Gabriella stood panting near us. His lean frame and pockmarked face triggered a memory.

"You there!" I said. "You brought the last injured man here. Do you remember where the ice cellar is?"

He gave a floppy nod.

"Go fetch some ice and take it to the surgery. It will slow infection."

He nodded and jogged off with his hand pressed to his side.

What else did we need? I turned to Gabriella. She stared at the wounded man with a pained expression on her face. "Gabriella, make sure the servants put water on to boil and place the candles where they'll give the most light."

"Yes, Alexandria." She took two steps and then stopped at a horrible cry coming up the lane.

"Jimmy! Jimmy!" A woman in a drab blue dress wailed as she stumbled toward us. Behind her jogged a chubby boy about ten years old.

I groaned. Peace from distraught wives was another thing we offered the patient, and more importantly, the surgeon.

The woman screamed like a banshee when she reached her husband, and then collapsed onto the gravel lane. The boy caught her round the shoulders and managed to keep her senseless head from hitting the ground.

It wasn't the usual method of establishing peace from distraught wives, but it would work.

I yanked the handbag off my wrist. "Gabriella, never mind about the hot water. They should know to do that. Take this. There's some lavender water in it. It will help keep the woman calm after she wakes. Have the servants take her and the boy to the morning room. It should be far enough away from the surgery so they won't hear any … noises."

Gabriella gave me a weak smile as she took the handbag. She knelt and helped the boy lift his mother into a sitting position.

A loud neigh and the clatter of hooves moving at breakneck speed down the lane announced the surgeon's arrival. He reined in his horse, sending gravel flying.

I watched as the horse pranced under the surgeon's firm hand, grateful the man's love for the theatric was tempered by the principles of his profession—he always made sure no one was in range of the spewed gravel.

He dismounted and handed the reins to a stable boy watching the excitement. He tipped his hat to me and walked alongside the bearers.

I joined them, and the surgeon turned from his patient to me. "Is everything ready, Lady Alexandria?"

"It should be, or very nearly, at least."

"Is the duke here?"

"No, Sir Guy. Mama's not either."

He paused and studied my face. "Would you help me? I'll need an extra pair of hands, and the duke says you have a cool head and steady hands."

My hands weren't steady enough to untie the knot in my stomach, but I couldn't deny that like all Floraisons, I could handle blood and stress when I needed to. "Of course I will."

He patted my shoulder. "Good girl. I knew I could count on you."

We guided the bearers to the surgery and placed the patient on the table. I showed the men to the morning room and then collected a bottle of brandy to ease the patient's pain. As I hurried back down the hallway someone careened around a corner and slammed me into the wall. The bottle slipped from my hands and shattered on the floor.

I glared at the imbecilic oaf still pressing me to the wall.

Marcel Ellsworth.

Why was I not surprised?

"Forgive me, Lady Alexandria." He pulled me hastily from the wall.

I stumbled forward a step before getting my balance. "Release me, sir, before you do more harm. What is the meaning of this?"

"That's what I want to know. I mean, your father sent me to fetch something, and I hear yelling and see blood on the ground outside. I was so worried. Is Lady Gab—everyone in the family well?"

"A peasant's been hurt. We're about to do surgery, and you've broken the pain relief."

His eyes widened as he looked at the spilled brandy. "I'm s-so very, very s-sorry." He took a step back and slipped on the wet floor.

I caught him by the arm, and he righted himself. Red blotches popped out all over his face.

"I'm s-sorry again. And th-thank you. Is there anything I can do to help? Comfort the family? Get your father? I'm so happy your family is well."

"No—yes, fetch another bottle of brandy and meet me in the surgery."

Gabriella asked that I give him a chance. This would be it; after all, a member of the Floraison family, by birth or marriage, should be able to handle all situations with poise and confidence.

His eyes bugged, but he nodded.

And stood there.

"The brandy, Lord Ellsworth. Hurry." I shooed him away and returned to the patient.

Marcel went deathly pale the moment he entered the surgery, swayed alarmingly a few times during the operation, and thrice dropped the sterilized instruments he should have put in my hands.

The third time I barely stopped a pair of forceps from landing inside the patient, I lost my composure. "You're worse than useless, Ellsworth. Leave."

Sir Guy looked up at me and raised a gray eyebrow.

"I apologize for my harsh tongue, Lord Ellsworth. Not everyone is fit for the sickroom." Or my family. "You've done enough here. Go get some fresh air."

He glanced from me to Sir Guy, who nodded his okay, and then made his exit.

When the patient's wounds were stitched up and he was sleeping quietly, Sir Guy sent a servant to the man's family with the good news.

Humming, he rolled down his shirtsleeves. I removed my apron, which had done a less-than-satisfactory job of protecting my clothing, and washed my hands and arms.

"You did an excellent job, sir. I feared we would need to amputate his leg."

"I was rather concerned about that too—at first. Infection is my only worry now." He sank into a chair and gave a satisfied sigh. "I'll sit with him for a while. Why don't you go do whatever it is fine young ladies typically do of an afternoon?" He waved his hand in a shooing motion.

I curtsied and opened the door.

"Lady Alexandria."

I turned.

He smiled. "You did a satisfactory job yourself. I appreciate it."

Suppressing a grin, I nodded and left.

Once the surgery door closed behind me, I took a deep breath, placed my hands on my hips, and stretched my tense back. Damp blood stained my fingers where they'd touched my dress.

"That peasant ruined my gown," I whined.

"For a few minutes you treated that peasant as another person. Now he's just a stain on your fashionable gown. You must have a lung of stone."

I jumped, my eyes darting to the wall. Marcel slumped against it. The fresh air had done little to bring the color back to his face or sense to his speech.

"You mean a heart of stone?" With a contemptuous smile, I brushed past him.

I had given him a chance, and he had failed. Though not a bad man, he wasn't up to Floraison standards. I hoped Gabriella realized that.

And I did not have a heart of stone. I didn't regret helping, just ruining my gown.

◈

The day before Papa's birthday was unusually wet, and as the downstairs was full of his visitors, Mama and I retreated to an upstairs room. She moved her needle with fluid motion through the fabric of the pillow she was embroidering. I stood near a window and surveyed one of the garden walks. There was something inviting about this particular path, especially on damp, gray days. Whether it was the stillness of the sunken walk, the glistening water droplets that clung like tiny crystals to the vines, or the way the water changed the color of the stone walls and released the fragrance of damp earth, I didn't know. Whatever it was, it was appealing.

As I gazed at the garden, a couple, taking advantage of the lull between showers, strolled into view. The young man caught my attention as he gallantly stepped forward to raise a fallen vine out of his companion's way. He took care not to shake any of the loosely clinging droplets onto her fair head. When he attempted to tuck the stray vine behind a limb, it revolted and flew into his face.

Marcel. Only he could be so clumsy.

His companion's cloak hid her identity. She raised her hand to her mouth, as if to hide a laugh. Marcel grinned and secured the vine to the limb. She took out her handkerchief and wiped his check. Her hood slipped back and uncovered silky blond hair.

Gabriella.

How could my sister, a Floraison, have tender feelings for someone like Marcel? His rank and fortune weren't high enough to make up for half of his defects.

"What are you staring at so intently? Is anything the matter?" Mama's voice surprised me.

Gabriella's choice would be scorned by all, and rightly, but I didn't want her to be hurt by the family's rejection. Perhaps I could do something about the situation before anyone else noticed. "Some limbs have grown out over the garden path. I must remember to speak to the head gardener about them."

⚜

I intended to have a serious talk with Gabriella the next day, but my words of wisdom weren't needed then. Eva and one of my aunts had seen her walking with Marcel. A bevy of enraged and offended relatives descended upon Gabriella that evening. She listened to them with tears in her eyes, but she refused to speak, except for one phrase, spoken mostly to herself: "There are two kinds of beauty; beware which one you treasure, for lasting beauty lies within."

Marcel, like most of the other guests, left before the close of the next day, as Papa's birthday celebration marked the end of the mentoring season. Marcel either did not ask for permission to correspond with my sister, as was customary for a man interested in a lady too young for courting, or had been denied, for Gabriella sadly admitted she never expected to hear from him again.

The few remaining guests departed within the week, and we resumed our normal daily routine. We were to have two months to ourselves before the next big occasion—my twenty-first birthday. Aunts, uncles, cousins, friends, and hopeful suitors would join us for an all-day gala complete with musicians, outdoor games, a pavilion of the finest foods of the season, pleasure-boat rides along the river, and, of course, a grand ball. And roses—everywhere. All enchanted by my parents to be in full bloom on my birthday.

Two weeks later, I learned our time alone would be limited to one month. Three young cousins would join us for the four weeks preceding my birthday. A young man who wished to be mentored by my father was also due to arrive at the same time. As I doubted he would be up to family standards, I hoped, for Gabriella's sake, he was married. Or at least had a pug nose. Surely even she couldn't fall in love with someone who had a pug nose.

CHAPTER 2

WALKING WAS ONE of my favorite occupations. The beauty of sunlit meadows and shadowy glades drew me from the house almost every day, for winter had blossomed into spring in the month since my father's birthday.

My favorite path led to a grove of beech trees bordering a bend in the river near our house, but this day, for a change, I chose the lane leading from our manor to the village. A charming, rock-bottomed stream escorted the tree-lined avenue most of the way.

A mile or so before the village, and just off the lane, sat a large and inviting rock perfectly positioned to give a good view of a bubbling cascade. I laid my bonnet and handbag on the rock and sat down. Tucking my knees under my chin, I drank in the enchanting sight. Violets and trilliums graced the stream's banks. Colorful song masters flitted through the boughs above me, and spring-green leaves raced over water-polished rocks, spun around eddies, and glided serenely downstream.

"Ain't this a lovely spot, my lady?"

An old woman with a hooked nose, shabby clothes, and stringy gray hair lowered herself onto a tree stump a few feet away.

"Sorry to startle you." Her smile was as yellow as a sunflower.

"Yes, it is lovely." I focused my attention on the droplets of water spraying over the moss-covered rocks jutting from the bank.

"I come here a lot."

Was her presence not enough of an intrusion—and an affront to the scenery—that she should insist on speaking as well?

"My children was fond of this spot when they was young." She gazed at the water with a slight smile, as if remembering her children splashing around in it. "They live far away now, but I often come here to feel close to them. Did my lady ever play here as a girl?"

"Certainly not." We played in a spot nearer to the manor house and not frequented by peasants. I grabbed my bonnet and handbag, took a few coins from the latter, and stood.

She stared at me as I held out the coins, and then she slowly reached out her hand to receive them. "Thank you, my lady. Sorry to have troubled you."

From the way she murmured and looked down at the dirt path, one would think she was disappointed with my generous gift. Wasn't that why she spoke to me?

As I strolled home, the rattle of carriage wheels drew my attention from the wildflowers blooming along the roadside. I recognized the livery as my uncle's. Three pairs of hands waved excitedly from the carriage. It rolled to a stop beside me, and a seven-year-old girl and a five-year-old boy scrambled out.

"Aunt Alexandria!" they cried and clung to my skirts.

"Guinevere. Jean. This is a pleasant surprise." I bent to give them each a hug.

"This certainly is." Uncle Claude leaned out the window.

"Hello, Alexandria." Aunt Penelope waved at me from the corner of the carriage. She moved two-year-old Madeline's chubby hand in hers.

Uncle Claude nodded at his two oldest children. "It's been a long ride, Alexandria. Would you let them walk to the manor house with you?" His smile was hopeful.

A twinge of panic erased my smile. He was leaving me alone with two children who had been cooped up for hours?

"Yippee! We're free!" Jean grabbed my hand and jumped up and down. "I'll protect you from the highwaymen." Clearly concerned for my safety, he proceeded to dash down the road.

Guinevere followed.

Uncle Claude shrugged his shoulders. "Would you like a ride? We'll walk the horses and pick up the children when they tire."

❧

I left my aunt, uncle, and the children with my parents in the drawing room and went to fetch Eva and Gabriella. I found Eva reading in her room. "The little ones have arrived."

She closed her book with a sigh. "It's going to be a long month, but a good one, I hope."

"Me too. Have you seen Gabriella? She wasn't in her room."

"No, I haven't seen her." She laid the book on her dresser and followed me out the doorway.

"I'll continue searching. You'd better go downstairs before Aunt Penelope and Uncle Claude think we're avoiding them."

Chuckling, she changed direction. "All right, then."

Gabriella was in the library. She practically jumped out of

her chair when I entered. She moved her hand to her chest and then pulled her shawl from where it was draped over the chair arm to bunch it in her lap. "You gave me quite a start. Has Papa's guest arrived?"

"No. Aunt Penelope and Uncle Claude have."

"Oh. Wonderful! Tell them I'll be with them in a moment." Her hands fidgeted in her lap.

I arched an eyebrow. She met my stare with an innocent smile. Perhaps she wanted to finish whatever daydream she had been engaged in when I interrupted her. Some of her dreams made for interesting stories. "I'll tell them you're on your way."

❧

My aunt and uncle were to leave the next morning on a pleasure trip around the kingdom. To make the most of our time together, we ladies left the children with their nurse and took ourselves out to the gardens for a walk. As we strolled, I heard the rumble of carriage wheels but paid little heed. We would meet the stranger at dinner. Gabriella's eyes were turned toward the sound, though a tall hedge blocked the view of the drive. I hoped he had a pug nose. And bucked teeth, for good measure.

❧

He didn't have a pug nose. Or buck teeth. Or any other fault that I could see. Giles Bête stood shoulder to shoulder with Papa and even rivaled him for the manly good looks for which Papa was known. The hereditary title of prince only added to his charms.

Prince Giles's striking blue eyes held mine with well-bred ease as Papa made the introduction. I curtsied, and he sketched a graceful bow. Papa led him around the drawing room and completed the introductions. My two-year-old niece climbed into my lap, and I agreed to her jumbled words as my eyes followed Giles from beneath lowered lashes. He moved with a certain grace and poise, and he spoke with confidence and intelligence. I smiled to myself. Here was a man who would fit into our family.

I felt eyes on me as I bent to retrieve my niece's doll from the floor. Giles, standing with my father and uncle next to the fire, regarded me with a serious expression I knew not how to interpret. Our eyes met, and he shifted to face Papa.

The butler soon announced dinner. As the eldest daughter, I was the one Giles escorted into the dining room, but Papa was the one he was seated beside. For once, I wasn't happy for my father to monopolize his guest.

Fortunately, Mama wasted no time in securing Giles's attention to the general audience when the gentlemen joined us again after the after-dinner separation.

"How was your journey, Prince Giles? Have you ever been in this part of the country before?" Her eyes, one sky blue, one sea green, had a bewitching effect on men. She motioned for him to join her, and he obediently came.

"The journey followed the pattern of most journeys, my lady." He chose the chair between Mama and me. "The ride was long and tiring, but the sights were fresh and interesting. And, no, I have never been in this part of the country before, though I have heard much of its beauty, and I must add that not only the beauty of its scenery was praised." He glanced at Eva, Gabriella, and me, a charming smile playing on his lips.

Gabriella, seated across from me, looked away, presumably to hide the pink tint of her cheeks.

What reason did she have to blush? We were often praised in like manner.

"I would have arrived earlier this afternoon," Giles apologized, "but, being afraid I had lost my way and spying an old woman walking along the lane, I stopped to ask directions of her." He studied each of us. "We ended up having a pleasant chat. I do believe the poor woman was lonely. I gathered someone slighted her earlier today, though she didn't say it outright." His gaze rested on me.

Something told me she was the same beggar woman who had accosted me. "I'm surprised you would've wasted time in such a manner. I don't see the necessity of stopping to converse with everyone one meets, especially if one is expected elsewhere."

"Is it wasting time to give an old woman the comfort of a listening ear?" His blue eyes searched my face. "A kind word is as much an act of charity as the gift of a few coins."

"What's an old hag to me?" The hint of defensiveness in my voice surprised me.

His eyes darkened and his lips fell from their smile.

That was a reproving glance if ever I saw one. I turned to talk to Eva. Giles was a handsome man, but he had strange notions.

❦

Gabriella's laughter welcomed me as I entered the breakfast room. She and Giles filled their plates from the platters of food on the sideboard.

"Good morning, Alexandria." Gabriella greeted me with a smile as bright as her golden gown. "Did you manage to catch Aunt Penelope and Uncle Claude before they left?"

"Good morning, Lady Alexandria." Giles bowed. His smile was polite.

"Yes, barely." I kissed Gabriella's cheek and then faced Giles. "I trust your room is to your liking, Prince Giles?"

"Perfectly." He laid his plate down and slid a chair back from the table for Gabriella.

Her smile dimmed as she glanced from him to me, perhaps as chilled by his coolness as I was. "Alexandria, have you heard how the man injured by the wild boar is doing? Has he fully recovered yet?"

I picked up one of the white plates rimmed with gold and decorated with a floral design and began to fill it. "I spoke to Sir Guy about him after church last week. His injuries have healed. He will in all probability walk with a limp, but at least there was never any infection."

"Thanks to your expert help during surgery, no doubt." Gabriella raised her glass to me.

Chuckling, I added some fruit to my plate and walked to the table. "The surgeon may have something to say about that."

"Who was this man? The son of a nearby nobleman?" Giles pulled back a chair for me. I took my place at the table, and he began to slide the chair underneath me.

"No, a villager."

The chair jerked to a halt.

Giles cocked his head and looked at me. "You actually inquired about a peasant?"

Was it unseemly for the daughter of a duke to be concerned about a peasant? "He was my patient."

The chair slid forward again, finally enough for me to sit.

"Of course. You needed to know for your records."

"Really, Prince Giles. You make Alexandria sound quite heartless." Gabriella glared at him.

"Nonsense. I'm sure Lady Alexandria has a heart." Giles took a seat, murmuring as he moved his eggs about on his plate. "She's just particular about the type of people who can touch it."

"I don't keep records, Prince Giles. I was genuinely interested in the man's well-being."

He looked up and held my gaze for a moment. His expression softened. "I apologize, Lady Alexandria. Traveling has made me irritable." He smiled, his blue eyes twinkling. "Forgive me?"

Who could resist such a charming smile in such a handsome face? I let my lips curve slightly—I wouldn't give him too big of a smile—and nodded.

Gabriella's furrowed brow relaxed. "When you came in, Prince Giles was telling me of the time he was abducted by highwaymen."

I made a concerted effort not to let my mouth hang open as I sought the truth of the statement in his face. He returned my surprised stare with a mischievous grin. I narrowed my eyes.

His grin widened, and he raised his hands, palms toward me. "On my honor, Lady Alexandria. I was captured by a group of the roving villains when I was a lad of ten. My father paid a handsome price to get me back."

Visions of silly young women gasping and begging him to tell them every detail of the story flashed through my mind. But something told me that wasn't the sort of woman who would capture his attention.

"What a terrifying experience for your mother. Pass the marmalade, won't you, Gabriella." I gave him a sideways glance as I accepted the dish from Gabriella.

He watched me with a raised eyebrow, but then one corner of his mouth tilted up suspiciously as if it wanted to smile.

❧

After the midday meal, and after refusing the company of my sisters, who often complained I kept too fast a pace, I set out for a long walk. I started for a delightful, flower-filled meadow but ended up skirting the meadow and hugging the creek that flowed beside the village lane. At a shallow spot, I lifted my gown and hopped from stone to stone until reaching the other side. I made my way to the packed dirt lane and walked along it for a quarter of a mile before reaching my unintentional destination—the little cascade.

Once again, I assumed the rock seat and prepared to enjoy the spot without disturbance. Yet, with each leaf crunched by a hopping bird and each twig jostled by a chipmunk, I glanced around half expecting to meet the old woman.

This will never do. Think of pleasant things.

My skin obeyed and told me of the cool breeze caressing a few loose strands of hair, my ears conveyed the cheerful calls of birds, my nose the fragrance of wildflowers, and my eyes the perfect positioning of lines, shapes, and colors in the scene before me. My eyes were those of an artist, and they saw nothing to improve. This idea of visual perfection directed my thoughts to another example, an even more pleasant one —Giles.

At breakfast, he had expressed a hope of being able to go riding with my sisters and me soon, though his eyes were on me as he spoke. Would he stay until my birthday celebration? Surely, he would. Hopefully, he would.

A twig cracked, and I looked around. I didn't see the old woman, but Giles's look of reproof flashed before me. My mood changed from admiration to irritation as the previous night's reproving glance replaced the morning's smile. *Why should I have stayed and talked with her? I gave her money, which I'm sure she needed. You may look at me however you like, Giles Bête, but if I saw her today, I would act the same.*

As if to prove my point, I marched home along the road,

barely even looking at the one beggar man I passed, though I did throw him a few coins.

❦

Three voices calling my name brought me out of my reverie as I neared the house.

"Alexandria, did you leave your ears behind you? We've called your name several times." Eva waved at me from the path to the gardens. Gabriella and Giles stood beside her.

Returning her wave, I joined them on the gravel walk. "My thoughts must have muffled the sound." I cast a quick look at Giles. I had walked off my ill mood, but even if I hadn't, it would have melted away before him. But why wasn't he with Papa?

He seemed to sense my question. "Your father was called away on business, leaving me alone for the afternoon." His eyes held a mischievous glint. "He suggested I make good use of my free time."

I gave him an arch look. "By becoming better acquainted with his daughters?"

He grinned. "I can't think of a better occupation. Won't you join us for a walk?"

Both of his arms were taken by my sisters, but I gladly accepted Gabriella's free arm and the three of us gave him a tour of the pleasure gardens, which he praised as genuinely and tastefully as even I could wish.

CHAPTER 3

THE HOPED-FOR RIDE happened a few days later. It was my parents' anniversary, and Papa declared, as he did every year on this day, that he would devote his attention to his bride and to no one else. With a smile, he banished Giles to the care of Eva, Gabriella, and me; the four of us set out for Caveless Lake.

"You have an older brother, do you not?" Giles asked as we passed one of the farms along the way.

My gaze left the field of sprouting grain and settled on him. "Yes, Frederick is away at the university."

"Surely you've noticed how Cook looks in on us during dinner and then heaves a sigh when she sees you?" Eva said.

Giles cocked his head. "Yes, I have."

"You're sitting in Frederick's usual seat, and you remind her of him."

He chuckled. "Is that all? I was beginning to think she didn't like me."

I joined in his laughter. "She likes you. She just misses her 'mischievous imp.'"

"Her imp?" Giles gave me a grin that made me think the title had been used on him quite often.

"Prince Giles." Gabriella claimed our attention. "Do you think they'll be able to get that wagon out?"

She pointed to a group of three or four men gathered around a wagon sitting deep in a muddy path between two fields. The horse attached to the wagon strained ineffectually to scramble out of the mud as a man pulled on its bridle. The group of men shifted, revealing a woman holding the hem of her simple white gown off the ground. I took another look at the wagon. It was filled with furniture and two small trunks.

Giles reined in his horse and examined the scene. "Not without unloading it. Wouldn't do the items in the wagon any good, not as muddy as the ground is."

Gabriella gestured to the woman as she talked with the man who had been working with the horse. "That would be a sad beginning to your wedding day, cleaning mud off of all your belongings." She locked gazes with me, and I groaned as I realized what she wanted.

Giles looked at her questioningly.

"Many of the peasants get married on my parents' anniversary because Papa gives them the day off," Eva explained.

Giles urged his horse forward. "You're right. No one should spend their wedding day cleaning. I'll see what I can do."

Sighing, I nodded to Gabriella. "Prince Giles, wait."

He brought his horse around to face me.

I took a deep breath. I didn't mind him knowing, but I didn't care for all the peasants to know. "My family has the power of enchantment."

He furrowed his brow. "This is no time for confession, Lady Alexandria."

"What she means, Prince Giles," Gabriella said, "is that we can help."

His lips twitched, possibly at the thought of us lifting furniture or wiping mud from spindly chair legs. He noticed my serious expression and cleared his throat. "How?" His question came out in a contrary tone that, though I suspected it was feigned, annoyed me.

I raised my chin. "I never divulge my methods."

Gabriella glanced at us and sighed. "By using our powers—Alexandria's the best of us at spells. However, we don't want to make a scene before the villagers. We will need your help."

"What kind of help?"

"We need a diversion."

He quirked an eyebrow. "You want a diversion so you won't make a scene?"

I grinned at the irony. "Yes."

He leaned forward in a bow, and his lips spread to form a smile—a decidedly impish one. "Lady Alexandria, I would consider it a privilege to rescue you should your horse happen to run away with you."

My cheeks caught fire. I would sooner die than descend to such a cheap trick to get a man's attention. Though, I wouldn't mind being rescued by a handsome prince if I were in real need, especially if the prince happened to have blue eyes. "Your gallantry is inspiring, Your Highness, but I was thinking of something less dramatic."

He made a sweeping gesture with his hand. "Your wish is my command, my lady."

"Go talk to them. Make certain they are all facing you and standing well away from the wagon."

"At once, my lady." With another bow and a grin, Giles trotted over to the peasants, who were standing about ten yards away.

Gabriella and Eva followed.

I smoothed out the folds of my skirt near my left hip until I found the long, slender pocket. Since the days of the great war between the enchanters and the evil, power-hungry sorcerers, enchanters never went anywhere without a wand. Though we seldom used them, my family continued the tradition. I slipped my wand from its hiding place and ran my fingers along it. It grew warm at my touch, and the engraved rose vines encircling it burned red against its silver body.

I glanced at the group by the wagon. They were laughing with Giles. The man certainly had a way with people.

A few whispered words, a flick of the wand, and the wagon became the size of a child's wagon. The startled horse plunged forward through the mud and gained the firmer road.

"Would you look at that?" Giles said in a loud voice.

I raised my wand again but stopped, my heart in my throat as he pointed where the wagon had been.

I tightened my grip on the wand. He had been called an imp before. If he wasn't my father's guest I'd ...

But he swung his arm up and gestured at a formation of birds flying overhead. I let my breath out slowly and glared at the side of his head.

He glanced over at me and winked.

My scowl lasted until he looked away. Then it curved into a grin. Shaking my head, I refocused on the horse and child-size wagon and then made small circles in the air with the wand. On the third loop, I jerked the wand toward me, bringing the spell with it. The full-sized wagon reappeared.

With a feeling of satisfaction, I slipped the wand back in its pocket and urged my horse into a trot. Giles greeted me with a knowing look and began to introduce the peasants to me. I greeted each of them, wished the young couple a joyous marriage, and suggested we be on our way.

Giles frowned, but he and my sisters wished the peasants a good day and followed my lead down the road.

He caught up and rode abreast of me. "Are you always eager to avoid conversation?"

I stared at him with raised eyebrows. Who wasn't eager to escape conversation with a peasant? Except another peasant, of course.

Frowning, he turned to Gabriella as she rode up beside him. "So, in addition to remarkable beauty and intelligence, your family possesses the power of enchantment? Do you have any other secrets I should know?"

"Nay." She laughed. "We don't, and our powers are no secret —just little known. We don't want to be bothered by novelty seekers who would pester us to make impressive fireworks." Her lips curled up. "Or to turn people into toads and back again."

"Or not back again," Eva added.

"Or for our neighbors and the villagers to constantly ask us for favors."

"What sort of favors?" Giles asked.

I flattened out my smile. "Oh, the usual kind. Cure warts, provide a potion to make a horse win a race, turn straw into gold." I shrugged. "That sort of thing."

Giles rubbed his chin, but didn't quite cover his smile. "I can see why you don't publicize it. What do you do with it?"

"Do with it?" I shooed a fly away from my mare's chestnut mane and looked ahead. The road angled to the right and increased in slope. We were nearing our destination.

"Mama and Alexandria developed a spell to prevent flowers from freezing," Gabriella said. "And another one to induce them to bloom any time we desire—such as for Alexandria's birthday celebration."

"My mother would love to know that spell," Giles said.

"Papa is more practical. He's a master of the 'magical art of penmanship.'" I led them off the road, and we continued single file along a path through the woods.

Giles chuckled. "Master of what?"

"His quill will, on its own, take dictation."

"Indeed?"

"Indeed. Papa says it's more efficient and mannerly than most secretaries."

"Those are entertaining uses, but surely you exercise your gifts in some other way as well?"

"We don't go scouring the countryside for wagons to pull out of the mud, if that's what you mean."

"No," Giles said slowly, his eyes intent on me, "but if you should see some way it would benefit others, you would use your powers?"

"If I see it, yes."

"And I'm sure you would agree that there's a difference between seeing a need and seeing yourself as part of the solution?"

"Of course."

He frowned and added softly, "Unfortunately, the latter can be much more of a challenge than pulling a wagon out of the mud."

"Why do you look at me with such a speculative expression?" Did he not think me capable of reflecting on a need deeply enough to see myself in its cure? I suddenly had the unsettling feeling he saw a need in me and was contemplating how to fix it.

"Here we are," Gabriella said, preempting Giles's reply.

The trail opened into a clearing, and we dismounted and led our horses to the edge of the hillside overlook. The blue fingers of Caveless Lake gleamed up at us.

"Lovely. Say, is that a cave down there? It looks like steps going into the water." Giles pointed to the upper right edge of the lake where the water met a rock outcropping.

"No, that's the reflection of the underside of the rock above it. But it does resemble natural stairs and has deceived many people, hence the name."

"How very curious, but I suppose reflections aren't always what they seem."

My horse nudged my shoulder, and I stroked her soft muzzle as I watched the clouds drift among the ripples in the lake. "Speaking of reflections, Papa is also the keeper of a collection of enchanted mirrors."

"Do they tell you that you are the fairest one of all?" Eyes twinkling, Giles stooped to pick a dandelion seed head.

Smirking, I accepted it from him. "I've never thought to ask." I ran my finger over the soft, puffy sphere and then dispersed the seeds with a breath. "To tell the truth, Prince Giles, I've never known the mirrors to present actual reflections."

He refilled my hand with a young dandelion in golden glory. "I imagined their reflections would be considerably different than those of other mirrors, but what do they show?" He clicked to his horse, and we walked on, following Eva and Gabriella across the bright clearing to the edge of the shadowed forest.

"The Rappelez-vous mirror reveals memories." Eager to see his face light with amusement at the Fête mirror, I stopped in pretense of wanting to pick some violets. He stopped as well, taking the reins from me. "The Fête mirror—whose back sometimes mimics tablecloth designs—shows the kitchen and dining room of our house as well as those of our neighbors and the villagers."

Giles burst out laughing, rewarding me for my ploy. "Is that how you make sure the cook washes her hands properly?"

Joining in his laughter, I noted how he was even more handsome when smiling. "No. But Cook occasionally borrows it when she wants fresh menu or table décor ideas, or when Lady Tannon has a dinner party. Lady Tannon's cook is her arch nemesis."

Still chuckling, Giles guided the horses forward. "Most interesting and useful mirrors you have."

"Hurry up, you two." Eva and Gabriella waved at us from the trail leading down to the lake.

Warmth touched my cheeks as I noticed that their horses were already tied to tree limbs and that they were several yards into the forest. Giles quickly secured our horses' reins to a limb.

"Magic mirrors, indeed." His whispered scoff as he followed me onto the narrow trail drew my attention.

Though eager to catch up with my sisters, I was unwilling to let the comment pass. Slowing my pace, I twisted slightly to look at him. "You'd be surprised, you know, about the usefulness of the mirrors. My brother, Frederick, actually bewitched the Fête mirror once."

"For what purpose?"

"To convince Cook that Lady Tannon's children were served custard for lunch every day. No vegetables, just custard."

"A noble purpose. Did he succeed?"

"Yes and no. Cook believed it, but she haughtily declared she didn't care what that 'flaky ex-confectioner' fed her children, we still had to eat our vegetables." *But he proved the mirrors could be tampered with.* "She was furious when she found out he'd deceived her. She walloped him with her largest wooden spoon, and Papa made him apologize to her." I chuckled. "And he's been her favorite ever since."

"As my father says, 'Women are an unfathomable mystery.'" Giles stepped around me and helped me down where the path dipped suddenly. "Does your father have any other mirrors?"

"One more, but it's no toy. The De—"

Gabriella stepped to me and whispered, "Look over there."

My eyes followed the direction of her pointing finger. A doe stared at us from among the trees. She raised her white tail and bounded gracefully away, leading our way down to the lake's edge.

❧

The next few days were quiet and uneventful. Giles and Papa left us for a week to attend a meeting in a nearby city. It was mid-afternoon when they returned. A servant fetched me from my room and then left me to find my sisters, neither of whom, she remarked, were in their rooms. As I descended the stairs, it occurred to me that Gabriella might be in the library, as she had been when my uncle and aunt arrived.

I rapped on the library door before swinging it open. My hand tightened around the metal knob as I looked on the scene before me.

Gabriella, curled up in a comfortable chair, held the Demandez à Voir mirror close to her smiling face. "What happened then?" she asked of the mirror.

"Gabriella, whatever are you doing? You know we aren't supposed to use the mirror for entertainment."

Her head jerked up, and she made as if to conceal the mirror with her shawl. Her shawl fell from her lap to the floor instead, uncovering the mirror. A blush overtook her cheeks, and she blurted out, "Oh, Alexandria, you don't think he's so unsuitable, do you?"

My mouth fell open. Gabriella had been watching Marcel? She'd been disappearing at this time every day for a while now, hadn't she?

I finally found my voice, as well as a new respect for the mirror's power. "Have you been communicating with Lord Ellsworth using the mirror?"

Nodding slowly, she picked up the shawl and then arranged it neatly on her lap before looking up at me. She nodded again, more firmly this time. "I missed him so much that, a few weeks after he left, I asked the mirror to show him to me. He was sitting in a chair holding a mirror rather like this one." A sparkle lit her eyes and she held up the Demandez à Voir mirror. "He was turning it over in his hands as if deciding whether or not to look in it. I don't know why, but I called his name." Giggling, she hugged the mirror to her chest. "He heard me, Alexandria! He nearly dropped the mirror in fright. I don't know how, but the two mirrors allow us to hear one another. We talk every day now."

Uncurling her legs, she sat up straight in the chair, her merry gaze becoming intent. "But you didn't answer my question. You said nothing at the family conference when everyone else was degrading him and scolding me. You don't think so poorly of him, do you?"

A strange sickness washed over me. Why did she have to ask a question whose answer would pain us both?

"Gabriella, you know the family standards and expectations. I hate to disappoint you, but I agree with the others. He is not suited to our family."

She drew back. "How can you say that? There's nothing lacking in his intelligence or his character. He is as wonderful a person as I've ever met. You'll think better of him once you know him more."

Wonderful? Awkward and little more than plain were all I could say for him. And I had no reason to suppose I would ever see him again.

"You're not still pining over that scarecrow are you, Gabriella?" Eva startled us both as she slipped past me into the room. "You are a strange one. Aunt Helene says the Floraison blood is watered down in you. Maybe she's right. After all, you're the only reputable person who thinks highly of Marcel Ellsworth."

I grimaced at Eva's statement. At seventeen, she was very impressionable and spent far too much time with Aunt Helene, who even I recognized as proud and unfeeling. Aunt Helene, the family leader of the crusade against unsuitable young men, had at one time disapproved of Papa marrying Mama because of her differing eye colors, though Mama was remarkably beautiful and gracious. But, in Eva's defense, she wasn't intentionally hurtful, just thoughtless.

"Why should I care what Aunt Helene thinks?" Gabriella's face shone as red as a robin's breast. "Prince Giles thinks highly of Marcel, and I consider him to be a better judge than any Floraison, especially that busybody Aunt Helene!" Gabriella thrust the mirror at me and stormed out of the room.

What was Marcel to Giles?

"I don't understand her." Eva flopped into a chair. "How can she think of Marcel with someone like Prince Giles around? Aunt Helene will be disappointed. She thought she had cured Gabriella of this foolish, youthful fancy."

My fingers tightened around the mirror's handle, and I glared at my youngest sister. "Leave Aunt Helene out of this. I'll worry about Gabriella." Aunt Helene wasn't going to harass Gabriella any more if I could help it. But how?

CHAPTER 4

A LEXANDRIA, DEAR." PAPA stopped me as I passed his study. He and Giles stood just inside the doorway. "Prince Giles suggested a walk to the village. Won't you come with us? I know how you love walking—and you won't have to slow your pace for us."

"Please do." Giles stepped forward. "It's a beautiful morning for a walk, and I'm sure you will find mingling with the villagers enlightening."

A walk to the village? To mingle with the scratched clay pots that lived there? My family never visited the village, except for an occasional shopping excursion. What interest could Giles or Papa have in it? Out of curiosity, I decided to accompany them.

"If you promise not to lag behind, I'll join you," I replied with a teasing smile.

"Anything for the company of a lovely young woman." Papa tucked my arm under his.

The threat of the common vessels awaiting me in the village didn't spoil my trip there. The weather was pleasant, the exercise refreshing, and the company delightful. Papa was full of information. I always enjoyed listening to him, and Giles proved to be more than commonly knowledgeable and humorous. I was sad to reach the village and lose their attention.

The villagers were surprised to see us, but they treated us politely in their simple fashion, doffing their caps and saying, "Lovely morning, ain't it, Your Grace?"

I said very little. Bad grammar always gave me a headache, not to mention the eyesore of drably dressed, sunburned women and weather-beaten men with dirty hands.

Giles, on the other hand, seemed quite at ease and conversed merrily with the baker, a farmer, a tinker, the innkeeper, and an outgoing peasant girl with two frizzy, brown braids and a multitude of freckles. Papa followed all the conversations with interest but rarely joined in.

We were about to leave the village when someone caught Giles's attention. At first I thought he waved to a beech tree, but then I noticed the beech gave shade to a bench on which rested an old woman in a worn dress.

"Mrs. Potter! How are you today?" Giles addressed her with the warmth of an old friend.

"Fair to middling, Your Highness, though I'm doing all the better for seeing you." She rose and took the hand he offered her. Her teeth were as yellow as a lemon.

"Mrs. Potter, may I have the honor of introducing to you the Duke of Henly, Alfred Floraison, and his amiable daughter, the Lady Alexandria?"

No one had ever introduced me as amiable before. Beautiful and charming, yes, but just amiable, never. That epithet was reserved for plain women with nothing to recommend them beyond the ability to smile when someone looked their way.

"I'm pleased to meet you, Your Grace. Your ladyship." The old woman gave a faltering curtsy.

"It's a pleasure to meet you, Mrs. Potter," Papa replied.

I returned her curtsy, though mine was much more graceful.

"Is your rheumatism any better?" Giles asked her.

"Aye, it's much improved. Thank you kindly for asking, Your Highness. I've been taking your advice. It's been a world of help."

"That's wonderful, Mrs. Potter," Giles said.

After a few more comments and inquiries, we parted.

"What an unpleasant creature," Papa remarked when we were out of earshot.

"I beg your pardon. 'What an unpleasant *looking* creature,'" Giles responded. "She has a charming personality. I find her friendly and amusing, despite the shortcomings of her appearance."

After a moment of thought, Papa slowly nodded his head. "It was only her appearance that was repulsive. Her conversation was not of an intellectual bent but kind-hearted." He walked on quietly, his chin dipping in that manner peculiar to him when his concentration was not on his surroundings.

While Papa assimilated whatever thought had struck him, Giles leaned toward me and said, with a grin, "Be careful, Lady Alexandria, a smile might break that pure porcelain face of yours. You wouldn't want to crack up in front of these common vessels, would you?"

I gave him a severe look. I had suspected it before, but I was now certain—the "amiable" comment had been satirical.

"What is it about this woman that offends you so? Has she been rude to you? Has she not shown you enough attention?"

"Her yellow teeth," I replied, curtly.

He arched an eyebrow and smiled, as if unconvinced. When I didn't elaborate, he looked at me intently. Those blue eyes seemed to search my very heart. I'm not sure what he found, but an expression of sadness, mixed with frustration, clouded his face.

"I'm sorry. What have we been talking about?" Papa asked as he came out of his reverie.

"We were speaking on the subject of beauty," Giles said. "Believe it or not, my grandfather was uncommonly unpleasant looking when my grandmother first met him. He was hairy with pointy teeth, terrible manners, and an extremely unsociable disposition."

Papa chuckled. "She cleaned him up and turned him into quite a handsome and charming prince before she married him, no doubt?"

Giles laughed. "You're exactly right. She did just that."

❧

My fingers trailed along the fountain's edge as I rambled through the gardens a few days later. The stone was cool and slightly rough under my fingertips. It seemed a fitting comparison to my relationship with Giles of late. He didn't think very highly of me, I was sure of it, but I would admit no wrongdoing.

An ache weighed on my chest, and I sank onto the wrought iron bench beside the fountain. If he didn't have the sense to value a Floraison, what was it to me? When did I ever care about the opinions of others?

I pushed off the bench and strode toward the rose garden, snagging a petite leaf from the hedge lining the walk. I picked at the leaf, tearing it into strips.

But it was something to me. More than I cared to admit. I valued his opinion. That he could see my beauty, laugh with me in witty conversation, admire the house and grounds—evidence of our family's wealth and status—and not be satisfied, stung. I did not understand him.

I flung the shredded leaf aside. Just because my grandmother's clippings concerned the Floraison family and the Bête family didn't mean that I, as her namesake, would marry into the Bête family as she had the Floraison. It was a ridiculous notion. Giles had such un-Floraison-like ideas, after all.

Yet I'd never met a more attractive man, or a more enjoyable companion.

Sighing, I wrapped my hand around a slender rosebud on the vine scaling the garden wall. I didn't know whether to win this prince's heart or ignore him like a bug-eaten flower.

Did he even care what I thought of him?

The buzz of bees' wings broke my musings, and I stepped away from the wall to better take in this particular chamber of the garden. Roses climbed the walls and over arbors and grew in dense bushes. And all were covered with tight green buds, all enchanted by my parents to be in full bloom on my birthday, a week away. It was the loveliest gift they could give their lovely daughter they said.

I drew in a deep breath of the lavender-scented air. It would be beautiful. My shawl slipped off my shoulder, and as I straightened it, a hint of color peeking out from one of the buds brought a smile. What would this chamber, all the garden, look like when all of the roses, plus the many other flowers, were in bloom?

With an effort, I left my concerns behind and strolled through the gardens, stopping often to search the buds for gaps in the green coverings hoping to discover the color of the developing blossoms.

As I dawdled at the crossing of two paths, lacing a stray vine into the lattice of the arbor soon to be covered in flat-faced white blossoms, a deep blue suddenly invaded my view. I stepped back, instinctively raising my hand to cover my heart, for the foolish thing was fluttering like a leaf in a spring gale. My gaze traveled from the gold buttons of the elegant blue jacket before me to the handsome face I wasn't certain I wanted to see.

"I do beg your pardon, Lady Alexandria." Giles tipped his hat. "People really should whistle before going around sharp corners like that, especially if they walk as fast as I do." The concern in his eyes was every bit as attractive as the teasing light that so often entered them.

Be sensible, Alexandria. He's talking to you.

"Your father received a letter on a business matter that required his immediate attention," his lips curved ever so slightly, "which, in case you're wondering, is why I'm roaming around frightening young ladies."

I forced my hand down to my side and straightened my shoulders. "You are mistaken, Prince Giles. You didn't frighten me. I just didn't expect to meet anyone on this path."

He regarded me for a moment. "You've been avoiding me lately. Why?"

My hand scrunched the fabric of my gown. "Nonsense. Why would I avoid you?"

"That's what I want to know."

My fingers grabbed another handful of my gown, and I was forced to give myself a mental shake. *A Floraison does not lose her composure.* I stretched my fingers, smoothed my crinkled gown, and met Giles's gaze. "I've been busy helping Mama entertain my cousins."

"They've been here as long as I have. Why this sudden interest?"

"I felt guilty for not spending much time with them. They are my cousins, after all, and are to leave soon after my birthday."

My answer seemed to please him, for he smiled warmly. "Take a walk with me."

The confident way he said it, not asked it, piqued, and

tempted my pride to say, "No, thank you," and walk independently back inside. But Giles didn't give it the opportunity. Before I could reply, he slipped my arm through his and pulled me along with him down the garden path. He kept up the conversation by himself for several minutes, not allowing me the opportunity to excuse myself. The desire to do so soon blended with the greenery and was forgotten.

When we reached the sunken garden walk he slowed his pace, and we strolled through it wondering aloud what made it such an enchanting spot.

A rose-covered bridge arched over our path. Heavily laden vines floated gracefully above us. A bit of deep crimson in a fat bud caught my eye. I captured the bud as it moved in the breeze and stroked the sliver of silky petal no longer hidden by its rough, green guardian. "This one is a bit further along than its sisters."

Giles cocked his head and studied the vines and then the rose bushes near the path, all covered in tight buds. He whispered "oh" as if remembering Gabriella's comment about our enchanted roses.

Smiling at him, I released the bud back to the breeze. "Yes. They do this for me every year. I enjoy watching the progress of the buds almost as much as the sight of them all in full bloom."

He looked up at the sky with its fast-moving clouds and then removed a penknife from his pocket and cut the plump bud from the vine. "I believe it's going to rain for the next couple of days, and there's no sense in you getting wet checking your roses when you can keep one with you." He broke off the thorns and handed the bud to me.

"It's lovely, Prince Giles. Thank you." I unpinned my grandmother's cameo brooch and used it to attach the rose to my shawl. Made especially for my grandmother, the cameo was a rose in bloom instead of a woman's profile.

We left the gardens and rambled for a while, ending up in a flower-filled meadow. Daisies, goldenrod, bee balm, and other wild beauties bowed and rose in the wind. I picked a couple of daisies, relishing the feel of their soft petals. "These are Mama's favorite wildflower."

"She has excellent taste. Do you often pick her bouquets?"

"Only occasionally." I added a golden sunflower to my collection.

Giles handed me another. "My sister once told me I had no talent for picking bouquets. She seemed to think pinecones, clover, and dandelions did not make a lovely arrangement." His blue eyes twinkled. "My mother liked it."

I couldn't help but grin at the image of a young Giles proudly handing his mother that bouquet. "Of course, she would."

"Do you think one's skills improve with age? Do you think your mother would like a bouquet I picked?"

"It's possible." I smiled archly. "There are no pinecones here."

"That's a great comfort. I feel confident already. In fact, if we both picked her a bouquet, I think mine would be lovelier than yours."

"I doubt that."

"We shall see."

We raced around the meadow searching for the best of its flowers. I spotted an attractive lobelia and was about to pick it, thinking how well its spiky form and blue flowers would contrast with my goldenrod and daisies, when I noticed I was not alone in admiring the plant.

Lying on one of the lobelia's trumpet-shaped blooms, with the tips of its folded wings touching the stem and its body resting on the flower, was the finest midnight moon moth I had ever seen. It lay motionless, not a hint of movement in its soft body or along the velvety black tips of its golden wings. It saddened me to behold so gorgeous a creature so still, as if it were laid out dead upon a couch of blue.

"Poor little thing," Giles said as he walked up beside me.

In the vain hope the moth was only caught, I unpinned my rose and used its stem to nudge the moth's wings away from the lobelia's central stem. The little moth fluttered its wings, rose into the air, and danced away in delight for its freedom. My heart joined in its rejoicing.

"Oh, Prince Giles, it's alive." I believe I may have actually clapped my hands, and possibly given a little—but only a very little—hop.

Giles laughed and called me "the noble rescuer of the moth."

My cheeks grew warm at my little jubilee. "I hate to see beautiful things dead or trapped."

"I hope you hate to see poor, ugly things in that condition as well." He spoke in a jesting manner, but somehow I felt it was a sincere wish that had accidentally slipped out. I was the defender of the beautiful and the perfect. He was the defender of the ugly and the imperfect and wanted me to be too.

The rose fell from my hand as I saw Giles clearly for the first time. My happy mood shattered into dozens of sharp, shiny fragments, each one reflecting a memory: Giles silently admonishing me for not talking to the old woman, Giles suggesting a walk to the village to talk to the peasants and then calling them pleasant and charming, Gabriella declaring Giles a friend of Marcel's, Giles paying me flattering attentions—me, the eldest daughter and the one most likely to have influence with Papa.

The razor-sharp fragments cut my heart. And my pride. Giles had come to our house on Marcel's behalf, to convince us to approve of him as Gabriella's suitor. He wasn't interested in learning from Papa or in getting to know me.

Giles picked up the rose and held it out to me.

I took it from him and pinned it to my shawl, which I pulled closer. A chill came over me from the inside out. "I despise lowly things. Let's return to the house."

❧

I shut myself in my room and curled up in my favorite chair. A tiny part of me wanted to throw myself on the bed and cry, but the rest of me scorned that foolish, overly romantic part of myself. I needed to think, not weep. Giles Bête's visit was nothing more than subterfuge, and I didn't want him around anymore. He was here on Marcel's behalf, so if Gabriella voluntarily and irrevocably cast off Marcel, Giles would have no reason to stay. I had said I would do something about that situation. Well, I wasn't going to put it off any longer. But how could I convince her to give him up? His unsuitableness, his lack of poise, and his plain face hadn't hindered her forming an attachment to him.

I couldn't imagine it happening, but what if another woman showed an interest in him? Would Gabriella respond in anger and accuse him of encouraging it? Possibly. Or the twinge of jealousy might prove how dear he was to her.

I wrapped my arms around my waist, hugging myself, trying to quiet the ache in my chest. My eyes fastened on the bouquet resting on my dressing table. I'd forgotten to give it to Mama. I didn't know the fire of jealousy, but I was beginning to understand the pain of deception.

I fell into a sleep of vivid dreams. I stood amidst the shrubbery on a castle lawn. A dark-haired man paced the drive. Giles. Must he haunt even my dreams?

I stepped forward, eager to take him to task for lying to me, but catching sight of a hideous old woman on the drive, I retreated to the shrubbery lest he force me to converse with her.

Running my hand along the smooth shaft of my wand, I waited as the woman shuffled forward.

"Forgive me, Your Highness." The woman's voice was as cracked as parched earth. "I'm exhausted from a long journey and lack of proper food. Might I warm myself by the fire in your kitchen and spend the night there? I will gladly do whatever I can to repay you for a little hospitality and food."

"Let a repulsive creature like you in my home? Not for a sack of golden crowns." The sneer on Giles's face made me grimace.

What had come over him? Where was his unaccountable fondness for the ugly and lowly?

Undeterred, the hag offered him a rose—the one Giles had given me earlier. "Not even for the beauty of an enchanted rose?"

"An enchanted rose? It was spirited out of someone's garden, no doubt." Giles looked away and impatiently tapped his whip against his leg.

She stared at him and then straightened her shoulders as much as a crooked old woman could. "There are two kinds of beauty, Your Highness; beware which one you treasure, for lasting beauty lies within." She took a step forward, her disgracefully muddy shoes showing under her shabby dress. "Will you not help me?"

"Why do you bother me so, old hag? Be gone." He swiveled to face the castle. "Where is that blasted man with my horse?"

Would it be so difficult for him to order his servants to give her a glass of water and a loaf of bread before sending her away?

The wand flared hot in my hand, as did the desire for justice in my heart. No, not so much a desire as a command. Trembling, I looked from the wand to the old hag to the handsome prince. The memory of another hag, this one near a stream, came to mind, and I shifted uncomfortably.

Certainly the prince could have been more charitable, but,

obviously, he was in a hurry. What was the woman doing accosting him anyway? The ugly thing should have gone to the kitchen to ask the servants instead of bothering the prince. The prince, undoubtedly, meant for her to ask *them* for assistance.

I shoved my wand into its pocket in the folds of my dress.

I ate dinner quietly, pretending to be oblivious to Giles's attempts to catch my attention.

"You've been silent, Alexandria." Gabriella studied me from across the table. "Aren't you feeling well?"

I made an effort to smile and was pleased by the result. Curving my lips into a happy expression actually lifted my spirits a little. "I am well. I took a nap this afternoon and simply haven't woken completely."

She accepted my answer with an understanding nod, and I looked past her to the mirror hanging on the wall. In it, I could see everyone seated at the table. Giles was leaning toward Papa, intent on whatever Papa was saying. He seemed genuinely interested and respectful, but, as he'd said before, "Reflections aren't always what they seem."

The dining room door swished open, and Cook peeped in, sighing when she saw Giles. My eyes flitted between her, Giles, and Gabriella. *Reflections ... Frederick and the mirror.*

Endeavoring to appear normal, I added in a word here and there to my neighbors' conversations, but my mind was busily engaged elsewhere. It appeared I had a use for my powers after all—to separate Gabriella and Marcel and rid myself of an unwanted prince.

Eva knocked on my door as I was putting the finishing touches on my plan that night.

"Why the secret conference, Alexandria?" She came in and shut the door softly behind her.

"What would you do if you saw the man you thought was in love with you walking hand-in-hand with a beautiful woman wearing an engagement ring?" I pushed aside a few pillows and sat at the head of my bed and motioned for Eva to join me.

"I'd assume he'd played me for a fool and would break off the acquaintance immediately. Why?" Eva stretched across the foot of my bed.

"Because that's why Gabriella is going to sever her friendship with Marcel."

She gaped at me. "Marcel's engaged? Surely, there aren't two women—"

"No, but we can make Gabriella think that the same way Frederick made Cook believe Lady Tannon's cook always served custard for lunch, only we'll use the Demandez à Voir mirror."

Eva sat up and wrapped her hands around the bedpost. "We couldn't possibly enchant the Demandez à Voir mirror to do that."

"Why not?"

"Because …" She paused and then shrugged her shoulders. "I don't know. Papa treats it as an extra-special mirror. I'm afraid to touch it. Plus, as Papa says, it's been terribly cranky since its mate disappeared seventy years ago."

"Eva, do you know the reason Prince Giles is here?"

"To be mentored by Papa. Why?"

"That's not the real reason. He's here on Marcel's behalf, to soften us toward those not matching our standards."

Her eyes went wide. "Are you certain?"

"Yes. You remember Gabriella declaring that Giles thinks

highly of Marcel, don't you? And isn't Giles constantly encouraging us to talk to the villagers?"

Eva sat in thought, her fingers rubbing the decorative carvings on my bedpost. When she spoke, her voice was sad, but tinged with anger. "I believe you're correct. I've always felt that Giles and Gabriella had some sort of understanding. Now I know what." Eva looked with doubtful eyes at the ordinary handheld mirror on my dressing table. "But tampering with the Demandez à Voir mirror could be difficult."

"We can manage." My heart ached at the thought of the pain it would cause Gabriella, but it was for her own good. If we didn't succeed, Aunt Helene was sure to find out somehow, and Gabriella would be subjected to another of her "family conferences" and then forbidden from ever speaking to Marcel again. The former scenario would leave her brokenhearted for a while; the latter would leave her brokenhearted and pining for who knew how long, for she had a loyal heart. "I'll deal with the mirror. I need you to write a detailed description of the scene we are to conjure."

The next morning Eva and I ascertained that everyone was occupied outside or in some other part of the house and then stole away to the library. Ignoring the sinking feeling in my stomach, I used my key to open the drawer where the mirror was kept and slowly picked it up. The rose-decorated back felt cool against my hand, but the sensation did little to calm me. It was a lovely mirror. Lovely and powerful.

Why hadn't it disappeared along with its mate? Why take one and leave the other? A nervous laugh tickled my throat. Perhaps I should ask it to show me the Magic Collectors? If one believed the legends, then they were, in all probability, behind the mirror's vanishing act. Enchanted objects often found their way into the Magic Collectors' keeping to be a source of power they could wield. They had no powers of their own, as we enchanters and the evil sorcerers did. Oddly enough, it was the few tales and the many conjectures about the mysterious Magic Collectors—rather than the stories of sorcerers and the enchanters who defeated them—that captured my attention as a child.

I shook my head and scolded myself back to the present. Eva and I chose seats in the corner of the room and then began tampering with the mirror. In other words, I requested the image of Marcel, told it the image it showed was incorrect, and described the image I wanted it to show—that of Marcel walking hand-in-hand with a beautiful woman wearing a diamond-encrusted ring on her ring finger. After many repetitions, our image appeared whenever Marcel's was requested.

The next day was long and anxious. Eva and I checked the mirror several times. I cringed each time Gabriella left my sight, fearing she would seek out the mirror and yet hoping to have it over with. Once, I almost decided to clear the mirror of its false reflection, but Aunt Helene came to visit us, and I hated to think what she would say if she found out about Gabriella and Marcel's secret communication. This trick of mine would hurt Gabriella, but it would be better for her in the long run.

After Aunt Helene left, it began to rain. Eva and I retired to the sitting room to knit. Giles joined us a few minutes later and, without saying much, settled down with a book.

Rain splattered on the window. The winding race of the droplets down it entertained me until I noticed a movement in the reflections loaning color to the glass.

Giles shifted in his chair and looked at my reflection. "How are your roses getting along, Lady Alexandria?"

I glanced at the bud still pinned to my shawl, a delicate, lacy shawl I often wore because I was fond of it, rather than because I was cold. The enchanted flower had lost its green covering and pointed tip and was now a plump collection of dark crimson petals, all huddled together with their tips curved out ever so slightly, as if each petal were awaiting the sign to take a graceful backwards dive.

"It's coming along splendidly," I replied to his image in the window and then focused on my knitting.

"Giles! Giles." The cry preceded Gabriella into the room. She clutched the Demandez à Voir mirror to her chest as she ran to him.

His book slapped the floor as he sprang up and took hold of her arm. "Gabriella, whatever is the matter?"

"He—" She suddenly glanced at us, as if finally realizing we were there, and then pressed her lips together and faced Giles again. "Is Marcel engaged?"

Guilt pricked my heart at the tears threatening to streak Gabriella's cheeks. She blinked hard against them.

"What? My cousin isn't engaged to anyone. Where did you hear that? Did he send you a letter telling you that?"

His cousin. That explained his meddling.

"No, I saw him, or them really, in the mirror. Who is she?" Gabriella handed Giles the mirror, her voice hardening in anger.

He turned the mirror over in his hand and ran his fingers along the silver roses. "You have a Demandez à Voir mirror?"

"Yes, it's how we communicate."

"Mirror to mirror?"

"Yes."

Giles frowned. "I should have known nothing so ordinary, so common, as post or carrier pigeon would be used by this family."

Gabriella tapped the mirror. "You just tell it who you wish to see."

No. I clutched the arm of my chair. My tongue stuck to the roof of my mouth and refused to say anything to prevent him.

"I know how it works." Giles positioned the mirror so both he and Gabriella could see it. "Show me Marcel." His eyes widened, and he glanced from the mirror to Gabriella and then back to the mirror. He clenched his jaw. "I don't believe it. I've never seen this woman before. Mar—"

"I knew it." Gabriella grabbed his arm. "Marcel's far too honorable to do such a thing. He's been bewitched, I'm sure. This … this"—she jabbed a finger at the mirror—"woman has the look of magic about her, and Marcel's walk is too fast and strutting. Something is dreadfully wrong. We must save him, Giles."

Giles squeezed Gabriella's hand and took another look in the mirror. "Something's not right, I agree, but I'm not sure what. Marcel loves you, Gabriella, and he's not the type to lose his head over every attractive woman he meets. Enough, mirror." Giles lowered the mirror to his side. Brow furrowed, he looked up, his gaze sliding over Eva and me as he seemingly searched the room for an answer. His eyes quickly found their way back to us.

Eva was as pale as a snowdrop. I stood beside her, wringing my hands, torn between the desire to comfort Gabriella and a sense of guilt for being the cause of her distress.

A strange expression came over Giles's face. He turned his gaze back to the mirror. "Show me Marcel." He narrowed his eyes, shot a glance at us, and handed the mirror to Gabriella. "Is this what you saw earlier?"

"Yes, it's as if they've been walking in circles, and we always come in at the same spot."

Giles pointed at the image in the mirror. "They're not walking in circles, and she's not walking at all."

There was anger in his blue eyes, and, unfortunately, they were fastened on me. I stood straighter and returned his gaze with defiance. I had done this for Gabriella, and no one, in the family at least, would disapprove of the anticipated result.

He held the mirror out to me. "Ask it to show you Marcel."

I crossed my arms. "What else do you expect to see? The mirror obviously wants everyone to see that scene."

"Are you sure it's not what you want us to see?" He thrust the mirror at me again.

"Take the mirror, Alexandria." Papa's stern voice sent a bolt of fear through me. When had he and Mama entered the room?

I uncrossed my arms and forced my hand to accept the offending mirror. I might as well have been accepting a blindfold for my execution.

"Ask to see Marcel. The real Marcel," Papa commanded.

I gripped the mirror tightly, feeling the weight of everyone's eyes upon me. Giles's clenched jaw said he was still furious with me, though there was a strange expression of foreboding in his eyes. Mama watched me anxiously as she held a comforting arm around Gabriella. Eva, trembling as she sat, glanced frantically between Papa and me. Papa's look was the worst, for he wore the look of a parent disappointed in the child he loves. There was also a sense of resignation about him, as if some doom were approaching and he could do nothing about it.

I took courage and held up the mirror. "Show me Marcel." My invented image appeared.

"Again," Papa ordered.

"Show me Marcel." The same image appeared, and I held it out to him. Maybe they would believe the image now or think the mirror was playing games on us all.

"Again."

Or maybe they wouldn't. There was no hope of escape for me. "Show me Marcel. No, not that. He should be sitting indoors near another mirror." I admitted my guilt slowly, repeating the request two more times before I beheld Marcel's lanky figure hunched over a desk on which lay a handheld mirror. Unable to bear the tension any longer, I threw the mirror onto the seat of one of the thickly cushioned chairs. "Here's what you want to see."

Gabriella scooped up the mirror, glanced at it, and then back at me with confusion on her face.

Papa looked at me sadly. "Child, do you know what you have done? You have forced the mirror to lie and used it for a deceitful purpose. The Demandez à Voir mirror is not an ordinary mirror, not even an ordinary enchanted mirror."

His words hung in the air. Giles's foreboding look and Papa's depressed countenance began to make sense. Misuse of the mirror must result in punishment. But what kind of punishment?

Gabriella screamed and threw the mirror onto the chair's seat. Its silver surface, where Marcel's image should have been, was now black, but not a solid, smooth black like polished ebony. It was a threatening, swirling black, like a mass of thunderclouds driven by a furious wind.

My heart trembled as the mirror's surface churned and a mass of black smoke tumbled over its silver lip and cascaded to the floor, slowly rolling toward Eva and me. The distance wasn't far, but time seemed to expand that short space into miles. I felt like a queen waiting as the Black Death moved through her city house by house, knowing the castle gate could not keep it out. Like her, I saw destruction approaching but could do nothing but wait for it to reach me.

And so I waited. Its leading edge swirled as some invisible breeze blew against it and divided it in two. One half curled away toward Eva and the other slithered toward me. Eva, her knuckles white from clutching the arms of her chair, looked more frightened than I thought anyone could ever look. I pitied her and feared for her as well as for myself. It would reach her before it did me.

"Stop," I heard myself saying. "It was I who commanded the mirror to lie. Leave her out of this. It was my doing."

The darkness stopped near Eva's chair as if considering. Then, it slowly withdrew and re-gathered itself into one and continued toward me. Over the thumping of my heart, I heard Papa beg it to reconsider and tell it I was only young and foolish and had meant no real harm. But it ignored him and curled about my feet and began to twine about my skirts. I broke my gaze from it and took a last look on my family and Giles. Horror and helplessness were carved into their pale faces. As darkness blotted out my vision, I heard someone cry out my name with an anguish and despair I'd never before heard in it.

"Alexandria!"

CHAPTER 5

Aᴸᴸ ᵂᴬˢ ᴮᴸᴬᶜᴷ and cold. A rushing noise broke the silence as the darkness with its cold fingers took hold of me. It dragged me down, down, down. Its grasp grew painfully tight and sharp, and I felt as if I were being torn apart and rearranged piece by piece with each piece replaced opposite of its normal location.

Over the rush and the pain I heard voices—one arguing, the other decided.

"But she tampered with the mirror. You know the punishment for that," said a voice that sounded flat, but not in the unemotional sense.

"Yes, but she was willing to take all the consequences to save the other girl," replied an airy voice.

"You saw her haughty look of defiance. She's not repentant."

"She will suffer, but justice will be tempered with mercy. She has been given a task to perform, as you well know. Her fate will be tied to his as his will be forever changed by hers."

"Oh, very well," sighed the first voice.

The rushing noise died down during the conversation.

Though I was no longer being pulled apart and put back together like the decorations on a hat, I felt completely backwards and rather flat. I looked around and tried to find the speakers, but I couldn't see anything. Then, the rushing sound began again, and I once more went through the painful sensation of being separated and having my parts put back together, only this time they were put back in their proper places.

"No, not like that. I gave you the instructions," the airy voice said.

The flat voice grumbled, and I was mashed and smoothed like a lump of clay being formed into a figurine by a potter with very large hands.

"Won't she be surprised," the flat voice said with a chuckle.

My world flipped upside down, and I fell through the nothingness.

❦

I woke stiff and sore, my experience a vague memory that felt more like a fantastic dream than an actual occurrence. Sunlight sprinkled down on me through the red and orange leaves of an unfamiliar forest. Closing my eyes, I listened to the birds twittering overhead.

So I hadn't been killed or made a prisoner of the mirror. No granting wishes like the genie or answering questions like "Who is the fairest one of all?" My lips curled into a smile, and I breathed in the soothing smells of tree bark and rich earth. My punishment seemed to be no more than a long walk home and the missing of my birthday celebration. The explanations for my absence would be most embarrassing.

Men's voices carried to me on the breeze. How would I get home? I scrambled up and followed the sound, but instead of finding someone who could show me the way, the trees grew thicker around me, and the voices faded into whispers in the wind.

I continued on, panic hurrying my steps as limb after limb slapped me. At last, I came to a stream and was about to quench my thirst when voices again came to me through the woods, only this time I distinguished several speakers. Forgetting my thirst, I pushed through the laurels lining the stream and followed its edge toward the men. The shrubbery suddenly stopped, and I rejoiced as my feet hit a dirt road. Not twenty yards in front of me four young men joked around as they led a heavily laden mule down the road.

So intent on the men was I that I forgot to watch my step. One foot hit a rock. The other sunk into something damp, thick, and slippery. I screamed and fell headlong into a mud puddle.

The men raced to where I lay and pulled me to my feet. "What's the matter, mother? Did a bear or wild hog chase you out of the woods? Where is it?"

Mother! I wasn't some old woman that they should call me that.

I wiped some of the mess off my face. "I'm covered in mud. I can't show myself in town like this." I sounded petulant even to myself.

One of the men sneered at me. "She's mighty particular about her appearance for an old hag."

"Aye, scaring us half to death with a scream like she's dying just because of a little mud," said another.

I clenched my fist. Old hag! I might not have been looking my best after the hike and the mud bath, but I certainly wasn't an old hag. Why were these men so insulting? I glowered at them. "Where's the nearest town where I might rent a horse or carriage?"

They stared wide-eyed at me and then pointed down the

road in the direction from which they had come. "The town's about a mile that way."

I nodded in reply and marched back to the stream. A rickety wooden bridge stretched across it.

The men's laughter followed me. "She's funny in the head all right, but she's healthy enough. She'll make it to town okay."

Kneeling beside the stream, I washed the mud off my hands. I gasped at the chilly water and then choked at the sight of my skin. I jerked up my sleeves and scrubbed my arms and face again, a sick feeling in my stomach. Hadn't the voice in the darkness snickered "Won't she be surprised?"

Let it be my imagination. Please, let it be my imagination.

My heart slowed as I looked at my hands and arms again. My skin was tight and rough and covered with ugly brown sunspots and disfigured by moles and protruding veins. I leaned over the water and touched my cheek. The reflection of an old woman with wrinkled skin, a crooked nose, a hideous wart on her forehead, and grizzled hair poked her cheek.

I reeled back.

This was the revenge of the mirror—to turn me into an old hag. Black spots danced before my eyes, and I knew nothing for some time.

When I regained consciousness, my first thought was of longing for a hug from my mother. But she had vanished with my youth and beauty. I pulled a threadbare handkerchief from my handbag and cringed at the sight of the coarse gray dress and scuffed boots I wore. Instinctively, I pulled my cloak closer about me. Was that a patch? Was there no way to hide my disgraceful attire?

I pushed the cloak back toward my shoulders. A bit of color captured my eye. The rose Giles gave me rested snugly between a gaudy, silver-and-red rose blossom pin and my cloak. I glared at it. How had it and the pin remained free of dust and mud? Mama and Papa would know how its enchantment worked …

I wiped my eyes and struggled back to my aged feet. *A Floraison does not wallow in self-pity.* I resolved not to think about loneliness or my condition, or to glance into anything reflective. Surely my parents could undo the spell when I returned home.

I brushed off the dried mud as well as I could and made my way back to the road and followed it in the direction the men had indicated. The outline of a village came into view, and it occurred to me I would need money for food and traveling expenses. A quick inventory revealed my jewelry had vanished or been replaced by cheap substitutes, as in the case of the pin holding my rose. My wand, as I suspected it would be, was also gone. My handbag was empty except for some coins, and there were barely enough to create a jingle. I had never bought food at a village market before, but I doubted my few coins would get me much.

❦

The village was even smaller than the one near Henly Manor. There was little to tempt me to spend my scant funds unwisely. No novelty shops or pastry shops or bookshops. I did manage to find a small bakery, which doubled as a primitive restaurant. In addition to bread, they sold cheese and ale. Careful to maintain a safe distance, I walked up behind a dirty, roguish-looking man—a pig farmer if my nose was any judge—standing at the counter. He ordered a loaf of bread, a small hunk of cheese, and a large glass of ale. His bill was slightly more than what my purse could handle. I ordered a small loaf of bread and a small hunk of cheese. I sighed as I walked away. It was poor fair indeed for a Floraison. Oh, how I longed for creamy butter and sweet meats and fruits.

Nonetheless, my stomach was glad of the few morsels, which I washed down with water I pumped from the village well. After I ate, I rested beside the well and watched the villagers. Did any of them possess a map, either physical or mental, of whatever land in which I now traveled?

After a few minutes of observation, despair shrouded my hopes like clouds the sky on a stormy day. None who passed me had the look of a well-informed traveler or scholar. I doubted many of the people had been farther from their farm than this small village or maybe the next. Perhaps the owners of the general store had traveled to purchase merchandise.

I located the general store, walked in, and stood a few feet in front of the door. Nothing happened. A few people glanced at me but quickly looked away. No one rushed up to offer me a chair and ask what I desired. There were no courteous salesladies pampering me. Were the owners insane? What shop-keeper would snub the daughter of a duke?

I spun around and started for the door, but the reflection in the storefront window arrested me. They weren't snubbing a wealthy noblewoman. They were ignoring a ragged old woman who didn't have any patronage to give.

The store windows were large, enabling me to see more of my reflection—I couldn't bring myself to say "more of me"—than in the stream. I stood there several minutes, unable to look away from the revolting creature staring wide-eyed back at me. I was still Lady Alexandria Floraison, wasn't I, underneath this façade?

How would people treat me now?

An ungracious "Is there anything I can do for you?" answered my question. The shopkeeper stood beside me, though not too closely. I daresay she thought age and ugliness were contagious.

"Yes." A quick glance revealed no other patrons in the store, the obvious reason for the shopkeeper's notice of me now. A small portrait of a silver-haired king ornamented one wall. I had seen a similar one during my history lessons. I smiled. At least I was in Sonser. "I have been traveling for some time and have lost my way. What village is this and what is the name of the nearest city?"

"This is Oak Glen. Gilden is the nearest city." Her smirk implied I was a waste of her time and that she had anticipated as much.

"I've not heard of those. Do you have a map here? Or are you familiar with Florenburg?"

"We have no maps here. I suggest you go to the city and try there." She said "the city" as if Gilden were the only city and all the others bearing that label were unworthy of it.

"How do I get there?"

"Go out of the village toward the mountains and follow the signs." She put her hands on her hips and looked around the store, as if searching for a shelf to dust or something else preferable to conversing with me.

I persevered despite her lack of interest. "How long is the journey?"

"I wouldn't know. I've never been there. You'll have to excuse me. I must attend to my customers now." She strode off to greet a couple who had just entered the store.

I glared at the woman's broad back and stringy hair and left the store. Outrage at my treatment alone prevented despair from getting a firm hold on me. Instead of learning where I was and how to get home, I discovered I would have to journey many days to simply find out where I was in relation to my home. And I had no food or money for the journey. Or money to sustain myself in the village while waiting for a letter to reach home and a carriage to come for me. Not that I had money to send a message via a special courier. The common-rate post was sadly unreliable in Sonser. I kicked a pebble as I started down the street.

"Did you hear what happened to Tom coming back from the city?" asked the tallest of a group of men standing outside the store.

No, but I wanted to hear. I ducked around the corner of the building.

"He was taking a drink outta a stream when his horse got spooked by a snake. The darn horse broke free and ran off, leaving Tom stranded in the woods miles from nowhere. I told him it was dangerous to travel so far."

"How'd he make it home?"

"He walked until he got to Briary Village. Then he rented a horse."

"Aye. They say he survived by eating berries and nuts and by sleeping under a pile of leaves for warmth."

"You don't say. I'll bet his feet were mighty sore by the time he reached the village."

"His wife was pretty worried about him by the time he got home too. You see his horse got back three days before he did!"

"I've heard tell of a shortcut not far from Briary. Why didn't he take it? Maybe he could've gotten some help."

"Aye, but from the tales I've heard, he wouldn't have gotten help from him that lives there. Leastwise, no more help than the rattler gave him."

The men's chuckles faded as I left my hiding place and walked to the well. Poor Tom. But at least I'd learned how to reach the city—by foraging for nuts and berries along the way. I would rather starve than beg, but I would rather eat than starve, and now I knew how I could eat honorably.

I pumped the lever on the well until the water flowed. I took a long drink and then headed down the muddy lane toward that mysterious city, "the city," which lay at the end of the road.

I amused myself for a while by imagining what sort of city it was. It might be a city of majestic buildings, magnificent cathedrals, and rows and rows of interesting shops where the fashionable elite gathered. I would be pleased with that city. Yet, it might be a murky city with dilapidated buildings and grimy children running around crowded, stinking streets. This was probably nearer the truth. Or, just maybe, it was an exotic city filled with the smell of spices and the voices of foreigners hawking their wares above the calls of richly plumaged birds. Perhaps it was clothed by brightly colored fabrics hanging from vendors' stalls and ornamented by flower markets and gardens such as I had never seen. Maybe gardenias and roses grew on the side of the street as abundantly as weeds did here, and orchids of every variety sprouted from every crevice in the stone walls until the air hung heavy with their fragrance and the polished streets reflected their glory.

I would love to see that city. Perhaps there would be a great enchanter living there, and, on beholding me in the street, he would recognize me for who I was. He would remove my curse and restore my youth and beauty. Perhaps he would fall in love with me and I with him.

Wouldn't everyone be surprised if I returned home married to a great enchanter, the ruler of a large city? How would they react? Would they be happy for me? Would they be envious? Would they be sad to lose me to a faraway city?

Of course, Giles wouldn't care. He probably loathed me for trying to spoil his cousin's romance.

As I walked, the shadows lengthened and the sunlight dwindled, like my energy. The city of unrivaled beauty and romance became a dingy, filthy, stinking population center.

I wandered off the road into the woods to look for dinner. Avoiding a bush with bright red berries, I picked huckleberries and then cracked a few hickory nuts between two rocks. I looked at my broken nail and stained fingers with pride. Floraisons were not helpless.

In the dim light I spotted an ancient oak with great, raised roots. After moving a few twigs and acorns aside, I settled down between two of the roots. A poet once said, "A night beneath the stars with the moon as thy lamp and the grass as thy mattress is as pleasant as the first bloom of spring after a long winter." Hopefully, he hadn't exaggerated too much. Using one arm as a pillow, I lay down to sleep.

A few hours later, I awoke with a start. Light from a full moon highlighted the edges of leaves and the water dripping from the furry chin of a doe walking gracefully past me, her steps barely audible over the tree frogs and the rush of a nearby stream.

A wolf howled, and the doe bounded deeper into the woods. Why did I choose a bedroom near a popular route to a watering hole—and thus a good place to hunt?

With anxious glances and a thundering heart, I grabbed my handbag and crept back toward the road. The moon played games with me as I went, often darting behind a cloud to leave me in utter darkness and then reappearing suddenly, announcing its presence by casting eerie shadows before me.

I stepped onto the road, empty except for the cold glow of moonlight hanging in the air and glittering among the gravel. My chest tightened at the open loneliness of it. I retraced my steps to the edge of the forest and leaned against the smooth trunk of a sycamore for comfort. What could I do?

The call of a whippoorwill answered me. I looked around for a place to roost. A tree with low limbs stood a few feet away, and I walked to it.

Wouldn't everyone laugh to see me climb a tree? Especially with this old body. I raised my foot to the lowest limb and reached for a branch overhead. My arms trembled under my weight, my foot slipped, and I plummeted to the leafy ground. The wind rustled through the leaves, carrying a snickering sound with it. Even the squirrels were laughing at me. Grunting, I pushed myself to my feet and reached for the branch again. A wolf howled and leaves crunched. Five seconds later I was perched ten feet up, hugging the rough tree trunk.

⚜

The sun's rays warmed my face. Blinking, I tried to sit up. My makeshift harness jerked me to a halt, and I grabbed the trunk to steady myself. The bits of bark clinging to my hands scratched my face as I rubbed the sleep out of it. I brushed off my hands and untied my cloak from around the tree.

My muscles ached as I stepped from limb to limb until slipping and falling the last two feet to the ground. Groaning, I picked myself up and followed the sound of the stream, my skin itching for a hot, soapy bath and clean clothes. A shiver shot down my spine as I touched the frigid stream water. No bath for me. I splashed my face and arms and headed to the road, eating what I could find along the way.

"After a light and healthy breakfast of nuts and berries, the Lady Alexandria set out for a pleasant stroll in the early morning light," I said aloud as I reached the road. I wasn't entirely sure if I meant the comment to be cynical or if I was making light of the situation, but it was comforting to hear a human voice, even if it was my own. Alas, my voice was as hoarse and scratchy as, well, an old hag's.

Ahead of me, the road led high into rising mountains. My spirits lifted at the sight of the majestic trees and peaks, but my feet brought my spirits down to earth, reminding me they would pay the toll for this path.

They mumbled complaints every step that weary day, but I

Ignored them, my thoughts generally drifting from reviews of my father's botany lessons to considering how I would paint a particular scene to another trip to my imaginary, exotic city. This time I saved the city from a terrible danger, and, in gratitude, the great enchanter released me from my curse. I went home, and I never saw Giles or Marcel again.

Whenever a berry-laden bush or fallen nuts caught my eye, I stopped to eat and rest. Few travelers passed me that day, and when they did, I left the road to avoid them, as much to hide my disgraceful condition as for safety reasons. When the only sunlight was that reflected by the moon, I gathered my courage and looked about me for a place to bed down for the night. Near the forest's edge sat an abandoned wagon missing one wheel. I crawled underneath it, spread out my cloak, and lay down.

Exhausted as I was, hunger and aching muscles kept me awake, or so I told myself. "Floraisons are not weak, sniveling quitters," I said aloud, for emphasis and for company. "Other families might give up and lie weeping beside the road, but I will not." I wiped a tear from my cheek. If solely by pure pride and stubborn determination, I was going to make it home.

╋

On the third day, my journey transitioned from uncomfortable to decidedly unpleasant. Clouds obscured the sky when I awoke and by noon the earth itself was blurred by a heavy rain. The wind whipped the rain and drove it under the trees where I took shelter. *Might as well walk wet as sit wet. At least it's a warmer bath than the stream.* Sighing, I pulled the hood of my cloak down to shield my eyes and stepped back out onto the road. I was too low on supplies to lengthen my journey anyway.

I was forced to return to the forest that night for the slight shelter of a large cedar. The only other option was to sleep under a bridge, but I was too afraid the stream might swell and carry me away as I slept.

The next day I woke shivering in my undergarments. Cringing, I slipped on my dress, still cold and soggy after a night drying on a limb. Sensing it would be a useless endeavor, I gathered twigs and branches and piled them together for kindling. If only my wand hadn't vanished with my youth and beauty. I picked up two pebbles from the road and struck them together near the twigs. Fifteen minutes later, I threw the pebbles against a tree. They hit with a satisfying thud. Holding my head in my hands, I rocked back and forth until flies began to buzz around me. I swatted at them, took a deep breath, and trudged to the road.

It was riddled with muddy puddles. I smiled grimly. At least most of them were shallow. As I jumped over a large pothole, a vision of my father pulling me from one I had fallen in as a child came to mind.

I had cried as the chill water seeped through my stockings and the muddy bottom refused to release me. It made slurping noises every time I tried to raise my little booted feet. "The pothole is hungry and wants to eat you," Frederick had said. When I began to wail, Papa shushed Frederick and pulled me out. I clung to him all the way home.

Home.

My sight shifted and everything seemed a little closer to me. *Maybe this whole experience is a dream, and I am really in my comfortable chair at home.*

I shook my head and focused on the real pain of the blisters on my feet.

I soon stopped to gather nuts, using a stone against a boulder at the road's edge to crack them. The crunch of the shells couldn't cover the rumbling of my stomach or my growl of frustration as I struggled to dig the meat out of the opened shells. I tried to ignore the noises but they soon grew too loud and too much like a carriage.

A carriage?

Dropping my mid-day meal, I raced around the boulder, but I was too late to avoid the spray of muck as the carriage sped by me.

I wiped my face with my hand and shook the mud off with an angry flick of my wrist. *If they knew who I was, they would have felt privileged to convey me wherever I asked.* I wiped my face on the relatively clean inside of my cloak. The cheap fabric brushed roughly against my skin. *They would have stopped for who you were but not for who you are—a penniless, repugnant wanderer.*

Muddy water dripped from my motionless fingers. *I shouldn't think such things. I must divert my thoughts.* I tried to hum, but I choked on the tune. What I had said was true. I was one of those vile creatures no one wished to associate with and whose misery no one pitied. I clenched my fist and dug my fingernails into the palm of my hand. *It's not fair. I'm not really one of those people. Unfortunate circumstances only make me appear as one.*

That part of me that so often brought up unpleasant ideas spoke up with malicious intent. *Perhaps the old woman with yellow teeth whom Giles was so fond of but you slighted couldn't help her unattractive appearance. Maybe she wanted a helping hand and a friendly smile as much as you do, though you're too proud to admit it. Maybe she—*

Oh, mind your own business! I am under a spell, and she is not and has no excuse.

I marched down the road and concentrated on avoiding the puddles.

The skies cleared in the late afternoon, and the unseasonably warm weather that had preceded the rain left with it. I shivered all night under my cloak.

The next day the sun was bright and the sky clear, but the wind was fierce. It whipped my cloak about me, tugged at a few wisps of loose hair, and plastered me with leaves. I shuddered each time I caught a glimpse of my gray hair.

By late afternoon, my face burned with fever and my body trembled from the chills. Too ill to continue, I lay down beside a fallen log bordered on either end by bushes. Content that I was fairly well hidden from the view of casual passersby, I slept, disturbed only by feverish dreams.

One dream was so real I could smell the scent of sweaty horses and feel the touch of gloved hands. It began with hooves thudding down the road. They slowed beside my hiding place, and I heard two thumps and then soft steps. I pried my heavy eyes open to watch the dream unfold. The dim light of the waning moon shone on a stocky, middle-aged man with a thick mustache. His companion, a good fifteen years younger, had a build as scraggly as the hair jutting from under his cap.

They stared down at me.

I almost asked, "How did you find me? I thought I was hidden," but my mouth didn't seem to want to open. They knelt beside me.

"An enchantress!" Scraggly hissed. He drew a knife and raised it above me.

Would I wake from this dream now? Or just before the knife pierced my chest?

Stocky grabbed Scraggly's arm and lowered it to his side. "I don't hold with killing defenseless women, even enchantresses. Look at the way she stares. She's feverish or asleep."

"You call that a woman? She's hideous."

Stocky grunted. "Are you blind? It's no wonder the Collector's Council wouldn't let you on that committee." He placed his companion's free hand on the back of my hand.

Scraggly's eyes widened, and he jerked back. "What sorcery is this?"

"Do you still think she's hideous?"

"No. She's the most beautiful woman I've ever seen." He raised the knife again. "She likely intends to shed this disguise and enchant some man with her beauty."

My breath caught at the hate in his eyes.

Stocky gave him a scornful look. "You are a fool. Don't you feel it?"

Scraggly scowled at him but lowered his weapon.

"She's wrapped in a powerful spell, more powerful than any I've ever come across—even the Amasser himself couldn't control it." Stocky pointed at me. "If we kill her now, we'll lose it. My intuition tells me it's a shedding spell—that after a certain amount of time or a certain action on her part, a portion of the spell will leave. It might be manageable then. We'll tell the council about her. Perhaps in the future we can collect the power of the spell that remains cast over her." He rose to his feet. "And with that, what power she herself possesses."

The horses cantered down the road, carrying the men away, but the cold and chills didn't let me relax for some time.

The next morning, as I stumbled around collecting a handful of berries, I noticed two sets of hoofprints deviating off the road near my hiding place. Too miserable to consider what that meant, I collapsed behind the log again, hoping sunlight and a day of sleep would purge me of my illness.

My fever did drop, and over the next couple of days I managed to walk a few miles between rests.

On the morning of the third day, the woods thinned out and were replaced in part by cultivated land. When I came to a stream, I clambered down its grassy bank to the water to wash some of the dirt off and make myself more presentable. A gust of wind dislodged leaves from the colorful maple trees guarding the opposite bank. The leaves fluttered to the stream. Sunlight hit them and cast a red glow on the clouds reflected in the water.

CHAPTER 6

A s I passed one of the farms, I noticed a brown-and-black, evil-eyed mutt sprawled out under a tree. His master sat indolently on a bench outside of a ramshackle house.

The dog barked viciously at me, his bared teeth gleaming in the light. I kept walking but feared to look away. The barks grew more intense as he sprang up and gave chase. A quick glance at the man showed he would utter no word of restraint. Lifting my skirts, I sprinted down the road, the varmint snapping at my heels. Its hot breath burned my ankles, and I pleaded with my feet to move faster.

A whistle split the air, and, jumping at the shrill sound, I stumbled and hit the ground.

The dog, dribbling drool, leaped over me, and lumbered back to his master. I scrambled up and ran lest he change his mind about letting me go. The malevolent farmer's laughter rang through the air, sounding even louder than the thundering of my heart and the thump-thump of my boots on the dirt road.

As soon as I was out of sight of the house, I slumped against the weathered husk of a dead tree and slid to the ground. My right hand trembled as I brushed hair from my face. I slammed my fist into the tree. I'd never been pursued by a dog in my life. What kind of people were these who would allow their pets to harass harmless passersby? My family or neighbors would never allow it.

This trip of mine was certainly full of new experiences, and none of them pleasant. If I had known any curse words, I might have used them on that man, and if I still had the power to enchant, I would've turned him into a chipmunk to be chased by his own hound.

My breath, which must have walked instead of ran, finally caught up with me, and we resumed the road together. Half an hour later the two-storied half-timbered homes and shops of a village came into view. My heart sank. I still hadn't reached the city?

A group of boys played marbles on a smooth patch of the road as I entered the village. A marble hit the dirt and a puff of dust floated to me. The boys' eyes followed it. They pointed at me and laughed. I walked faster.

"Old hag. Old hag," they jeered. "Were you hiding in a nook when they passed out looks? Bet you were the cook for the paupers' ball."

Clenching my fists, I looked away. I'd turn them into goldfish and put them in a shallow bowl in a house tenanted by cats.

Their chants faded as I walked down the narrow streets shaded by tall, flat-faced shops. As usual, I made my way to the village well to drink and wash. As I dried my face on a corner of my cloak, men's voices drifted across the street to me along with the unpleasant sensation that I was the topic of discussion. Looking around, I noticed a group of young men loitering outside the tavern.

"There's a pretty one over there, Johnny. Why don't you ask her to the social?" A tall young man pointed at me.

Sandy-haired Johnny raised his hands, palms out, and stepped back. "No, thank you. I'd rather miss the social than dance with her. If you like her so much, Eddy, why don't you ask her?"

I glared at the two.

"I already have a partner." Eddy smirked. "I was only trying to be helpful."

"Hey, Frank needs a girl," said the paunchy young man standing beside Eddy.

"Yeah, but they favor a lot. They might be related."

They all laughed except one skinny lad standing on the outskirts of the group. He had an angular face, a pug nose, buck teeth, too many freckles to count, and limp dirty blond hair.

Frank.

My cheeks burned and then went cold at the realization that they had meant to insult him. I'd turn them into mice and keep them in a barn where the owls met at night and the cats played during the day. Except Frank. He didn't laugh at their jests against me. I couldn't make him handsome without giving him an entirely new face, but I could make him a little less ridiculous by giving volume to his hair, removing his freckles, and straightening his teeth.

The men looked at me, and I glowered at them to let them know I heard their comments. They quickly looked at the ground and then moved away.

I smoothed my hair, shook the dust from my dress, and hunted up the general store.

A bell jingled as I entered. A customer stood at the counter completing her transaction and another lady perused the ribbon section. I waited near the front window, prepared to be ignored until no other customers remained. When the door shut behind the last customer, I sought out the shopkeeper.

Her gaze skimmed over me, and she began to straighten the dresses on the mannequins. Eyebrows raised haughtily and thin lips pinched together, she tweaked the dresses in an obsessive manner, occasionally glancing my way as if to let me know I was being snubbed.

I pushed down my frustration and humiliation and walked to her. "Excuse me; do you have a map of Sonser?"

She looked me over and gave a scoffing grunt. "What? Can you read? Barely half of the folks here who know how to bathe know how to read. I certainly wouldn't have expected it of you."

"I asked you if you had a map, not if you thought I could read it." Such insolence. I had cleaned up as much as I could without soap, privacy, and a bathtub.

"There's no need to take offense."

No need for me to take offense? I took a deep breath and tried again. "Do you have a map?"

"I heard you the first time. Why do you need a map?" Her eyes held a cold gleam, rather like that of a cat eyeing a mouse.

"To get directions to Florenburg, though I don't know what business it is of yours."

"It's my map you're asking to see, though I doubt you're willing or able to buy it. You certainly have a high and mighty attitude for such a dirty, old thing."

I glared at her through narrowed eyes and then walked to the front door. She called out as my hand closed around the knob.

"I have a map. I'll let you see it if ..."

She leaned behind the counter and grabbed a broom. "If you sweep up the mud you've tracked into my clean store."

I stood still, locked in place by a tug-of-war between the

anger urging me to leave with my pride and my desperation to reach home.

With a smug, sadistic smile, she held out the broom.

I gripped the knob hard. I wanted to snatch the broom and throw it back at her, but I dared not. I needed the map. I never hated anyone so much as I hated her that moment. I didn't hate the mirror for transforming me. Maybe because it was only a magic mirror and had been given certain orders, or maybe because I knew I had to be punished for misusing it and was relieved, though not so much at the moment, just to be alive. My Floraison pride must have shown through my rags, or she would never have taken so much pleasure in humbling me.

Releasing the doorknob, I grabbed the broom with a seething look and swept the few traces of mud in my path out the door—I had wiped my feet before entering the store.

I propped the broom against the wall when I finished, but she inspected the floor, made a tsk-tsk sound, and motioned for me to sweep again. And then again. We repeated the process until not one speck of dust or hair or anything else remained on the wooden floor.

Finally, she took the broom and condescended to show me the map, leading me to a small room behind the main area. She took the map from a box and spread it out on a low table. She didn't offer me a chair, so I leaned over the table. She stood close beside me, most likely to ensure no dirt from my hands soiled the map and to let me know she didn't trust me not to abscond with it.

My heart sank when I saw the title and scale of the map. It wasn't of the entire kingdom of Sonser but of this small section. Still, it was better than nothing. I scanned it for a familiar name or landmark but saw none other than Gilden, the city the other shopkeeper had mentioned. An X marked my current village. I traced the distance between it and Gilden. A week's journey, at least.

Not far from the village, the road made a sizable loop as it skirted a forest with a castle at its center. A footpath led from the village side of the loop through the forest to the castle. A proper lane led from the castle to the road on the far side of the loop.

Was that the shortcut the men talked about? Was it worth taking?

I bent closer to the map.

"You've seen it now. I must be getting back out front." The matron rolled up the map.

I opened my mouth to protest but shut it when I noticed the eager look in her eye. My fingernails dug into my fisted hands. She wanted me to make a fuss so she could belittle me even more. Raising my chin, I strode back through the store and out to the street.

A gnat. A little, insignificant gnat. In a dusty, old room with a large population of spiders and yards of sticky web. A spider would wind her up tightly on its web and leave her for when it had nothing better to devour. When she felt the web vibrate with the spider's movements, she would never know if it was coming for her or not.

I walked briskly down the cobblestone street for a few paces but then stopped and leaned against the corner of a building. Fighting hard to hold back the tears threatening to escape, I covered my mouth with my hand and took a few deep breaths. I pictured her as an annoying gnat, but, in reality, she was in possession of a stinger.

Straightening, I wiped my eyes. I might have sunk to the status of scullery maid, but I wasn't a worthless beggar. I was the Lady Alexandria Floraison, after all.

I was rich. I was beautiful. I was spotlessly clean.

At least I would be as soon as I returned to my family. They would welcome me. Wouldn't they welcome me? Aunt Helene was rude and thoughtless, but even she wasn't as bad as that venomous shopkeeper. I was family. They would love me despite … wouldn't they?

A man stared at me with a look of pity on his face. That piqued my spirit. I didn't want anyone's pity. I marched through the village. The group of boys who'd graced my entrance now played games in the village square. They heckled me once again, adding more insults to their chants. "She's fond of mud baths by the look of her. Too bad they haven't done her skin any good. She still favors a prune."

I ran out of the village. Old age soon forced me to stop. My chest burned for lack of air, my empty stomach was in knots, my eyes stung from tears trying to breach their defenses, my nose was runny, and my throat ached from my efforts to prevent an emotional display.

At the sound of a carriage, I stumbled to the edge of the road and watched it approach. It was decorated with a family crest and was drawn by elegant horses. A richly dressed woman gazed out the window with a bored expression on her face. When she saw me, she sighed and looked away, focusing on something in the carriage.

If only she had just turned away, I could have scorned her and maintained my narrowly-held composure. But no, her gaze returned to me, and small, gleaming objects sailed toward me. Several coins landed at my feet. The woman gazed out the carriage window again, not even bothering to notice where the coins had landed.

Bile rose in my throat. She'd tossed them at me as one tossed scraps to a dog. All that I had suffered, the insults, the snubs, the weariness, the utter degradation, all my buried hurt and shame rose before me. My fury increased with every thought until it was such that I trembled from head to toe and my vision blurred.

I looked at the coins. I wanted to hurl them right back into the grand lady's bored face. I didn't want her charity! I bent to pick up the ammunition, but being weak and shaky, I stumbled and fell, landing face first in the mud. My foot tangled in the hem of my dress as I tried to rise, and I fell again.

My Floraison pride broke at last. I was a wretched, starving, repulsive hag without friends or family. No one would claim me in my present form. I was doomed to lonely wanderings until death claimed me.

I crumpled under my anguish and wept.

Sunlight glinted off the scattered coins, hurting my eyes, which had long since given all their tears to my grief. I collected the coins and staggered up. What did it matter if the magnificent Lady Alexandria was reduced to the status of beggar?

I returned to the village and purchased bread and cheese, but I found no joy in the promise of a full stomach. Everything around me was dull—the colors, the sounds of customers talking. Even the smell of freshly baked bread barely registered. The rose bud, still pinned to my cloak, was as fresh and clean as always, but its beauty couldn't cheer me.

I left the village and wandered down the road for two days, rationing my meager food supply and sleeping, huddled under my cloak for warmth, beneath the trees. Desire to be with my family no longer fueled my steps. They would spurn me as everyone else did, but I continued toward the city anyway. I had to go somewhere.

The second afternoon, I left the road to rest a while in a meadow. Head bowed, I set my course for a thick-trunked tree rising above the tall grass in the center of the meadow The shadows of its branches were laid out before my feet when I heard a child's distant voice.

"Look, Mama, it's an old lady."

Startled, I looked up.

Before me stood a slim, pale woman. Her sad brown eyes peered into mine.

"Mother?" Her voice, a sweet and kind voice, seemed too lovely to be part of my world. She laid a gentle hand on my sleeve. "Won't you rest yourself under this tree? You must be tired." She motioned to the tree's raised roots.

My mouth opened, but I couldn't answer. If I'd been in the dark for days, I couldn't have been more dazzled by full sunlight than I was by her kindness.

She repeated the invitation.

I stammered a "thank you" and lowered myself onto a root. She sat on another one. A stocky man with curly brown hair led a chestnut-colored workhorse over to us. A little girl, about four years old, gazed down at me from the horse's back.

"My name's Belle. What's your name?" she asked.

My name? No one had cared to know my name since I left home. Who was I? I was no longer the Lady Alexandria Anastasia Floraison, daughter of the Duke of Henly. Even Alexandria sounded too grand for me.

"My name is Alexandria." I hadn't used my voice for two days, and it sounded shaky.

"Alexandria. That's a pretty name. I once had an aunt called that," the young woman replied. She touched my hand in a friendly manner as she spoke.

It was the first touch of another human and the only time my name had been spoken for weeks. I felt a warmth in my hand. It raced to my fingertips and then to my palm and spread throughout my body. The numbness that had enveloped me for the past few days melted away, and a glimmer of hope took its place.

"My husband, child, and I have been on a picnic. Would you —" She turned her face aside and coughed violently into a handkerchief. The dry coughs shook her slight frame. Her husband stepped forward with a concerned look.

"I'm sorry," she apologized weakly when she regained her breath.

I wasn't a physician or a psychic, but I knew the woman was seriously ill.

"You've been outside long enough, Anne." Her husband put his arm around her and turned to me. "If you'll excuse us, friend, I must get my wife home."

Anne nodded, and she took some bread, cheese, an apple, and a slice of cold meat from a picnic basket near her feet and placed the items in my lap. "I packed too much food. Please take what's left."

My breath caught. Here was a woman, obviously not wealthy—not impoverished, but not wealthy—and who was ill, going out of her way for me, a hag. And she did it with kindness. I could see it in her eyes and sense it in her touch.

Tears blurred my vision. For once, I was grateful for the offerings, for they were gifts of love and weren't given out of a sense of duty. A desire to give her something in return bubbled within me. But what? I had nothing of value, nothing of beauty. Except the enchanted rose. Anne, even by Floraison standards, was a lovely woman. The rose would look well on her or on her daughter, who greatly favored her.

It may have been my stiff, clumsy hands, disfigured by age and arthritis, or some enchantment on the flower, but I could not unpin it from my cloak. I only got several pricks and a few drops of blood for my trouble.

Anne smiled. "No, you keep it, Alexandria." She smoothed

the windblown wisps of hair away from my face with an almost wistful look.

She would never have gray hair. Perhaps she was thinking the same.

"God bless you, Alexandria." She squeezed my hand in farewell and returned to her family.

I would heal her, if I were still an enchantress.

I watched them leave and then slowly ate my feast, not forgetting to return thanks for it this day.

I spent the night leaning against the tree. It broke the wind and reminded me of my recent companions.

After a peaceful slumber, I woke to the sound of birds chirping as they flitted about the bare branches above me. No exuberant song rang in my heart, but a small hope flickered there. It grew during the next couple of days until I was able to laugh when I saw squirrels chase each other and to admire the moon as it rose round and golden to guard my slumber.

❦

The "shortcut," the trail leading through the forest to cut off the long loop of the road, had found me. It tempted me. "Leave the broad, open road for the companionship of songbirds and gentle doe and spare your blistered feet and worn shoes miles and miles of toil," it said. It didn't mention that I would have to leave the hard-to-lose road and give up any chance of help finding me, if I needed it, along the way. Even though I knew this, the familiar yearning to be surrounded by green leaves and moss-covered rocks that drove me from my house almost every morning before my exile enticed me toward the trail.

My stomach rumbled. It was decided. I would take the shortcut. There would be more chance of finding berries and nuts along the forest path than along the road.

It may have been a shortcut according to the map, but it was a long, miserable route. There was never enough food to satisfy my ever-shrinking stomach, and my body soon discovered that fall was merging with winter. No matter how often I tried, I could never produce so much as a spark by rubbing two stones together. My situation was desperate. Around every bend and over every hill the scene was always the same: trees, rhododendron, and fallen leaves. The only slight change was the occasional winding stream with a fallen log stretched across it as a bridge.

Sunlight and darkness. Walking and resting. Hunger and cold. That was my life.

The two days after I left the village I would have welcomed a leafy grave, but enough of my old self had returned for me to spurn the idea of dying of starvation or hypothermia in a lonely forest.

Lonely?

The mention of "him who lives there" returned to my mind. I had forgotten the castle in the wood. Perhaps he would help me. I could offer to work in return for food and shelter.

The afternoon of the third day since entering the forest I spotted what looked like a clearing in the woods. Summoning what little energy I had, I jogged toward it. Was it the castle lawn?

I broke through a ring of trees. My feet hit on something hard. I wasn't on grass but on a cobblestone drive, on the other side of which was another seemingly endless expanse of forest. Had I missed the castle and ended up on the main road?

A cold, merciless wind whipped at my ragged skirt. I sank to the road and stretched across the sun-heated stones. Starved and weary, that's what I was. Starved for food, starved for companionship. Weary of body and weary of life. I half wished I'd die there and that the bored lady who threw the coins would find me. A dead body would be just the thing to liven up her life.

Chirp! Chirp!

Chirp! Chirp!

Little claws scratched my hands and arms.

The scratching turned into pecking.

"Stop!"

I pushed myself up. Two plump blue birds scolded me for all they were worth. I made shooing motions with my arms, but they dodged my hands and dove in to nip at me like a dog nipping at his sheep.

"I'm going! I'm going!"

To where? Should I take my chance on the cobblestone drive or continue to traverse the forest? Two painful pecks on my right side determined my course. I ran down the cobblestone drive toward the heart of the forest.

CHAPTER 7

STORM CLOUDS GATHERED overhead. Soon, heavy raindrops and cold hail bombarded me as I shuffled forward. One peculiar cloud loomed tall and spiky above the treetops and didn't move with the wind. The rain and hail suddenly ceased, and a ray of sunlight fell upon the sedentary cloud. It shone like polished stone.

I lifted my weary feet higher and quickened my step. Half an hour later, I passed through the gate and into full view of the castle. It was a thing of beauty. Polished, white stone walls, storm-cloud blue shingles, towers and turrets that rose into the sky as majestically as any snow-capped mountain. Elegant statues adorned the corners and ledges, and countless windows blinked in the newly returned sunlight.

The beauty of the castle shamed my haggard appearance. I was a blot on the landscape, but I was a desperate blot. I trudged up the long driveway.

A man of great height and expensive clothes paced the drive in front of me. He kept looking toward the stables.

"Where's that man with my horse? Blast him!" He spun

around and glared at me. "Who the devil are you, and what do you want?"

My breath caught in my throat, and I retreated a step. The man looked so much like Giles they could have been brothers. The height, the build, the curly dark hair. Aside from age—Giles was a few years older than me while this man looked to be about nineteen or twenty—the main difference was the eyes. Though the same startling blue, his eyes lacked the warmth of Giles's.

"Stop staring at me, woman."

I curtsied. "Forgive me, my lord."

"Highness."

"Forgive me, Your Highness. I am exhausted from a long journey and lack of proper food. Might I warm myself by the fire in your kitchen and spend the night there? I will gladly do whatever I can to repay you for a little hospitality and food."

"Let a repulsive creature like you into my home? Not for a sack of golden crowns."

"Not even for the beauty of an enchanted rose?" I hastily unpinned it from my cloak, the clasp offering no resistance this time. My words and his sounded vaguely familiar.

"An enchanted rose?" He sneered as I held the crimson flower out to him. "It was spirited out of someone's garden, no doubt."

Hunger, exhaustion, and wretched appearance were all forgotten. A sort of righteous indignation burned within me. This man had everything—wealth, health, beauty. I had none of those and therefore he refused me.

Yet, he did lack something.

A heart.

Gabriella's words echoed in my ears and flowed from my mouth. "There are two kinds of beauty, Your Highness; beware which one you treasure, for lasting beauty lies within."

Clutching the rose and the pin to my chest, I implored the prince again. "Will you not help me?"

"Why do you bother me so, old hag? Be gone." He dismissed me with a wave of his hand and turned toward the castle. "Where is that blasted man with my horse?"

His words stung my soul. If I were still an enchantress, I'd turn him into a creature so ugly he would be scorned by all and helped by none. He would quickly learn the importance of love and kindness. My hand tingled. Something long and slender replaced the sharp pin beside the rose. I stared down at my silver wand.

The voices in the mirror said I had been given a mission, something to do with a *him* to whose future I would be linked. I glanced at the prince. Was this the *him*?

The wand grew warm in my hand as if in answer. Words came into my head, and I spoke them.

A blaze of dazzling colors burst from the wand and engulfed me. It came hot and rough against my skin and then left, taking the trappings of the hag with it. Where I had been old and withered and drably dressed, I was now young and straight and robed in a gown as lovely in its design and deep red color as the enchanted rose itself. I was once again the Lady Alexandria Floraison. Enchantress.

The prince fell to his knees. "O Great Enchantress, I beg you to forgive me. I was a fool not to realize who you were. Please, come inside and stay as long as you like."

I took a step forward. The wand pulsed in my hand. His personal graces and his position tempted me to excuse him, but I heard once again the voices in the mirror and realized I was an instrument of judgment. I dared not refuse. Why should I? He would have let me starve. Shame twisted my heart as I realized why the scene seemed so familiar. The hag begging for help in my dream had been me—and I had sided with the prince.

But not this time.

The wand trembling in my hand, I pronounced a curse on the prince. "Selfishness and unkindness, these traits you have chosen, and you shall reap their fruit. On you, your servants, and your lands, I pronounce a curse. You shall keep the comforts of your palace, but you shall keep them in loneliness. You shall have fur in place of fine clothes, claws in place of nails, and in place of a handsome face—a visage such as none could look at without revulsion. You shall trade beauty for ugliness and live as a beast!"

I raised my wand to seal the curse upon him, but the voice in the mirror had declared that justice should be tempered with mercy. *No, he deserves to be punished. He is selfish and totally without love.*

Wasn't I?

They showed me mercy—my life, my current restoration, and one brief moment of companionship. I could secure him some means of temporarily escaping his lonely state.

My fingers curled around the smooth handle of the Demandez à Voir mirror now magically in my hand.

Had I called it from its velvet-lined drawer at home?

I held it out to the prince. With a look of despair, he took it.

"You cannot leave your domain, and few shall dare to venture into it. This mirror shall show you any place or any person you desire to see, but use it wisely."

I raised my wand again, but I knew it was not enough. The sweet fragrance of my rose filled the air, bringing with it the bittersweet memory of a friendship that died and the sorrow of a birthday celebration missed. It was the one thing that survived my punishment unchanged, as if it had been waiting its turn.

I placed it in his hand. "This rose shall reach full bloom on your twenty-first birthday, and then petal by petal it shall wilt. If you can learn to love and be loved in return before the last petal falls, the curse shall be lifted. If not, you shall live and die a beast."

"Let it be so," I cried.

A cloud as dark as the one that had issued from the mirror to engulf me descended on the prince. It crashed over him like a wave and rushed to cover the castle and grounds. Cries of astonishment and anguish sounded all around as the curse took effect. The darkness lapped at my feet and tried to take hold of me.

Horrified, I turned and raced away. The paved lane became rough and uneven as I ran. Twice I nearly tripped, and once I thought I had left the lane before I finally saw the dim outline of the gates. A cry of panic escaped me. The gates were closing. I lifted my skirts higher and sprinted toward them, barely managing to slip between them before they closed with a sorrowful moan.

I ran until I could run no more. I stumbled off the path and sank to the ground beneath a gnarled oak. Even as I panted, I felt weak in a way I'd never experienced before—I was drained of my power of enchantment. It must have been locked up when I was a hag, waiting for this moment. Now, it was gone, and the wand was cold in my hand.

My heart leapt into my throat as a deafening roar, a roar of anger and anguish I understood all too well, filled the air. My task was complete. The darkness shrouding the castle crept toward me, thinning as it came, and I fell into a deep sleep.

CHAPTER 8

THE OLD GRANDFATHER clock patiently tick-tocked, tick-tocked as we stared at the mirror's ghastly black face. When the clock decided it was time, it chimed the half-hour to scold us into the present.

The Duke of Henly gently pushed his wife from her place leaning on his shoulder and picked up the mirror. He placed it in its velvet-lined home and shoved the drawer shut.

"Is there nothing we can do to get her back?" I asked.

"I have little hope there is, Prince Giles," he answered softly. "I will see what information I can find on … prisoners of enchanted mirrors." He patted my shoulder. "I think it's time we dressed for dinner." He left the room looking as old and sad as only a man who has lost a child can look.

I should have shunned the room, but after dinner I found myself standing outside the library. Had it really happened? I grasped the handle, and my stomach turned with it as I opened the door and slipped inside. The candles flickered as they cast their light across the room.

The duchess sat in the chair Alexandria usually occupied and wept over the silver Demandez à Voir mirror. The duke stood beside her, one hand resting on her shoulder. The resigned look in his eyes and the mournful slump of his shoulders said he had little comfort to give other than that of his presence. I stepped back, pulling the door with me.

He straightened his shoulders and stepped toward me. "Don't go, Prince Giles." His shoulders fell again. "I need you. There's a chance the mirror will reveal Alexandria to us, but neither my wife nor I have the courage to ask. Will you call up my daughter's image?"

Now my shoulders drooped. I wasn't sure I wanted to know what would happen to a person captured by an enchanted mirror, especially one wearing black. I rummaged around myself until I found a pretense of courage and then took the accursed thing from the duchess. I squeezed its cold handle. *She'd better be all right, or I'll break you into a thousand pieces, and then we'll see who has seven years of bad luck.* "Show me the Lady Alexandria Floraison." *Please.*

It didn't so much as blink.

"No, it can't mean … show me Marcel." Still nothing. I looked at the duke. "It gives no reply." *The black doesn't mean anything. It's just being bad-tempered. Right?*

What might have been a flicker of hope in his blue-green eyes died. "I didn't expect it to, but I wanted to be sure. It didn't respond for months after its mate disappeared seventy years ago. With the addition of this insult, it may never answer again, or at least not in my lifetime."

"Mate? It's one of a pair?"

"Yes, they come in pairs, for two people to communicate. There are only three sets in the world."

Sets? My family had a Demandez à Voir mirror, but only one. It'd been in the family for … seventy years. My pulse quickened. I turned the mirror over and ran my hand along the polished handle and rose-embellished back. Yes, it was the same design. "Are they all decorated with roses?"

"No. Each set was specially designed for its owner's family. Floraison—'blossoming.' The roses signify our family."

Aha. "Do you suppose the mirror would respond if reunited with its mate?"

The duke rubbed his temple but didn't complain about my questions. "It might, but we've never been able to trace it. For whatever reason, this mirror won't show the location of the missing one."

My lips surprised me by curving into a smile. *I hope he won't think I come from a family of thieves.* "I have its mate."

His hand stilled as he stared at me. The duchess raised her head. "What? How did you come by it?"

"It's been in the family for about seventy years. According to the story, an enchantress presented it to my grandfather, the one I mentioned who was so unsociable." Unsociable was putting it nicely.

The duchess regarded me earnestly. "You don't believe the story?"

"I must admit I've always been a little skeptical. It's difficult to imagine my grandfather as being other than amiable."

"Where is the mirror now?" The duke obviously wasn't interested in stories.

My heart lifted at the determination in his eyes. "At my family's home in Silvestris."

He looked down at his wife. "Such a long journey for a fool's hope."

She squeezed his hand and nodded an answer to some question he'd silently asked.

"I would like to try the other mirror, Giles. May I accompany you to your home with this one? I don't want to wait for you to return with the mate," he said.

"No."

He blinked.

"There's no need. If I leave now, I can return with the mirror by tomorrow." I paused, letting the implausible statement turn some of their sorrow into curiosity.

The Duke of Henly furrowed his brow. "How is that possible?"

My hand found its way to my jacket pocket and curled around a gold ring. My finger outlined my family seal. "I have a traveling ring. It was given to my some-odd great, great grandfather by King Geoffrey II along with the hereditary title of prince. It will only carry one person and not for far. I'll need a map to locate places to"—*hop, skip, and jump from as Marcel would say*—"to break my journey into manageable lengths."

He stared at me a moment before goading himself into action. "Yes, of course." He glanced around the library and then headed to the far right corner to an open cabinet stuffed with rolled parchments. He chose a parchment and spread it out on a table, pointing out Henly Manor.

I grimaced at the distance between it and the castle at Silvestris. There wasn't a limit on the number of consecutive times I could travel, was there?

My finger traced a path between our homes, tapping each village and city that marked the farthest I could hope to travel in one twist. *Let me see, Henly Manor to Cremsee, Cremsee to Dill, Dill to Alteirs, Alteirs to Mun.* I named the other stops, closed my eyes, and tried to repeat them. *Henly Manor to Cremsee, Cremsee to Dill, Dill to Mun. No, it was Cremsee to Mun, Mun to—Oh, blast. I'll just take the map.* I rolled it up and stuffed it in my inner jacket pocket, ignoring the end that stuck out and bumped my collarbone.

I slipped on the ring, the metal cold and refreshing against my skin. The duke put his arm back around his wife's shoulders, and the traditional family goodbye rolled off my tongue. "I'll be back in two twists." Though it would take more. "To Cremsee." *To some nice, deserted place where no one will scream when I suddenly appear.* I twisted the ring a quarter turn around my finger. Their sorrowful faces and the flickering candlelight disappeared.

By the time I returned, the ring felt warm and moist as if extensive traveling affected it the way exercise does us. It contrasted with the cool mirror in my hand. I pocketed the ring and laid the mirror and the map on a chair in the empty library. The mid-morning sunlight floated peacefully through the window. What kind of goodies would they have in the kitchen at this time? I needed sustenance before finding the Duke of Henly and facing two enchanted mirrors.

Soon, the duke and I shut ourselves in the library. I tightened my grip on my mirror, its face a blank silver, and then picked up his black-faced one. Nothing happened. I looked at the duke. He shrugged. It had thrown a fit when its mate disappeared seventy years ago, wasn't it at least going to acknowledge its return now? As if in response to my accusation, the ill-disposed mirror's face lightened to grayish-silver, but a few black specks remained as if to say it hadn't forgotten the crime committed against it.

The duke nudged my arm. "Go on. Ask it."

"Show me the Lady Alexandria Floraison."

"No."

I almost dropped it. They talked? "No, you will not or no, you cannot?"

The thing snickered. "No, I will not."

Just as I suspected. "Tell me, is she well?"

"She may not think so."

What had it done to her? "Will she return to us?"

"I'm not a crystal ball."

Perhaps flattery was my best option. "Will you take me to her? I know you have the power."

"You seek to retrieve her, even after she scorned your friend?"

"Yes. There's a kind heart under the Floraison pride."

"Harrumph. Pray she finds it. But it's fitting you should seek her, as your very life depends, partially at least, on her."

My life? This mirror wasn't quite right in the head. The head? Oh, why not? It had a face. "You'll allow me to bring her back?"

"Of course." It snickered. "If she'll come with you."

If …

Well, she hadn't exactly been pleased with me of late, but surely she would get over that if it meant going home.

"And I mean with you," it continued. "Not the handsome Prince Giles Bête."

Was there another me?

The duke laid a hand on my arm. "Giles, let me go. She's my daughter, my responsibility." His eyes had lost the age that sorrow had brought them and held a brave determination, and it cheered me.

Yet, I shook my head. Her displeasure with me had something to do with that stunt with the mirror, I was sure. And I wasn't going to let the most wonderful, though flawed, woman I knew stay mad at me for long, certainly not forever as would be the case if we never saw one another again. "For any other daughter, I would agree with you, but not for Alexandria."

"But—"

"Only the prince may go, Your Grace," the mirror said.

The duke glared at it but then sighed and took the quiet, silver-faced mirror from me.

The black specks on the cantankerous mirror grew larger. "There are two conditions, Your Highness," it said. "One—you mustn't tell her who you are."

"She'll recognize me."

"You'd be surprised."

Oh dear. "What's the other?"

"You can't join her until after the first phase of her punishment is complete. This won't be easy."

Good thing adventure was my middle name.

The duke pulled me close in a brief embrace. "Take care of yourself, Giles, and of Alexandria."

"I will, sir." *Even if I have to turn her over my knee to make her see reason.* He stepped away. "Right, mirror. Take me to her."

Gray light engulfed me. The voice of the mirror came to me over a rush of wind. "I'm afraid I wasn't quite clear earlier. She can't leave until she's regained the enchantment—until the spell on the prince ends. And only then if she's ready."

The gray light became daylight. My heart skipped a beat as I looked around. I was in the woods near Silvestris, standing next to a gnarled mulberry that had been cut down years ago.

CHAPTER 9

A HAZY CONSCIOUSNESS fought its way through the darkness. What was that shaking? Was I back in the mirror? Was I being sent home? I pried my heavy lids open.

A hairy monster with blue eyes stared down at me. I scrambled up and fell back against a tree.

"Take it easy now, miss. You've proved you're alive. There's no need to overdo it," the monster said.

Leaning against the tree, I rubbed some clear sight into my blurry eyes and looked at the hairy thing again. This time I saw a man, mid- to late-twenties, with longish, dark hair and a thick beard. A peasant judging by his clothes, but he had stunning blue eyes. Eyes rather like Giles's and the prince's. What impertinence for a commoner to have such fine eyes.

And to shake me awake.

"Well, what do you think?" he said in an amused tone of voice. "You've looked at me long enough to paint a portrait."

What nerve. Nonetheless, I blushed, and he chuckled. "I think you could easily be mistaken for a bear with all that hair." I straightened and tried to take a step away from this rude stranger, but my legs wobbled beneath me. How long had I been asleep? And how long had it been since I'd eaten a proper meal?

"You're an honest maiden, aren't you? And a weak one." He took hold of my arm and gently eased me down. "Sit before you fall. I'll fix us some grub."

My cheeks burned with the indignity of my situation—being weak as a baby and dependent on a stranger, and a peasant at that. Despite my time as a hag, I still had a large portion of the Floraison pride, and it was the strongest thing about me at that moment. Pride was a habit, and I fell back into it, being too weak and overwhelmed to fight it.

Giving him a scornful glance, I struggled up again.

He pushed me back down. "What? Too good to eat with the likes of me? I think I should be the judge of that, especially since it's my grub. What's your name?"

I bit back an angry squeal. "I am the Lady Alexandria Floraison, daughter of the Duke of Henly." How dare he push me around like a little child.

He took in my appearance with a sweeping glance. "The Lady Alexandria Floraison, huh?" He raised his eyebrows in an expression of disbelief and looked away. He murmured something about a head injury.

Panic took a chunk out of my stomach. Was I a hag again? I held out my arms. No. Thank goodness. I was still young.

He noticed me looking at myself. "You know if you cleaned up a bit and smiled occasionally, you'd be tolerably pretty. You'd be surprised what a smile can do for an otherwise plain face. Speaking of appearances, you look parched. Drink this."

He pressed a water canteen to my lips and forced me to drink. I almost choked in my anger. Water dribbled down my chin and neck, which only made everything worse. I pushed the canteen away and started coughing.

"I'm terribly sorry. Forgive me, Lady Alexandria." He handed me a handkerchief and patted my back.

There was a familiar ring to the way he said my name. I looked up at him in surprise.

He cleared his throat. "I'd better see about the grub." Slipping the canteen's strap over his shoulder, he moved away to a steaming cauldron sitting over an open fire. A gentle breeze curled the smoke rising into the leafy canopy above.

The coughing fit subsided, and I laid the handkerchief in my lap across a wrinkled, brown dress, the drab kind commoners often wore. Gone was the magnificent gown I'd worn those few moments at the castle. And gone was my lacy shawl. I unclasped a coarse gray cloak from around my shoulders and shook the dirt and leaves from it.

Turning away from my host, I discreetly examined my appearance. Though young, my skin was pale. No longer flawless, it was marred by freckles and a sprinkling of moles. Why couldn't the mirror have left me alone after I enchanted the prince? I put my hands on my hips. My bony hips. I had lost weight at the expense of my feminine curves. I had the distinct feeling I was what was commonly called a "faded beauty."

My foot hit something as I turned back around. I stooped to pick up my leaf-covered handbag and opened it. A scrap of fabric—presumably for use as a handkerchief—a few pennies, a needle and thread, and a quill were all it contained. Sighing, I ran my fingers over the quill's silver plume and shaft. The handkerchief wasn't as ragged as before, and the quill was decent, for a peasant. A repetitive design on the shaft caught my eye. Were those markings from stripped-off barbs? They looked rather like flowers.

The smell of food stole my attention. It had been a *very* long time since I had eaten properly.

My benefactor cut thick slices of bread as he knelt beside the cauldron. He must have set up camp and started the stew long before I awoke. Gratitude and hunger ate away at my pride.

"What brought you here?" I asked. I hadn't fallen along a major highway after all. I doubted he had business at the castle, at least I hoped he hadn't.

He dished up a bowl of stew and put a piece of bread on a plate and brought them to me as I sat on a tree stump. "I was looking for a treasure."

"Did you find it?" I asked, surprised.

He smiled at me strangely. "I found you and had to call off the search."

"I'm sorry."

"Don't be. There is satisfaction in helping those in need, whether or not they appreciate it."

"Thank you for your hospitality."

"My pleasure." He served himself and sat on a rock a couple of feet away from me.

We ate in silence. He may have made one or two attempts at conversation, but I was too focused on taking polite mouthfuls of food instead of shoveling it down to answer.

My stomach told me it was the best meal I had ever had. My memory didn't quite agree and brought up images of gourmet meals with melt-in-your-mouth desserts, but I settled the dispute by clarifying that it was the best tasting one I'd had in a long time.

As I finished my second bowl of stew—which my benefactor had apparently decided I needed since he refilled my bowl without me asking—the polite silence was broken by a loud slurping. My mouth fell open in shock but quickly closed in a disdainful frown.

The hairy man lowered the bowl from his lips and wiped his mouth on his sleeve. His lips twitched as he looked at me, almost as if he was suppressing a mischievous grin.

He raised the bowl toward me. "Bottom's up."

"What's the matter? Is the stew not to your liking?" he asked when I didn't follow his example. "Oh, I forgot. You're a grand lady and not used to the simple eating of common folk. I'll take my meal to the kitchen, where I belong. I'll be easier to ignore there."

He moved away to the campfire before I could protest. I wasn't that ungrateful.

◈

A misty twilight rolled in, bringing sleepiness with it. My offers to help clean up dinner were refused, and I was made to sit still and feel completely useless, rather like a pampered child. And made to think I was considered such, which spoiled the improvement in my mood that the food had brought about.

"It's time to get to bed now, my lady. We'll rise early tomorrow and get on our way." He unrolled a blanket and spread it out beside my seat.

An electric shock coursed through me. I hadn't even thought about tonight, much less tomorrow. How long would I be reduced to the object of this man's charity?

Was it only charity? I eyed him closely. He returned my gaze with confidence. *Maintains eye contact, a good sign. His stance is relaxed. His clothes, though plain, are tidy, and his fingernails are trimmed and clean.* I felt a tingle of relief—he looked safe enough.

He chuckled again. "Don't worry. I'll sleep in the servants' quarters when I'm not on guard duty. Wolves, you know."

Wolves? I scooted closer to the fire. He failed to suppress a grin, and those impertinent blue eyes twinkled at me.

"Well, get away to the servants' quarters or the watchtower or wherever you're going." I shooed him away and lay on the blanket. My fingers skimmed the folds of my skirt. No wand pocket. I hadn't expected there to be one. No matter. I would make it home without one.

❦

As my eyelids slipped shut, my mind slipped into a cold, dark abyss. I seemed to stay there for years. Fury and despair clouded the air and pressed against me until it drove me to hopelessness. I cried out, but my cry went unnoticed.

Suddenly, part of a room materialized around me. A gray stone floor spread out before me and then turned up and grew into a wall of the same comfortless stone. A portrait of the proud and heartless prince in the castle appeared on the wall. I reached out to touch the golden frame, but it melted away into a flurry of crimson rose petals. As the soft petals landed in my hand they shriveled into brittle, lifeless heaps. Horrified, I swung my hand through the air, hoping to free myself of the dead petals. I hit something as I moved and noticed for the first time a table standing beside me. On it rested a mirror with silver roses entwined about its handle. Unable to resist, I picked up the mirror and looked into it.

A scream sounded through the room, possibly coming from me, followed by a snicker, which definitely didn't come from me.

The snickering stopped. "View your companion, the partner of your fate."

"No!" I flung the mirror back onto the table.

"Oh, but yes. You have more in common than you think. More than just this prison."

With a clashing of metal against metal, prison bars joined together to form the remaining walls of the room.

I ran to the door. Curiously, the lock was on the inside.

"Is there no key?"

A low laugh echoed off the one wall. "There is a key. It is beauty."

"Beauty? There is no beauty in this desolate place."

More laughter. "You're right. There is no beauty in this place —or within you or your companion. Yet, you must find it in order to leave. Without it, the magic won't return to you."

"How do I find it?" My cry went unanswered.

I glanced again at the image in the mirror. There was no beauty there, for my companion was a beast.

I threw myself against the bars as sobs shook my body.

❧

"Wake up, Sleeping Beauty. More shuteye isn't going to do you any good," said a deep voice.

I opened my eyes. No stone walls, no prison bars. Only trees and bushes and twinkling blue eyes in a hairy face. I gave a sigh of relief.

"I suppose you don't say 'good morning' until after you've had breakfast in bed?" the hairy peasant said.

He was determined to think ill of me, which made me want to oblige him. "I don't recall you wishing me a good morning, and I don't take breakfast in bed."

"I'm glad to hear it, because I wasn't planning on serving it to you." He glanced at my rumpled dress and disheveled hair. "You look a sight. There's a stream a little ways off to the right. Go freshen up."

He pulled me unceremoniously to my feet and then held out a towel and a bar of soap.

I glared at him before snatching the towel and soap and marching off in search of the stream. Bossy and insolent and unkempt. He'd probably never used a comb or a razor in his life.

Breakfast was laid out when I returned.

My host brushed off a patch of ground with his hand and motioned for me to sit. "My lady."

I sat down curtly, offended by the mocking tone of his voice, but one sniff of breakfast reminded me of my manners. "Thank you for sharing your meals with me. It's very kind of you."

"My pleasure," he said. "As soon as we've finished breakfast and packed up, we'll be on our way. There's a village a few days journey from here. I'll see if I can find a job for you there."

"Employment? I thank you, but I'm not stopping at the village. I was on my way to the city of Gilden when ..." when I turned from a hag to an enchantress and turned a prince into a beast, "... when I lost my way."

"Gilden? Why are you going there?" he asked.

"To find my home."

"You don't know where your home is?"

"Of course I know where my home is." What was wrong with this man?

"If you know where your home is, why do you need to go to Gilden?"

"Because I don't know how to get there."

"You mean you don't know how to get to your home or how to get to Gilden?"

"To my home. That's why I must go to Gilden."

"But you said you got lost on your way to Gilden. It sounds

as if you don't know your way anywhere. You're helplessly lost. You'd better come with me."

I'd heard some people growled when frustrated. I understood why at that moment. I could barely keep myself from making that unseemly noise, especially when I noticed my thickheaded host's teasing grin. "And I suppose an introduction from you would get me into the highest society of … whatever this hamlet we're going to is called?"

"No, I'm afraid not. I wouldn't want to burden high society with the presence of a plain, irksome female. Shopkeepers were more the society I was thinking of."

Humph. What would he know about high society? He seemed to know about traveling though. "I must get home. Would you escort me to Florenburg? My father is the Duke of Henly. He would pay you handsomely for your troubles."

"Your father's the Duke of Henly?" He laughed as if he'd just seen his closest friend fall face first in the mud in his Sunday best. "Sorry, my lady. I may be a commoner, but I'm not a simpleton. You might be the cast-off lady's maid of a wealthy merchant's daughter—you have a bit of sophistication about you—but you're no daughter of a duke."

"How dare you! What would you know about the daughter of a duke? You're just a … a … what are you anyway?"

"I'm a woodsman. And even a woodsman knows the daughter of a duke doesn't sleep in the woods, particularly not in a faded dress like the one you're wearing. Now, eat up. You're going to wash the dishes this morning."

It was useless to argue, so I contented myself with an angry glance before returning my attention to breakfast. I wanted a fork to stab at something with, but all I had was a spoon and a bowl of runny porridge. But at least it wasn't nuts and berries.

Half an hour saw us cleaned up and packed. I looked longingly at the one horse, a bay with a silver streak in its mane. It was no thoroughbred, but riding a mule would be preferable to another day of walking.

The woodsman put a hand on the horse's bridle. "If you ask nicely, I might let you ride him. Mister's gentle enough for a fine lady such as yourself."

Why did he always have to make digs about me being a fine lady?

"That's very kind of you, but I wouldn't want to inconvenience you by depriving you of your horse. I'll walk. I'm accustomed to walking."

He shrugged his shoulders. "Suit yourself." He rubbed the horse's muzzle and took hold of the reins. "Come on, Mister." He led the horse forward.

I stared after them. "Aren't you going to ride him?"

"Certainly not. My mother raised me proper. I can't ride while a woman, even a stubborn one, walks."

Humph. I pulled my cloak closer about me and marched forward.

"Looks like you're getting off easy today, Mister." Whistling, the woodsman led us down the broad, overgrown path.

What had happened to the well-kept road? I spotted a dash of purple near the base of a tree. Violets. And to the approaching winter? How long had I been asleep under that tree?

The tree and everything beyond it to the castle still slept in dim, uneasy daylight.

⬥

The sycamore made for a lovely chair for a lunchtime picnic. A scaly root for a seat and a straight trunk of sleek white bark for a back.

Pity the rock ledge beside us was too high for a table. Goodness. What would Aunt Helene and the rest of my family say about me sitting at a table, even a rock one, eating a simple lunch with a rude woodsman? To whom I hadn't even been properly introduced.

"By the way, what is your name?"

He opened his mouth to speak and then shut it. A look of surprise and then of amusement crossed his face. He quickly replaced it with a stern look. "So you've finally condescended to ask, have you?"

"I should have asked before, but I—"

"Why should you have? What's my name to you? I'm only a woodsman, while you're the ex-maid of a fine lady. Of course, if I was someone else, say a knight or wealthy merchant, what interest would I have in your name?"

"If you wish to remain anonymous, just say so. You needn't insult me."

The blue eyes twinkled. "I don't know what this a-nony-mess means, but I'll tell you what—I'll let you call me Mr. Woodsman. Or, if you'd simply smile once in a while, I might let you call me Woodsman, maybe even My Woodsman."

"I'll call you no such thing."

"Suit yourself." He slurped his stew. On purpose. The tilt of his lips proved it.

"Do you refuse to introduce yourself to everyone or just to young ladies?"

"To everyone. I prefer to travel incognito." He flinched and dropped his spoon.

"Did you hurt yourself?" I asked, rather hopeful.

"Hurt myself? Oh. Ouch." He put a hand to his cheek and gave an exaggerated grimace. "It's nothing. You needn't concern yourself."

I couldn't help but smile. My Woodsman. Traveling incognito. He deserved to bite his cheek.

"Wait a minute. Traveling incognito? How does a woodsman who doesn't know what anonymous means throw words like 'incognito' around with ease?"

He flinched again. "I heard it in a play once."

"In what play?"

"In *The Prince Travels Incognito*. I saw it in Gilden. You needn't look so skeptical. Even a poor woodsman makes it into town every now and then for a bit of high-class entertainment."

I doubted it. He was muscular, but not as much as a common laborer should be, and his hands, though not exactly smooth, weren't that rough. He was probably the ex-servant of a nobleman and had likely been dismissed for insolence.

○●○

I hated to get back up, but lunch was over, and it was time to go. The blister on my left heel begged me to swallow my pride and ask permission to ride the horse. Mr. Woodsman must have heard it, for he walked over and abruptly pulled me to my feet.

"Mister's getting lazy. He was made to be a beast of burden. You'd better ride him." He put me on the horse before I could find my tongue. I wanted to find the sharp edge of it, but in the surprise of being manhandled, I could only find the dull end. A sarcastic "thank you" was all I could manage.

I had barely settled into the saddle when Mister began to fidget. "Pack horse. Be still. My situation is precarious enough without you dancing around beneath me." I tightened my grip on the reins.

The woodsman laid a hand on my arm. "Be quiet." There was an intensity to his voice that chilled me.

A snuffling sound, like things nosing around in the leaves, came from just down the trail. The snuffling creatures were heading in our direction.

"What is it?" I asked in a whisper.

"Wild boar."

My heart leapt in fear as images of the gored man brought to Henly Manor flashed through my mind.

Mister's fidgeting became nervous prancing. He reared. The woodsman grabbed me around the waist and pulled me to him. Mister bolted up the trail.

"Sensible horse. He knows when to run." The woodsman set my feet on the ground. "Our best option is to get above their reach." He pointed to the place where we ate lunch. Above the rock ledge, and accessible only by a steep bank, was a magnolia tree with low limbs. We sprinted toward it.

The snuffling became grunting.

Then I did what everyone wanted to do but should never do in a situation such as that. I looked back. Six or seven wild boars emerged from the trees.

The grunting became the pounding of heavy hoofs.

Perhaps dying of starvation alone in the woods wouldn't have been so bad.

"Hurry, Alexandria," Mr. Woodsman urged as we raced toward the bank.

My legs protested the ascent, but it was my feet that turned traitor. I slipped on the covering of dead leaves and fell to my knees, crushing a clump of violets.

The woodsman grabbed my arm, jerked me to my feet, and whisked me up the bank as if I were a waif. He didn't get me up the tree as if I were one, but he got me up, and himself up, about two blinks before the snuffling, grunting, pounding boars charged the tree. The thick-skulled brutes rammed the poor tree. Vibrations from the impact ran up my arms as I clung to the tree trunk.

"Maybe they'll get bored soon and go away," Mr. Woodsman said.

I knew he'd say something like that sooner or later.

"I said 'maybe they'll get *bored* and go away,'" he repeated.

"I heard you the first time."

"You're full of starch."

Better that than brainless puns.

The brutes eventually tired of the assault and moved on. We climbed down, and I lamented the tree's deep scars and the trampled wildflowers.

"Well, that was exciting, but we must be going. Come along." He whistled, and Mister trotted to us from whatever place of shelter he had disappeared to. Mr. Woodsman helped me onto the horse.

I looked from Mr. Woodsman to the battered tree and back. An unpleasant sensation nagged me, and I knew what I needed to do. My cheeks grew warm. I leaned forward and tapped him on the shoulder. "Thank you for saving me from the boars."

It was hard to tell under all that facial hair, but I thought he blushed.

"Yes, well, I can't stand the sight of blood. Come along, Mister. We don't want to be here when our friends come back through."

❧

"How long have you been gone from home?" Mr. Woodsman asked as we prepared dinner that night.

I had done such a good job washing the dishes after lunch that he had condescended to let me stir the stew. Floraisons valued self-sufficiency over being served, so I had no disdain of working when necessary.

"A while." Truth be told, I didn't know. I was ashamed to admit I'd sunk so far in misery as to not keep a mental calendar.

"Why did you leave?"

He was a nosy fellow.

"To search for the goose that lays the golden eggs."

"Oh, so you're a treasure hunter, also? Isn't this a coincidence? You must tell me all about your adventures."

Cheeky too.

"It's not a very interesting tale. I passed through a couple of villages with unpleasant inhabitants and ferocious dogs, met a beggar who offered to swap me three *magic* beans for my cloak—"

"You refused, of course?"

"Of course."

"Very sensible of you."

"I think so. And then I got lost in the woods and was rudely awakened by a stranger."

He was silent for a moment and then eyed me strangely. "You didn't stop by a castle did you? I've heard there's one hereabouts."

A shiver ran down my back. What would happen if people found out I'd enchanted the prince? "I may have passed it, but I certainly didn't stay there. I've heard the master of the castle isn't hospitable to strangers."

He contemplated me and then grabbed one of my hands. He flipped it over and examined it as a nursery maid examines her charges' hands before mealtime.

"I washed my hands." I tried to pull away. He held tight.

"You have the hands of a fine lady. That won't make you very popular in the village, particularly not with your highbred bearing and vocabulary."

He rubbed dirt and bits of bark into my hands and made me hold them in the cold stream for as long as I could stand it. If he wanted my hands to be red and chapped when we entered the village the next morning, he was certainly going to get his wish.

"I'm sorry to do this." He said it as if his hands were the ones being rubbed raw. "But no one will hire you if they think you've never worked a day in your life."

"Must I stay in the village?"

"We can't camp in the woods until our supplies run out. You've got to get a job, and I've got to get back to work."

The memory of my days of loneliness and hunger quickly stamped out any thoughts of rebellion. "Where do you work?"

"Around."

I cocked an eyebrow.

"Don't worry. I'll come by and check on you every now and then."

"That would be a great comfort," I said dryly.

CHAPTER 10

MIDMORNING WE DESCENDED a steep bank and came out of the woods onto a dirt road. Workers toiled in the green fields opposite us.

"We're not far from the village now." Mr. Woodsman patted Mister on the shoulder and looked up at me as I rode. "By the way, what can you do?"

I tilted my head to look at him. "Do?"

"Other than walk long distances. You've already said you could do that."

I drummed my fingers against the reins. "Well, I can sing, play half a dozen instruments, dance, embroider, knit, paint, intelligently discuss topics you've never heard of, manage a household—"

"That's wonderful, but I meant in the way of employment?"

"I'm a first rate lady's maid."

"I don't think any of the ladies here would want you. But you might make a decent schoolteacher. Can you cook? Oh, wait. Of course not. You've probably never been in a kitchen in your life." He rubbed his jaw.

"I can too cook. I also know how to sew, bake, and cultivate roses and other flowers." My mother had been of the opinion that in order to properly direct servants, we needed to know how to do their duties. I had a vast amount of theoretical knowledge on the subjects, some practical knowledge, but little practice, and that was a long time ago. But I wasn't going to admit it.

"I am duly impressed, milady." He made a surprisingly graceful bow. "But convincing the townsfolk of your accomplishments might be a little difficult. We'll check the school first." He gestured ahead to a cobblestone bridge over a canal. "Ah, here we are."

The village stretched out along the opposite side of the canal. It reminded me of the one near Henly Manor, only larger. Two- to three-story half-timbered homes and shops crowded together along narrow streets. Townsfolk strolled leisurely as they went about their business.

We crossed the bridge and Mr. Woodsman helped me dismount. I glanced around for a group of boys or young men who might harass me before I remembered my improvement in looks. Thank heavens.

"Excuse me, friend." Mr. Woodsman walked over to a short, balding man who had spent too much time in the sun. "Could you direct us to the schoolhouse?"

The man smiled. A friendly smile, despite the crooked teeth. "That, I can. The school's the last building on Goury Street." Buildings followed the canal for some distance down the waterway, and the man pointed to a group of houses a good quarter of a mile away. "But the head of the school board, Mr. Colter, owns the mercantile. If you'll just follow this road, you'll come to it. It's only a short walk."

"We'll go to the mercantile then. Much obliged." Mr. Woodsman touched his hat in farewell.

"Good luck to you." The local dipped his chin to me. "Good morning, miss." He smiled again and walked off.

We followed the road until we came to a two-story building with a freshly painted sign, which read "Mercantile," hanging above the door. A man with graying blond hair and an upturned nose rested on a wrought iron chair outside the store. His shopkeeper's apron and the familiar way he greeted people entering the store announced him as the owner.

"Remember, none of this daughter-of-a-duke stuff," the woodsman whispered as we approached the store.

"Good morning, Mr. Colter." The woodsman held out his hand to the man.

Mr. Colter stood up. Stoop shoulders ruined the air of authority his height and broad chest would have given him otherwise. "Morning. Do I know you?" he asked as they shook hands.

"No." The woodsman indicated me with a sweep of his hand. "This is Alexandria Floraison. She's new in town, and since she has a heap of book learning, we wondered if you could use her as a schoolteacher."

The man inspected me as an officer inspects his troops. Insolent man.

"I'm sorry but the position is full," Mr. Colter said when the inspection was over. I was surprised he didn't check to see if there was dirt under my fingernails.

"I don't suppose there's any chance of the young lady quitting soon to get married is there?" Mr. Woodsman persisted.

Mr. Colter didn't answer immediately but twisted to look toward the door as it swished open. A young woman with a wealth of blond curls and a slightly turned-up nose promenaded out and took him affectionately by the arm.

Mr. Colter's daughter I presumed. Her good looks, coupled to her father's business, doubtless put her among the most eligible females of the village. And she knew it. She gave Mr. Woodsman a coquettish smile. She wouldn't have even made the list in Florenburg.

I glanced over at my companion, half expecting him to either decamp or start stuttering in nervousness, but he kept his eyes fixed on Mr. Colter.

"The schoolteacher is a him." Mr. Colter gave his daughter's arm an affectionate pat. "We keep married schoolmasters. We don't hire married young women." He glanced at me.

"What a pity," Mr. Woodsman said hastily. "Thank you for your time, Mr. Colter. We'll try somewhere else."

The young woman looked disappointed.

"But we're not married," I said. There was no reason why Mr. Woodsman shouldn't be made a spectacle of too.

"Not that it matters since the position isn't open." There was a delightful hint of displeasure in Mr. Woodsman's eyes.

"You're brother and sister then?" Miss Colter gave Mr. Woodsman that smile again.

"No, we're not related." Mr. Woodsman rubbed his fingers through his hair and considered me. "She's sort of an inheritance left to me by a friend. He's no longer able to care for her, so he left her to me. I'm trying to find her a position so she can care for herself, and I can go on my way."

"But he said he would come by and check on me every now and then," I added.

Miss Colter's face brightened. "An orphan. How tragic. Papa, couldn't we find her a position in the shop so her noble provider doesn't have to worry about her?"

Mr. Colter considered me again and then did his officer's examination on the woodsman, who was scowling.

Mr. Colter patted his daughter's hand. "I'm sorry, my dear, but we can't use anyone just now. I'm sure the young woman can find employment elsewhere." He looked back at us. "Good day, Miss Floraison. Mr. ...?"

"Good day, sir. Miss. Sorry to have troubled you." Mr. Woodsman took my arm and directed me back the way we had come. "Come along, Miss Floraison."

"I don't think he approved of me," I said when we were out of earshot. I didn't even try to suppress the impish grin betraying the false sorrow in my words.

Mr. Woodsman gave me a dark look. "You mean you don't think he approved of me. I would be obliged if you would let me do the talking from now on."

"You know, if you shaved and cut your hair, you might be tolerably attractive—to more discerning people than the village coquette."

"I should have left you in the forest," he said gruffly. He ran a hand over his thick whiskers and said defensively, "Hairiness runs in my family, particularly at this time in the family history and in this close proximity to—" He stopped and tugged on the horse's bridle. "Come on, Mister. Pick up your feet. We don't have all day." He hurried us down the road.

"You'd be of absolutely no use at a blacksmith's or at the livery stable," he mused as we trudged along. "It was a 'no' at the mercantile and at the school. Aha. Here's a bakery. It's a reputable looking place. We'll try there."

Unfortunately, the bakery was much like the mercantile, only without the coquette. I was examined and dismissed "on account of us having all the hands we need at present." I wondered why they bothered to inspect me if they didn't need anyone.

We left the bakery and walked silently through the village until we came to a dressmaker's shop. The woodsman eyed me speculatively.

"Perhaps a new dress would help." He tied Mister's reins to a post.

"I haven't any money."

"That's all right. I have."

Food was one thing, and that was sore enough, but clothing was something else entirely. "I can't accept a dress from you."

"You can and you will." He took me firmly by the elbow and ushered me into the store. "You can pay me for it after you've worked a while, if you wish."

A bell rang as we entered, and a woman emerged from a back room. She had a small, round face on a long, lean body. Her close-set eyes and beak-like nose reminded me of a hawk, but at least her dress was as fashionable as one could expect of a place like this.

The woodsman, as he had said he wanted to, did all of the talking and choosing. Since I wasn't needed, I glanced around the store and flipped through a catalog, mentally preparing myself for a tasteless outfit of garish color. At least it would be clean, and I could pay him back for it.

But then he presented me with a pale yellow dress, the most fashionable of the ready-made garments and the one I would have chosen if given the opportunity.

"Thank you," I stammered. "It's ..." lovely was perhaps going too far for someone who had worn the gowns I had, "... very nice."

"Well, I rather fancied a purple and orange combination with lots of big bows, but Mrs. Sutton assured me that she doesn't carry anything of that description."

Bravo for Mrs. Sutton.

The discerning lady motioned to a dressing room, and I noticed the woodsman whispering to her before I disappeared into it.

I had never purchased a ready-made dress before, but I

doubted the dressmaker usually spent much time fretting over it. Mrs. Sutton, however, seemed in no hurry whatsoever and fussed over the hems and darts and made little alterations here and there until I was nearly driven to distraction. The fact the mirror confirmed that I was a "faded beauty" didn't help any.

At last she gathered up my old dress and told me to sit and rest while she wrapped it up for me.

I soaked up the peace and quiet for a few minutes before returning to the front of the store.

The woodsman chatted comfortably with Mrs. Sutton at the counter. He noticed me and smiled. "You look worlds better. We'll be on our way now. Thank you for everything, Mrs. Sutton." He took a wrapped package from her and headed toward the door.

Mrs. Sutton gave me a friendly smile. Pity she looked rather like a hawk, especially since she didn't resemble one otherwise.

I thanked her and followed the woodsman.

Two weary hours later we ate lunch and rested in a meadow at the edge of town. I reclined on a blanket in the shadow of a cedar tree. The darkness fit my mood. We had been to practically every establishment in the village—all the major ones at least—and every one had rejected me. One owner dared suggest we try the local tavern. Me, the daughter of a duke, become a tavern wench! As if I would accept the job no matter my birth. Mr. Woodsman's objections were no less strong than my own.

He was quite an enigma, this woodsman. He clearly thought me a plain, irksome female, yet he went to great lengths to take care of me. His kindness and efforts only added to my shame, and, as irrational as it might be, irritated me.

"Well, it didn't go so well this morning." He leaned against the tree and twisted blades of grass in his hand. "But there are still a few more places to try our luck."

In other words, a few more places for me to be sized up and

found lacking. A few more hours of this man's life wasted on my behalf, an increase in my debt to this hairy woodsman. A debt I couldn't repay. My insides felt like they were being squeezed by hot hands. I could bear it no longer. I stood, folded the blanket, and put it in Mister's saddlebag. I ran my fingers through the silver streak of mane near his ear, rubbed his muzzle in goodbye, and then marched past him to the road, heading away from the village.

I had gone several feet before the woodsman noticed. "Where are you going?" His steps quickened in my direction.

"To Gilden."

"Are you so anxious to leave me?"

That wasn't exactly the reply I expected. I stopped and pivoted to face him. "You've been very kind, and I thank you. I really do. But I can't stay here. I'm tired of being humiliated, of begging for a job, of being an object of charity, of being eyed like a horse at auction and rejected as unfit. Maybe Gilden has a position for a fine lady. You needn't trouble yourself with me any longer."

He reached out as if to take my hand, but let his own fall back to his side instead. "They say a little humiliation is good for one. And you're not the one begging for a job, I am. Don't be too hard on the townsfolk. You'd be an investment after all. They'd have to provide room and board and a small wage in exchange for services they don't know if you can give."

"Why do you go to so much trouble for me?"

"Because I found you. You're my responsibility." He grinned. "Besides, you need me."

"I do not, and I don't want to be your responsibility. You can find another burden for your horse, because I'm going to Gilden." I stormed away.

"Alexandria Floraison, you stop where you are, or I'll turn you over my knee."

I spun around. "You wouldn't dare."

He took a threatening step forward. "Oh, wouldn't I?"

He would. Obstinate man. Why wouldn't he leave me alone? I faced him squarely and tried to tell him by a defiant glare that he hadn't defeated me. I considered my options. But I had none, unless starving on the way to Gilden counted as an option.

A smile of victory spread slowly across his face. "My lady." He gestured back towards town.

I gave him an angry look and brushed passed him—going back to the town. He whistled a jaunty tune as he fetched Mister and caught up with me.

I bandaged the wound to my pride by considering what I would turn him into if I had my power of enchantment. All I could think of was a moth with velvety black tips on its golden wings. I doubted this prickly caterpillar would turn into a handsome moth.

⊹⊱◈⊰⊹

"Mrs. Sutton said the man who owns the bookstore doesn't need an assistant, but I don't think there's any harm in trying. She said he's a pleasant fellow."

"That would be a change," I murmured.

"That's what I like about you. You're extremely optimistic and always look for the good in people." The woodsman's blue eyes bored into me with the same reprimanding force that Giles's had at times. I turned away and decided to keep my comments to myself.

The smell of books greeted us as we entered the bookshop. It was perfume to me. Visions of Papa sitting in his favorite chair in our library floated before my eyes.

The sound of a book closing and a chair squeaking was

shortly followed by "Welcome to Peachtree's Bookstore. I'm Albert Peachtree. What can I do for you?"

A man a few inches taller than me walked around a bookcase to the front counter. He was clean-shaven, and his hair was cut close to his head, probably in an attempt to hide a deep widow's peak. Mid-forties and far from handsome, but he had a gentleman-like bearing.

"It's a pleasure to meet you, Mr. Peachtree," said the woodsman. "I have two matters of business to discuss with you. The first is … do you have any adventure books? I find I'd really like to read a good adventure."

Mr. Peachtree's eyebrows rose as if he were surprised. No wonder, most common laborers founded their pride on their hard work and skill. Reading was shameful idleness to them. Who was this woodsman?

"Don't you have adventure books here?" Mr. Woodsman prodded.

Mr. Peachtree blinked. "Forgive me. I have just the book for you. I ordered it for a particular customer, but she won't be wanting it now. She loved roses and adventure books, so I thought she would enjoy this one." He searched through books piled on the long counter and underneath on its shelves.

"Did something happen to the young lady?" The woodsman sounded concerned.

"I hope not." His voice echoed among the shelves. "They say she went to live with her aunt. Left a few days ago. Here's the book." Mr. Peachtree plopped a thick book on the counter. The book was titled *The Sword of the Rose Prince*.

"I love a good adventure," Mr. Woodsman said as he paid for it. He glanced at me. "I leave all the poetry and essays and biographies to her."

I felt it only a partial compliment, but Mr. Peachtree looked at me with admiration.

"Is the young lady well read? I would have wagered she preferred romances, as most of her sex do."

"The heroes are rarely up to her standards," the woodsman replied before I could clarify that I enjoyed a variety of genres, and not all of a strictly intellectual bent. "She's actually the other matter of business I came about," he continued. "I'm endeavoring, albeit unsuccessfully at the moment, to find Miss Floraison a respectable position. Do you know of a position suitable for a well-educated young woman?"

Mr. Peachtree considered for a moment. "I suppose you've tried the mercantile?"

"Yes, and the dressmaker's, and the hatter's, and the baker's."

"Hmmm. There's Miss Rosalie Lightwood's pastry shop. Have you tried there?"

"No. Where is it?"

"It's a few blocks down, set back a little from the other stores. Miss Lightwood's a kind, respectable woman. I can't promise she can take Miss Floraison, but it'd be worth asking her."

I sighed as the door shut behind us. That was the closest I had felt to intelligent society since leaving home.

Miss Lightwood's store was a two-story building with one good-sized window on the first level and two small windows on the second, which I assumed served as the living quarters. Clematis vines chased each other up the wall to rest on the steeply sloping roof. A couple of rose bushes and a gardenia were planted in baskets under the large window.

A plump woman with ill-arranged hair and dark circles under her eyes greeted us cheerfully as we entered. Certainly not a handsome face, which may have been one of the reasons she was on the wrong side of forty and still a Miss.

"Lovely day, isn't it? What can I do for you?" she asked with a smile.

"Good afternoon, Miss Lightwood." Mr. Woodsman removed his hat and smiled at her. "There are two things you can do for me. The first is that you can sell me two of your most scrumptious pastries, and the second is that you can listen to me pitch a sale. Mr. Peachtree suggested I try you."

Miss Lightwood's smile brightened. "Mr. Peachtree did? Well, sit yourselves down at a table, and I'll grab the pastries and join you."

Mr. Woodsman put a few coins on the counter and led the way to one of the unoccupied tables.

Miss Lightwood joined us. "I'm Miss Rosalie Lightwood, but you probably already guessed that. What are you two's names?"

"This is Miss Alexandria Floraison, and I'm a woodsman."

"I've never heard of the Woodsmans. You're not from around here?"

"Woodsman is more his profession and sobriquet than an actual family name. He prefers to travel incognito," I answered. His reluctance to give a name was most peculiar. I supposed he thought it amusing. Perhaps his name was Rumpelstiltskin.

Miss Lightwood looked confused and embarrassed.

"What Miss Floraison means is that woodsman is my trade and that I find the title a convenient name as well. Tell us about yourself, Miss Lightwood. How long have you been in business? What sorts of things do you sell other than these mouth-watering pastries?"

He was right about the mouth-watering pastries. They were quite good even by Floraison standards.

Miss Lightwood's smile faded. "When my father died I sold our farm and bought this shop. I do whatever I can to keep it going. I make pastries, grow a few flowers, and knit little toys and some warm things, like scarves and mittens, for men who don't have womenfolk to do it for them. I cook meals for a few of the single men, Mr. Peachtree in particular. It's a nice little shop I have, and I've gotten to know several of the townsfolk over the years, but it's a bit lonely after quitting time."

Mr. Woodsman smiled warmly and leaned forward as he listened. You would think he was listening to one of the magi. I certainly didn't think she was a magus, but I remembered my loneliness as a hag and sympathized with her.

"You seem to be doing well with the business," he said.

Her smile returned. "Pretty good, yes. I enjoy the work, though it's a bit tiring at times. I've a score of knitting requests to fill, a lot of mending, plus making lighter socks for warmer weather and that sort of thing. More than I can get too really, especially since my wrist hurts if I knit too long." She rubbed her left wrist.

"I'm sorry to hear that," Mr. Woodsman said. "One of my aunts has the same problem. She wraps her wrist up tight with a bandage. She says it helps. You might try it."

"A bandage? That's an idea," she answered. "But what was it that Mr. Peachtree suggested you try to sell me?"

"Sell isn't exactly the right word. The truth is it's fallen to my lot to look after Miss Floraison, but I can't exactly drag her about the countryside with me. I was hoping to find her a position here so I could check in on her every once in a while."

"The poor dear. Let me think a moment." Miss Lightwood picked at the tabletop. "It would be a big help to me to have someone to mind the store while I deliver the lunches and help keep up with the knitting. Some company would be most welcome too. I've an extra room upstairs, but it's rather small, and I couldn't give much for a wage."

"Your friendship would more than make up for a small wage. You'll take her, then?"

Miss Lightwood glanced at me. "Yes, I'd be glad of her help."

The sudden change in my fortune left me speechless. Should I be happy about this? Servant of a poor woman? I felt a pressure on my foot, the one nearest the woodsman. I guess I was. I smiled as cheerfully as I could. "That's very kind of you, Miss Lightwood. I will strive to please you."

She patted my hand. "I'm sure we'll get along fine, and before you know it, we'll be like two peas in a pod. After all, I know what it's like to be in a strange place without family."

What I always wanted to be, a common garden vegetable. Though that was preferable to no company at all. But how long would it be before I could repay the woodsman and earn enough to travel to Gilden and, from there, home?

"I'm sure you two will get along famously," Mr. Woodsman said. "I have a few errands to run, but, if it's convenient, I'd like to order my dinner from you tonight and whenever I'm in town. If the meals are half as good as your pastries, I'm in for a treat."

"Of course. I'll add your name to the pot."

"Wonderful." He stood. "I'll pay another visit to Mr. Peachtree and take my meal with him. That way you won't have to hunt for me. If Miss Floraison will grant me a private interview outside, I will leave you to your work."

I reluctantly followed him out. Thanks and goodbye were in order, and I disliked giving both.

"It's my pleasure," Mr. Woodsman said as he retrieved a paper-wrapped package from Mister's saddlebag.

I took the package. "What? What do you mean?"

"I mean helping you is my pleasure. You were about to give a lengthy speech on your gratitude for my kindness and generosity, but as that would embarrass us both, I thought I would cut to the 'you're welcome' bit."

"That's very considerate of you. Should I now turn and walk away to save us the trouble of awkward farewells?"

"That's an excellent idea." He took me by the shoulders,

swiveled me around, and gently pushed me toward the store. "Till we meet again, my lady."

A feeling of uncertainty fell on me as I walked back to the store. I hadn't been in one place longer than a night since leaving home. What would life be like as a shopkeeper's assistant?

I glanced at the woodsman. He was hairy and uncouth, but he had been kind to me. And I rather enjoyed trading sarcastic remarks with him.

CHAPTER 11

ROSALIE, AS SHE insisted I call her, chatted about the village inhabitants as she showed me around the store and the upstairs living area. She was detailing the Colter family history when we arrived at my room. The history faded as I took it in. The scullery maid's room at Henly Manor was larger and better furnished than this.

A bed with a thin mattress rested against the inside wall, and a trunk and a worn chair tried to hide in the far corner. A short chest of drawers squatted under the only window. The view from the window was the only consolation as it overlooked mountains and forests.

"And you've met Mrs. Sutton, the dressmaker." Rosalie's voice came back into focus.

How many villagers had I missed? "Yes, I have."

"She's a nice lady but busy with her shop and family. I wish she had more time for visiting. Well, how do you like your room? Goodness. It's a bit drab, isn't it?"

She scurried out and then back in a few minutes later with a multicolored quilt and a vase. "My mother made this quilt." She spread it over the bed. "It will add a little color and warmth." She put the vase, a cheap white thing with blue flowers painted on it, on the chest of drawers. "It still needs something. Ah. I know just the thing." She hurried out again and came back with a bouquet.

"Are those roses?"

She laughed at the excitement in my voice. "I wish they were, my dear. The only roses here are the ones I brought with me when I moved, and they're pathetic, flowerless bushes now. From what I've heard, the roses hereabouts caught the blight some fifteen years ago and died. These are crocheted."

"No roses?" It was unthinkable. Dreadful. Appalling. Un-Floraison-like. "Do you have many other flowers?"

"Oh, yes. As many as other places. Just no roses." Rosalie lovingly arranged the crocheted flowers in the vase. Her serene humming cut through my shock, reminding me that there were beautiful flowers besides roses.

A smile touched my lips as I watched her. A woman who loved roses enough to copy them in yarn, and copy them artfully, could not be too common. And, apparently, not unkind, for I suspected this gift came from her room. For a shopkeeper who couldn't afford fine paintings or many decorations at all, the handmade roses would light up the space like a patch of blue sky on a cloudy day.

"They are lovely. Your generosity is astonishing. I thank you."

She blushed. "You're quite welcome. Oh, and speaking of lovely, I forgot to mention Miss Belle Monroe and her father. He was once a wealthy merchant in the city. But he lost most of his fortune and used what little was left to buy a farm in a nearby village. This was some fifteen or sixteen years back. Poor man, he lost his wife to consumption a few years after that. He and Belle moved here then for a change of scenery. Miss

Belle's as lovely as a rose. In fact many folks call her Beauty. Very sweet girl, too, and bright. She's a great favorite of Mr. Peachtree's, his best customer. Always reading, she is. And she wants my roses to bloom as much as I do. Her poor father hasn't been quite the same since she left."

"Is this the young woman who went to live with her aunt? Mr. Peachtree mentioned her." I was sorry to have missed the company of an educated young woman.

"Yes, that's Belle. The single men are heartbroken, particularly that Louis, but the single women are joyful, on account of Louis. Such a strong and handsome fellow. Most folks wonder why she didn't marry him instead of going off to her aunt's."

I helped cook dinner that night by fetching water and chopping vegetables. When that was done, Rosalie kindly left me to bathe and settle in while she delivered the meals.

The wooden tub in the kitchen and the hot water on the stove—and no maid to frequently refresh it—were a bit of a shock and an unpleasant reminder of my lowly station in life.

I stopped my bitter lament and reminded myself that the first Lady Floraison had lived in even more primitive conditions in the army camps during the Caffin Wars. She had insisted on staying with her husband and was credited for the victory at the Battle of Florenburg. She initiated and oversaw the careful collecting and burning of poison ivy near the enemy camp. A good, steady wind, and two days later the enemy surrendered—the only condition of which was that they would be given Lady Floraison's special anti-itch potion. The surrender was the turning point in the war.

Woods, mansion, or village store, I wasn't going to be defeated. I thought through the things my servants did for me and sighed. There was no one to comb the tangles from my hair before I went to bed. No one to lay out a clean nightgown. I would have to wash my own few garments—two dresses and one set of underclothes.

I ran upstairs to get my old dress. The smell of lavender escaped as I unwrapped the brown paper parcel. I gasped. On top of my neatly folded dress lay a comb and a bar of lavender-scented soap. There was also a nightdress and a set of undergarments tucked in beside the gown. I remembered the woodsman whispering to Mrs. Sutton and the amount of time she spent with me—time enough for him to collect these things.

He was very thoughtful, this woodsman. I blushed at how thoughtful.

But I blessed him for all he did for me as I settled into bed warm and clean. The fact that the bed was only slightly less lumpy than the forest floor did not disturb my sleep.

❧

The next week was exhausting and irritating. Aside from learning that some people could make excellent pastries and some could not, no matter how talented their instructor, I discovered what life was like without servants.

Despite my forgetting to empty the bath water or to conserve the expensive candles or my other frustrating failures, Rosalie was kind and patient. Every night before we retired she smiled and said, "I'm glad you're here, Alexandria."

To which I politely replied, "Thank you for taking me in."

❧

The fickle spring weather couldn't decide if it wanted to run back to winter or continue toward summer. Personally, I was ready to shed my cloak and only carry firewood inside for cooking purposes.

"Alexandria, are you out here?" The back door banged as Rosalie rushed outside.

I dropped my armload of firewood. "Is something the matter?"

"No, my dear." Chuckling, Rosalie slowed her pace and came to a stop in front of me. "Nothing is wrong. I want you to meet someone."

She brushed the bits of bark off my dress and hurried me inside the shop. She discreetly pointed to the tallest of the men sitting at one of the tables.

Sleek black hair, a handsome face, well-defined muscles. The universally admired Louis, no doubt. The tallest, strongest, and toughest man in town. As well as the best hunter, the biggest eater, and the most listened-to talker.

The young men sitting beside him and the young women at the next table hung on his every word. And he had plenty to say, between mouthfuls of the pastries covering his plate.

"That buck never had a chance. He knew he was a goner as soon as he saw who was after him. I already know where I'll mount his antlers." Louis waved his hand over an imaginary wall.

"Why, that buck beats the record," said the pudgy man sitting next to Louis. "You'll have to hang it where your last record-breaking kill is."

"That's the place I had in mind, Harry."

"You're going to need a bigger house to hold all your trophies," added a youth at the table.

"I probably will." Louis washed down his pastries with a large glass of lemonade.

"And what lucky girl would you get to decorate that new house for you?" asked one of the other young men.

"Not Belle Monroe. She don't care for antlers," Harry said.

Louis glared at him. "She was only being coy. She really loves them."

Rosalie nudged me and smiled. I managed to tilt the corners of my lips a little. His physical appearance was up to Floraison standards, but that was all that was.

Rosalie eased an overfull tray of pastries into my hands and sent me to Louis's table to refill the men's plates. The young women glowered at me. The young men gave me a quick glance and then returned to their pastries.

A sharp pain shot through my chest. I truly had lost the Floraison beauty. Not that the admiration of commoners—or nobles, I reminded myself—was important, but it was still a blow. I looked at Louis. At least I wasn't a brainless bag of muscles. Physical appearance wasn't everything.

The bell over the door jingled and a broad-shouldered man with a gray mustache entered. The empty pastry tray I was holding clattered to the table.

"Watch it, girl," Louis scolded.

I scrambled to pick up the tray and then hurried behind the counter.

Choruses of "Good afternoon, Mr. Monroe" sounded through the room. Keeping a tight grip on the tray to hide the trembling of my hands, I watched Mr. Monroe sit at an empty table.

It was the same man, only older.

Mr. Monroe was the husband of the beautiful and kind Anne, my only friend as a hag. Even if Rosalie hadn't told me he was a widower, the sadness in his eyes would have. And the little girl, Belle, was now motherless—and grown up. I had slept a long time in the forest.

Tears burned my eyes as I crept out of the room.

Rosalie found me a couple of hours later working on the knitting requests.

"Alexandria, whatever is the matter? Your eyes are all red."

They were. Red for the loss of a friend, for the pain in her husband's eyes, for the loss of their daughter, though it was a different kind of loss. He was alone now, as I had been. As I would be. I must have been asleep in the forest about fifteen years. He had grown older. The little girl had grown up. Was it too late for me to go home?

"Oh, it's those young men, isn't it?" Rosalie patted my shoulder. "Don't you fret, my dear, if they don't pay you any attention at first. Once they get to know you, they'll be pestering you to let them come calling."

I bit back a retort about preferring death to the thought of marrying one of those peasant men. After all, Rosalie meant to be kind. I shouldn't scold her.

"It's nothing. Just silliness and has nothing to do with those men, I assure you." I put down my knitting and stood. "Do you need assistance preparing dinner?"

"No, I've already finished and was wondering if you wanted to accompany me on my rounds."

I fought the urge to rub my puffy eyes. I wasn't fit to be seen. "Thank you, but I will eat here and continue working on these socks."

"That's quite all right. Maybe next time. I'll see you later." Rosalie patted my shoulder and left.

Maybe next time? Except for Mr. Peachtree, the other gentlemen reliant on her meals were uncouth. I had no desire to participate in the few minutes of small talk that always accompanied the evening deliveries. I could almost feel Giles's blue eyes on me, admonishing me for not considering Rosalie. I sighed. If it would make Rosalie happy to have my company and help in carrying the meals, then I would go with her. But I expected no pleasure from it.

❦

The few coins jingled as I shook my hand. My first wages. Some colorful ribbons would be nice, something to improve my appearance. A brief glance in the small mirror above my dresser supported the wish, but I didn't have money for such frivolities. I owed Mr. Woodsman for a dress and other garments, but even that would have to wait.

Grimacing at its three frayed spots and the stain on the drawstring, I opened my handbag and dropped the coins inside.

"Do you have a moment?" Rosalie asked as I passed through the kitchen on my way out. She gestured with her rolling pin to a letter on the table. "Roger delivered that recipe from his mother. Will you read it to me?"

"Of course."

As I read, she stared at the ceiling, her forehead wrinkled.

"Hmm. Too much water in the recipe. That's the problem." Her face relaxing, she waved a flour-covered hand at me. "Thank you, dear. Enjoy your afternoon off."

I paused before the mercantile and sighed that I had to make a list of purchases to ensure I stayed within budget so I could afford paper and ink. Rosalie had a penknife and an inkwell. Strangely enough, I'd had to dig through a closet to find the inkwell, but she didn't have much family to write letters to.

Most of my remaining earnings would go toward mailing the letter. It was probably a waste of money. Sonser had remarkably poor cross-country postal service. The wealthy used special couriers, but that option wasn't open to me.

After purchasing the stationary items, I left the store and

walked through the village for exercise, composing my letter as I went. "I love you. I miss you. Please come get me" was the gist of my thoughts, but how to say it in an elegant way?

When I reached my room, I filled the inkwell, laid out the penknife, and then retrieved the quill pen from my handbag. To my surprise, the pen didn't need mending. Pulling out a sheet of paper, I dipped the quill in the ink.

Dearest Mama and Papa ...

"Alexandria." Rosalie's voice sounded strained.

I tucked my bonnet and the finished letter under my arm and walked to the kitchen.

"Alexandria, I'm sorry to bother you again on your afternoon off." Rosalie huffed out a breath as she lowered an overstuffed basket onto the kitchen table and then rubbed her wrist. "But Mr. Tinsler's brothers are staying with him this week, and with the extra meals, I simply can't carry everything."

Trapped.

Can't escape the evening pleasantries with peasants anymore. I forced a smile. "I'll move some of the meals to another basket and join you, but I must stop by the mercantile."

"Of course. I appreciate your help." Rosalie's smile made mine feel a little more genuine.

After two deliveries, we made a short detour to the mercantile.

"I'll send this with the first mail carrier or reliable group of merchants who come through, Miss Floraison." Mr. Colter slid the letter into his jacket pocket. "It may be a while before a response comes."

"Thank—" A heavily bearded man at the periphery of the store drew my attention. He ducked down an aisle. Mr. Woodsman? I quickly turned back to Mr. Colter. "—you. Good day, Mr. Colter."

Peering down that aisle, and the adjacent one, as I left revealed no one but a smooth-faced boy eyeing the display of hunting knives.

❧

I dreamed of a young woman crying. Curled up in a chair in an enormous library, she wept.

A shadow fell across her.

"Stop that noise. You chose to stay," said a deep, gruff voice.

"I did. But why couldn't you have let us both go? I'm so lonely," said the young woman. Sniffling, she stared at the chair arm as if determined not to look at her companion.

"What do you know of loneliness?"

She started, as I did, at the bitterness in his tone, and gave him a brief glance.

"You know nothing," he said. "Even my guests refuse to be my company."

"No," said the young woman. "You know nothing. My mother is dead. I may never see my father again. You may be lonely for the entertainment of company, but I am lonely for those I love. Something you wouldn't understand."

"Am I too hideous to be looked at, much less loved? Is that what you mean?" he roared.

"Yes! Your face fits your heart so well no one would ever be misled by it into thinking you lovable."

There was a pause and the shadow moved away. The woman cried until darkness shrouded the window behind her and invisible servants lit the lamps and straightened the books around her. Upon wiping her eyes, she found a silver mirror resting on the table beside her. A note was tucked underneath it.

. . .

Beauty,

Your father is well. Call his name and this mirror will show him, or anyone else, to you. May this ease your loneliness.

Sincerely,
  Beast

❦

Something was different. I could feel it in the air and see it in the rose bushes outside the pastry shop. Each of the bushes had three tiny buds, the first since Rosalie moved to the village.

Mr. Tinsler, one of Rosalie's meal takers, shook his gray head and pointed to the buds. "What's the world coming to when a few flower buds are the seven days wonder of a respectable village? I ask you, Alexia Floraison, what's the world coming to?" He leaned against the doorframe, puffing smoke rings from his prized, handmade pipe.

"To a more beautiful place, I hope, Mr. Tinsler."

Aunt Helene would faint at the thought of a retired barrel maker with wooden teeth and barely enough money to live on calling me by a nickname. But he had taken quite a liking to me the few weeks I had been accompanying Rosalie on her rounds. I had hated the impertinent nickname to begin with, but it didn't rub so raw now.

"Why, Miss Floraison, you're smiling. I must be seeing things," said a deep and familiar voice. "Doesn't the smile improve her looks, Mr. Tinsler?"

Mr. Woodsman's reflection grinned broadly at me in the window I was washing.

"It do, though she's right pretty without it." Mr. Tinsler knocked his pipe against the wall. The falling ashes danced in the gentle breeze. Fortunately, they danced away from my clean windows.

I dropped the rag into the bucket of water and wiped my hands on my apron, twisting to watch Mr. Woodsman greet Mr. Tinsler with a hearty handshake.

"True, but I prefer her with it." Mr. Woodsman's eyes twinkled as they met mine.

"I'll be sure to take that into consideration," I said dryly, disconcerted by the strange feeling of satisfaction that he was here. On a Wednesday, of all days. I'd only seen him on Sundays at church since we first came to town. "What are you doing here? I thought you had work to do?"

"I came to see how you were getting along, of course, but the thought of one of Miss Rosalie's meals didn't hurt the notion."

"Did someone call me?" Rosalie stepped through the open doorway. "Mr. Woodsman! How are you? Mr. Peachtree said to expect you sometime today."

"To tell the truth, Miss Rosalie, I'm feeling a little puny." He winked at her. "But I think one of your pastries would just about set me to rights. And if you can find one for each of us, I know I would be well again."

"You sure know the way to cure folk." Mr. Tinsler slapped Mr. Woodsman on the back.

Rosalie laughed merrily. "I'm sure I can spare four pastries."

When we were seated, Mr. Woodsman said to Rosalie, "How's your new assistant doing? Has she been behaving herself?"

Rosalie smiled at me. "To be sure, she's a wonderful girl and a great help, though she's a bit quiet. I still don't know a thing about her."

I shifted in my seat. I didn't quite know how to talk to someone with such a different background. I couldn't very well talk about my past. She would think I was lying or insane.

Mr. Woodsman glanced at me. "Miss Floraison doesn't like to talk about her family. Rather a sad topic. You see, she lost them in a puff of smoke."

"A fire! How dreadful. Poor thing. No wonder she doesn't like to talk about it."

I avoided her sympathetic look, remembering when they did disappear in a puff of smoke, a different smoke than the woodsman implied though. Loneliness gripped my heart. Even if fifteen years had passed, and even if I was only a remnant of my former self, I wanted to go home.

"I'm sure she could find something else to talk about, if she put her mind to it," Mr. Woodsman said. "She's a bright young lady."

CHAPTER 12

I DID PUT my mind toward conversing with Rosalie, but it ended in miserable failure. Since she and Mr. Peachtree were friends, I assumed she would've made use of his book collection. On our way to Mr. Peachtree's shop for Sunday dinner, which was our weekly custom, I asked Rosalie her opinion of the most well-known authors and poets I could think of.

She knew none of them. She became quiet and serious at the mere mention of books. I couldn't fathom that a kind, respectable woman, whom I approved of more than most in the village, was totally unfamiliar with literature.

She was quiet at dinner. Even Mr. Woodsman, who was now to be a regular attender of our Sunday dinners, had a difficult time getting more than a short sentence out of her.

"I was walking along the canal earlier," he said, "and noticed a peculiar little flower growing out of a crack in the wall. You don't have a book on plants do you, Albert? I'd like to look up that little flower." He glanced at Mr. Peachtree and then flicked his eyes in Rosalie's direction.

Mr. Peachtree cleared his throat. "I have one around somewhere, but it's such a lovely evening, why don't we take a walk to see it? I'm certain Miss Rosalie can tell you what you want to know."

Rosalie gave a little smile. "I can't promise I'll know what it is, but I'd like to see it."

"So you shall," Mr. Woodsman said and rose from the table.

I soon found myself walking beside Mr. Woodsman a few yards in front of Rosalie and Mr. Peachtree. The cool evening breeze was a refreshing addition to the charming scene of flowering shrubs, vines scrambling up half-timbered homes, and white swans swimming in the canal.

"Miss Rosalie doesn't seem her usual, cheerful self tonight." Mr. Woodsman's voice brought me back to attention.

"I noticed that as well. I don't know why. We haven't fought, if that's what you're thinking."

He looked surprised. "Fought? I wouldn't accuse you of ill will against anyone, of neglect or misguided intentions maybe, but not of ill will."

I cocked an eyebrow at the misguided intentions comment but was glad he didn't think I was deliberately unpleasant to Rosalie. Though why I cared, I didn't know. "I've tried not to neglect her. In fact, since I cannot speak of my past, I endeavored to have a conversation with her on books and poetry. She had very little to say."

He groaned. "So that's it."

"That's what?"

"Miss Rosalie barely knows her letters. She can't read as you and I read."

I gaped at him. "Are you sure?"

"She had to quit school to take care of her younger sister and the household after her mother died. Mr. Peachtree said she hasn't specified just how much she can read, but he guesses it's not much. She's sensitive about her lack of education."

I walked over to the low stone wall of the canal and stared dumbly at the water flowing by. How could I have been so blind? I thought she asked me to read things for her because her hands were full or covered in flour. I couldn't imagine what it would be like to be illiterate.

A swan with her young family glided down the canal, the cygnets not venturing far from her, as if still unsure of their abilities. "Do you think Rosalie would enjoy me reading to her? She could learn a little that way, at least of stories, though not of words."

Mr. Woodsman's eyebrows rose in surprise; then his face took on such a pleased expression that I couldn't help but be embarrassed and pleased too.

"I think this village agrees with you, Miss Floraison. That would be a very kind thing to do. I'm sure it would help Miss Rosalie's opinion of herself, especially where Mr. Peachtree is concerned. I fear she feels beneath him because of her lack of education. She is as fortunate to have you as a friend as you are to have her."

My face flushed with warmth. What would Aunt Helene think of the daughter of a duke being friends with a shopkeeper who was little more than illiterate? I wasn't sure I cared what she would think.

The swans disappeared from view, and we continued walking.

"This village must agree with you as well," I said. "I've seen you here at least once a week for the two months I've been resident. I thought you intended to travel for work?"

Mr. Woodsman cleared his throat. "There's plenty of work for a woodsman in this area. I travel during the week and return for church service and now also for Miss

Rosalie's excellent Sunday dinners. Have you met the famous Louis? I hear all of the women are madly in love with him."

Humph. I rolled my eyes at the memory of the silly girls who invariably followed him into the shop. "*Madly* in love is an accurate description."

"You don't care for him? He's held up as the image of physical perfection around here."

"He is uncommonly handsome, but that is the only uncommon trait he possesses."

"I see. He hasn't the birth and breeding to match his appearance, does he?" There was an accusation of snobbery in his tone that I didn't like.

"He does lack those. Not that that would be an issue for most of the women here." My thoughts rushed from Louis to the proud prince. He had physical beauty, birth, and breeding, yet I couldn't approve of him any more than I could of Louis, even if we were of the same social standing. "Louis lacks other qualities as well."

"What qualities?" Surprise, curiosity, no accusation of snobbery. My answer must have pleased him.

"Forgive me for interrupting, but could you give us directions to the Silvestris Inn?"

I jumped at the sound of the polished voice.

Two men fashionably dressed in dark suits walked up to us. The taller of the two met my gaze, his eyes widening. Quickly recovering, he tipped his hat. "I beg your pardon, miss, for alarming you. We have just arrived in the village and are having difficulty finding our lodgings."

I curtsied in acceptance of the apology, and Mr. Woodsman gave them directions to the inn.

"I am much obliged to you, sir." The men tipped their hats and moved on.

"I wonder what they're doing here," the woodsman mused when the two men had rounded a corner.

I must admit to being curious myself. Obviously of good birth and breeding, they didn't belong to this quaint village any more than I did. And we were not the only people around they could have asked directions of.

I stared after them. "Passing through, undoubtedly."

"What do you make of them?"

"Gentlemen of wealth and education." Handsome too.

"Yes, undoubtedly."

"Who were they?" Rosalie's face held her usual cheer as she and Mr. Peachtree joined us.

"A mystery. If a love of fine pastries brings them to your shop, Miss Rosalie, find out all you can about them. Miss Floraison is curious," Mr. Woodsman said, his thick beard not quite covering his mischievous smile.

"They were handsome, weren't they?" Rosalie gave me a significant look.

I ignored her. "The sun is about to set. I think it's time we return."

"But we haven't found the flower yet," Rosalie protested.

"Oh yes. The flower. I'd almost forgotten it." Mr. Woodsman looked around and then up the path. "It's still a little ways ahead, if I remember correctly."

He took my arm and set a fast pace, quickly putting distance between us and Rosalie and Mr. Peachtree.

"Is there a flower?" I asked when I was certain we wouldn't be overheard.

"Of course there is." His eyes never left the canal wall. "Fortunately. Ah. Here it is."

I scanned the wall. I didn't see any peculiar flowers. Just common ones. "Where?"

"You don't see it?" he asked in a tone of mock astonishment.

"No."

"You have no eye for beauty."

My mouth fell open. *Ooh. If I had my wand ...*

The laughter in his eyes brought me back to my senses. I was not going to let a peasant make me angry. No matter how hard he tried.

He pointed to a small, purple flower with a long protrusion curving out behind it.

I put one hand on my hip and gestured toward the flower with the other. "Why, this is only a—"

"Miss Rosalie, what do you think of this flower? Rather unique, isn't it?" he interrupted.

Rosalie walked up and took one look at the flower. "Why, that's a long-spurred violet. I thought you meant you found something rare."

He glanced at me with a mischievous grin. "I never said it was rare, just peculiar."

Mr. Peachtree and Mr. Woodsman walked us home via the bookshop so we could collect our things. At the door of the pastry shop, Mr. Woodsman stepped close beside me and slipped a book into my hands.

"For Miss Rosalie's entertainment and education," he whispered and then left.

❧

Mr. Woodsman had slipped me his book *The Sword of the Rose Prince*. Unfortunately, the adventure book contained a number of "fancy" words, words Mr. Peachtree and I would use with ease but which would confuse most of the villagers, including Rosalie.

I perceived the predicament quickly thanks to a neighbor's

young daughter who spent a couple of days with us while her mother was ill.

"Is it story time yet, Miss Rosalie? When is Miss Alexia going to read to us?" Little Marie asked a dozen times before night came and we finally sat down to our knitting and reading.

I put the book on a stand and worked on a scarf as I read. "The man you need to find goes by the sobriquet of Gabe Feathers—"

"What's a soob-ri-kay?" Little Marie asked.

My wide eyes sought Rosalie's. Did children normally interrupt readings? But she seemed to be waiting on the answer to Little Marie's question.

"It's a false name, sort of a nickname," I answered and then continued. "'Gabe Feathers? Why do I need to find him?' the prince asked.

'You want to find out what happened to your grandfather, don't you? Well, Gabe can be rather loquacious at times.' Pierre twirled the brandy-filled glass in his hand."

"What's low-k-cee-us?" Little Marie asked. She and Rosalie had the same eager, questioning look in their eyes.

"It means talkative."

"Like me?" Little Marie said.

With a laugh, I closed the book. "Yes, like you. This story is full of big words. I think we'll need a dictionary to get through it. Why don't I tell you one of the stories my father told me when I was growing up?"

"Please story." Little Marie scooted closer to me, and I put aside my knitting and pulled her into my lap. With my arms around her, my mind went back to the days when I would sit in my mother's or father's lap and listen to stories.

"On clear nights when sitting beside a cheerful fire," I began, "you hear stories of mighty enchanters who use their powers for noble purposes, like defeating dragons and rescuing princesses.

On dark, stormy nights, in the light of flickering candles, you hear of sorcerers who use their powers for evil deeds—to kill, bewitch, and conquer. But, on gray nights, when you can't see the tree beside your house for the fog, those are the nights you would hear stories of the Magic Collectors, but they are too mysterious even for fireside tales.

"No one knows who they are or even what they look like. Some say they look like spiders, tall and lanky with cold, dark eyes, while others say they are short and hairy like foxes. Others say they look just like us. Yet, they aren't like us. They're not like enchanters or sorcerers, for they do not possess the power of enchantment. Or like ordinary people, because they can sense magic and wield its power, if given the chance. And that's the chance they want.

"After the Caffin Wars—when the enchanters drove the sorcerers away from this part of the world—mirrors, rings, wands, and other enchanted objects began to disappear from their places of safekeeping. People first thought the sorcerers stole them, but the sorcerers would have bragged about it and used the objects for their evil schemes.

"Then we heard whispers of a people known as the Magic Collectors. No one has ever been able to discover who they are or what they plan to do with their stolen magic. Or even to what lengths they will go to collect it."

Little Marie gasped. "Have you ever seen a Magic Collector, Miss Alexia?"

"She wouldn't know it if she had," Rosalie answered. "That's the scariest thing about them. But since we're not enchantresses, we have nothing to worry about."

Forcing a smile, I held Little Marie tighter. She and Rosalie had nothing to worry about. Enchanters seldom publicly displayed their powers, and, consequently, were slipping into legend in the minds of many. But we weren't legends. Neither were the Magic Collectors. They'd probably give a life—someone else's—to have the magic shrouding the prince-beast and his castle.

The mirror and rose I had given to the prince, the wand had disappeared as mysteriously as it appeared, and no one knew I'd enchanted the prince. I was safe. Wasn't I?

The clip-clop of a horse passing the shop sent shivers down my spine. Once more, I felt the burning of my fever, the cold hate in the two travelers' eyes, and my own fear at the raised dagger. Had it been a dream? Or had I nearly been the victim of Magic Collectors on that lonely road so long ago?

❦

The merry ringing of the bell and the familiar aroma of books greeted me as I entered Mr. Peachtree's shop.

"Miss Floraison, this is a lovely surprise. What can I do for you?" He slid a ribbon between the open pages of a book.

"Good morning. I was wondering if I could impose on your friendship with Miss Rosalie by making a request of you."

Chuckling, he deposited the book on the counter as he walked around it to me. "You're my friend too. I hope, anyway. But you may make a request on whichever friendship you choose."

My heart warmed at his easy acceptance of me. "Thank you. My request has to do with both of us, actually. Might I borrow a dictionary? The book Mr. Woodsman kindly lent Miss Rosalie and me contains many uncommon words; I thought it would be helpful if she and I were to look up the words in the dictionary."

Mr. Peachtree's brow furrowed and then relaxed. "Yes, a quick mind could learn a great deal of vocabulary and pronunciation that way. I would be happy to lend you a dictionary. Actually, I'm glad you came. I wanted to speak with you on another matter. Mrs. Janus's daughter was ill for several weeks and fell behind in school, particularly in reading." He glanced up as the doorbell rang, greeted the newcomers, and turned back to me.

"Mrs. Janus asked if I would tutor her daughter," he continued, "but it's difficult enough for me to keep the lessons straight for the children I'm tutoring now. Would you be willing to tutor the girl? I know Miss Lightwood enjoys having children around." He paused. "Mrs. Janus would pay, of course."

My mind shifted from framing an excuse to composing an acceptance. I could save the money toward repaying Mr. Woodsman and traveling to Gilden. And perhaps more than one person could benefit from the lessons. "Unless Miss Rosalie objects, I'd be happy to tutor the girl."

"Excellent. I'll fetch that dictionary for you."

Mr. Peachtree returned in a moment with the heavy book. I took it, turned, and walked straight into a well-dressed man. The dictionary slipped from my hands, and I did a little dance to keep it from educating my toes.

"I do beg your pardon," the man said. He picked up the book and handed it to me.

"You'll have to excuse him. He runs into everything," said another gentleman as he walked up to us. The surprise I felt showed in his face. "Devryn, you need to be more careful. This young woman and her friend gave us directions to our inn. Practically kept us from being homeless in this large village— and you repay her by running into her."

Recognition of the two handsome men heightened my embarrassment, but it was quickly swallowed by curiosity. These men belonged more to my world than to this village. Who were they, and why were they here? Despite my curiosity, I wouldn't stoop to nosiness.

"I am happy to know you found your inn safely. Good day,

sir." I curtsied and stepped away, but the taller of the two men, the one called Devryn, touched my arm to stop me.

"Forgive me, miss, it's presumptuous, I know, but one of the first things my brother and I do upon arriving in a village is to hunt up the bookstore. He doesn't care what he reads, so long as it passes the time, but I am more fastidious. I like to have the opinion of another reader, as well as the bookstore owner's, before I purchase a book."

He was rather presumptuous, but his smile had a boyish quality that prevented censure.

"You must have a great deal of faith in the patrons of bookstores," I said.

"It has seldom led me astray. I am a good judge of readers."

"In that case, I would be happy to give you my opinion."

"Excellent." He turned to Mr. Peachtree. "What books do you recommend?"

"*The Man from Deaden Downs* is popular right now, as are Gray's *Essays on the Morning*, and Manhern's *Second Collection of Poems*. Or so the dealers from Gilden tell me, my lord."

I expected this out-of-the-way bookshop to be a little behind, but this was ridiculous. Those suggestions were decades old. There must have been a revival of interest in older works since I'd left home.

"Those are all excellent," I replied. "Gray's 'The Rising Mist' is a particularly thought-provoking essay. If you like suspense, *The Man from Deaden Downs* will certainly please you, but be sure to keep your room well lit if you read at night."

"Well lit? You don't seem the type to frighten easily." There was a bit of a sparkle in Devryn's dark eyes.

"I try to avoid having cause to be frightened."

"You're a wise young woman." He looked past me to Mr. Peachtree. "I'll take all three of your suggestions." He turned back to me with a smile. "And to whom should I complain if I find these books unsatisfactory?"

My lips curved up slightly. "You may complain to me if you do not like them, though it would be admitting your taste is lacking."

His smile widened. "In that case, whom should I thank for the recommendation?"

I longed to say Lady Alexandria Floraison and declare my position as their equal, but who would believe me? I was dressed as a shopkeeper's assistant. I curtsied. "Miss Alexandria Floraison."

"Lord Devryn Collins. And this is my brother, Lord Leandre." He bowed and motioned to his companion.

Lord Leandre bowed. "Floraison? That is a name of nobility, is it not?"

Mr. Peachtree looked up.

"Yes, I … am proud to bear the same name as the Duke of Henly." It burned my heart not to be able to claim my own family. "Forgive me for running away, my lords, but I must leave. I am late as it is."

"Nay, Miss Floraison. Forgive us for detaining you. I wish you a good day." Lord Devryn held up the books Mr. Peachtree had just handed him. "And thank you for your advice."

CHAPTER 13

Too sour. Cringing, I added more sugar to the lemonade and then hurried back out to the front. While I was refilling Mr. Monroe's glass, Louis and several of his friends strode into the shop. They hung their rain gear on the coat rack. Water dripped from the coats to the bucket on the floor, disrupting the soothing sound of the steady rain outside.

"Good day, Harry, Oscar, Herbert. Roger." Rosalie's voice fell flat on "Roger." She'd had to ask him to leave once because of disruptive behavior. I hadn't cared for him before that—it was rumored he was involved in dog fighting. "And Louis. I haven't seen you around in while. What can I do for you today?"

"Louis's been hanging around with those swells from beyond Gilden. He doesn't have time for us peasants anymore." Herbert slipped into a chair.

I swallowed a reprimand. It was an indignity to refer to such gentlemen as Lord Devryn and Lord Leandre as *swells*.

"I'll take the usual." Louis pulled out his chair and sat heavily.

"They've got a handsome carriage and team of horses stabled

over at the livery." Oscar, the son of the livery owner, stood aside for Rosalie to set out their glasses. "I wonder what they're doing here." He looked pointedly at Louis. "Louis?"

"They've come to hunt. I'm their guide."

Roger opened his mouth but shut it at a glare from Louis.

I served the pastries and filled their glasses. Louis didn't acknowledge me, which wasn't unusual. He was unusually silent though. No tales of his exploits and spectacular new additions to his taxidermy collection?

"To hunt? You'd be the best guide then." Oscar reached for a powdered sugar–covered pastry as he slipped into his seat.

"I know it." Louis crammed an entire pastry into his mouth, the powdered sugar puffing out to dust his cheeks.

"Shot anything yet?"

"Shot the biggest boar I've ever seen." Harry stretched his arms wide to give an estimation of the boar's size.

"They've got themselves a trophy already then," Herbert said.

Louis washed the pastry down with a half-glass gulp of lemonade. "They don't want it. I'm having it mounted. I brought it down, after all."

"They didn't want it?"

"That's not the kind of trophy they're interested in."

"Strange folk." Oscar chuckled and leaned back in his chair. "Pay you to take them hunting and then let you keep the spoils. If this keeps up, you *will* need a bigger house for all your kills."

"Yeah, one as big as the squire's might do." Herbert laughed.

"Maybe even bigger than that." Harry nodded toward Mr. Monroe, and whispered, "She'll change her mind and come back quick then."

The next thing that escaped Harry's lips was "Ouch!" His eyes flew to Louis's stern face and then fell to his plate. "I mean a big place like that might hold everything."

"Even a few pretty maids." Roger winked.

I wrinkled my nose as I passed him. The stench of alcohol fought with his typical odor of dog. *He'd better not cause any trouble today.*

"They wouldn't be as pretty as Belle Monroe. She'd be the queen in my dream house." Oscar sighed, then coughed and sat up straighter at Louis's scowl.

I wiped down the nearby tables and took the dirty dishes to the kitchen. It still felt odd being the one to clean the tables rather than dirty them. But I had a table, food, and youth. And for that, I was grateful. Even if I had to put up with Roger, Louis, and the like.

"Why don't you rest a minute?" Rosalie waved at me as I returned from the kitchen, her firm gesture guiding me to the table where she and Mr. Monroe were sitting.

"What's your opinion of Louis?" Mr. Monroe spoke in a low, serious voice as he glanced back at the men.

"He's handsome but has more arrogance than brains."

Rosalie's head jerked up from her inspection of a pastry experiment. "Really, Alexandria. That's harsh."

"It is harsh, but I agree with her." Mr. Monroe frowned. "His opinion of himself has always been quite high, though it seems higher of late." He paused, his eyes focused on a faraway sight only he could see. "Despite that, I sometimes regret Belle rejected his proposal." His voice was almost a whisper.

Rosalie and I exchanged glances. She seemed as confused as I was.

He shook his head and forced a smile. "The squire invited me to his manor not long ago. He wanted my opinion on some matters of business. While I was there he asked if any new people were in town. I mentioned Mr. Woodsman and the young lords, all of whom were unknown to me at the time. It appears the squire is missing some of his larger game. He carefully manages his stock and has been disappointed in his take recently. He asked me to give him more information about Mr. Woodsman."

"Surely he doesn't suspect Mr. Woodsman of being a poacher? I would no sooner suspect him than I would Mr. Peachtree." What an idea.

Mr. Monroe gave a slight smile. "Miss Rosalie shares your opinion, and after meeting Mr. Woodsman, so do I. He has an air of mystery and yet of openness about him."

"He does. His past is his own, but his character is open for all to see," Rosalie said.

"You are as wise a woman, Miss Rosalie, as Mr. Peachtree says you are."

Rosalie blushed and picked at the half-eaten pastry on her plate.

Roger chose that moment to stroll over. I didn't like the look in his eye. Did he harbor hard feelings toward Rosalie?

"There's color in your cheeks today, Miss Lightwood. Did someone ask you to the dance?" He sneered.

Rosalie's cheeks took on a different shade of pink. "Dance?"

"Yes, what dance?" Oscar called out.

"Flier was put out yesterday. I got a copy of it. Why don't you read it to us, Miss Rosalie?" Roger pushed the flier toward her.

Rosalie went pale.

That malicious drunk. I'd turn him into a worm and stick him in a jar of preservative.

I snatched the flier from him. "Rosalie's hands are sticky from the pastries." I scanned the announcement. "The dance is one week from today, at eight in the evening, at the Carters' barn."

I thrust the paper at him with a warning look. He retreated to his seat. How did he find out? Oh. The notes from his mother about cooking advice. He must have noticed Rosalie always asked me to read them and write her reply.

Mr. Monroe raised his eyebrows.

"That man reeks of alcohol. Do you have any theories about the disappearance of the squire's wild game?"

He glanced around at the table of men.

"I don't believe you two would gossip, but I should keep my wild speculations to myself."

That night I cut several sheets of paper into small rectangles and then took them and my quill pen around the kitchen and living area and labeled almost everything.

Rosalie looked at me quizzically.

"Evie Janus spends half of her time looking around when I tutor her. I might as well make that time productive." To emphasize my point, I took out a whole sheet of paper. "W-I-N-D-O-W. Window," I said as I wrote. I hung it in the middle of said object.

Rosalie chuckled and stepped closer to the sign. "Window," she repeated somberly as she studied the letters, perhaps remembering the lessons she had as a young girl.

Rosalie's vocabulary had improved since I started reading to her and using "my, what a funny sounding word" as an excuse to look up words in the dictionary. The reading was slow and somewhat painful but, at least, she was learning. It didn't improve her reading. The signs would help her as well as Evie. That was my hope, anyway.

I pulled the thin bedsheet up to my chin that night and relaxed my aching muscles. Spring had already turned to summer and my muscles were still adjusting to their chores. In the top drawer of my chest of drawers was a pouch with the few coins I had earned. It wasn't enough to repay Mr. Woodsman, much less travel to Gilden.

I fell asleep thinking of my family but dreamed of the castle I'd enchanted. A cheery light shown from one of its windows, but it cast an eerie gleam on the garish statues ornamenting the castle towers. Through the window, I could see a large dining room. At one end of the table sat the prince—the beast. At the other sat the girl he called Beauty. If her profile was any indication of her face, she deserved the name. Their conversation was slow and awkward at first, and the girl would scarce lift her eyes to the prince. As dinner progressed, the conversation grew easier and they even laughed together.

In another room, an ornate vase sat atop a small table. Draped over the lip of the vase was a wilted rose. Several of its dark crimson petals lay on the polished wood of the tabletop.

The fallen petals filled me with despair. Was this just a dream? Or was it a vision? If it was, then the prince's time was running out. His fate was sure and terrible if he didn't win this girl's affection.

❧

"I'll only give these back to you on one condition, Alexia." Mr. Tinsler held the plates above his head. We always collected the dishes from the previous week's deliveries on Sunday.

"Really, Mr. Tinsler. This is hardly fair." I made an unsuccessful grab for the dishes. He was awfully tall and spritely for an old peasant. His teasing grin revealed yellow teeth.

"You'll never get it that way, Alexia." He grinned yellow again.

I almost grimaced, but his friendly teasing made me smile instead. "But why must I agree to attend the dance?"

"Because a lovely young woman, such as yourself, should be out dancing with a respectable young man, not sitting at home cooking for crusty old men."

"I'm not sure how Rosalie would feel about it. I don't know many people here."

"These dances are a great way to meet people. I'll be there to introduce you to folks, and I'm sure Miss Rosalie is wanting to go."

The Lady Alexandria at a country ball? Dancing with peasant men? Or maybe not dancing with peasant men. They may not ask me, which would be preferable.

I made another grab for the plates, but someone beat me to them. My heart thundered. Who had snuck so close beside me?

Mr. Tinsler burst out laughing and slapped his leg. "That was a good one, Woodsman. You should see your face, Alexia."

The woodsman's rich laughter joined Mr. Tinsler's. "Sorry to startle you, Miss Floraison."

Somehow, I wasn't convinced.

"It must be nice to be so easily amused." Hands on hips, I spun around to face him.

"It is, rather." Mr. Woodsman held the dishes out to me. Amusement still twinkled in his eyes.

I couldn't help but grin as I took the plates. It had been a week since I'd seen him. "They say laughter is good for the soul, don't they?"

"They do. And whoever *they* are, they're right." He continued to smile at me.

There was something contagious about his smile. What on earth was the matter with me? Standing in the street smiling at a peasant man?

I quickly picked up my basket and set the dishes in it. "I must be going now. Good afternoon, Mr. Tinsler, Mr. Woodsman."

"Wait. I'm coming with you." Mr. Woodsman stepped toward me.

"But didn't you come to see Mr. Tinsler?"

"No offense to him, but I came to see you." He glanced at Mr. Tinsler, who winked.

"No offense taken, Woodsman."

"How did you know I was here?"

Mr. Woodsman leaned close and said in a low voice, "The village is full of my spies."

"Really, Mr. Woodsman." He was the most exasperating man I had ever met.

"Yes, really." He relieved me of the basket and nodded to Mr. Tinsler. "Good afternoon, friend. I'll see that Miss Floraison gets home safely. And gets to that dance." He took my elbow and guided me back to the main street.

"Mr. Woodsman, I have no desire to go to the dance."

"Of course you don't. No one as dignified and sophisticated as you would be able to enjoy a simple country dance."

"You insult me."

"That's for you to decide. I was merely stating my personal opinion. But let's not waste a lovely afternoon arguing. You don't want to go to the dance, and that's that."

"Thank you."

"My pleasure. I'll even change the subject. What do you think of the weather? It's a lovely day, isn't it?"

It was a lovely day, and I quickly began to enjoy the walk.

"I made the acquaintance of Mr. Monroe recently." Mr. Woodsman steered me around the two-wheeled carts and heavy wagons creeping down the crowded street.

"So he said. I'm glad. He's very much a gentleman."

"He is. There's such a sad expression in his eyes, though," he said.

"I believe he's lonely. His wife was exceptionally kind and beautiful." The thought of her loss and his loneliness still saddened me.

"Did you know his wife?" Mr. Woodsman asked, a look of surprise on his face.

I bit my tongue at my carelessness. "His sad history is common knowledge."

"I suppose it is. They say his daughter Belle is as beautiful as her mother was." He looked at me slyly. "It's little wonder she went to live with her aunt. No doubt she wanted to escape those boorish peasants who were chasing after her."

"Probably so, though I don't see why her father didn't go with her instead of staying here to be lonely." Loneliness had been biting at my soul all day. It was Gabriella's birthday.

Mr. Woodsman gently tugged on my arm until I looked up at him. He gave me an encouraging smile, which pulled me out of the self-pity trap I was falling into.

I straightened and pushed a few loose wisps of hair from my face. "He was a little concerned you were a poacher."

"Was he really?" Mr. Woodsman said in mock surprise. "I can't say I blame him, me being a suspicious character." He stroked his beard expressively. "And new to town. Fortunately, Mr. Monroe saw through me. We're good friends now. He told me he mentioned the poaching suspicions to you and that you were adamant in your assertion of my innocence."

My cheeks felt unpleasantly warm. "You don't fit my idea of a poacher, that's all."

"Really? If I don't fit your idea of a poacher, then you must have some other idea of me. I should like to know what it is." He tilted his head so as to look straight into my eyes.

The temperature of my cheeks rose. "My idea of a poacher is

someone who is desperate to feed himself or his family. Or someone who merely enjoys breaking the law."

Mr. Woodsman chuckled. "I'm certainly glad to know you don't think me impoverished or a hoodlum. Actually, I don't think the poaching has to do with desperate need or a pleasure in law breaking, not in this case, anyway. The squire's poaching problem likely has more to do with pride and the sense of being above the law that often comes with pride."

We paused beside the mercantile to watch a group of children use sticks to race large hoops down the street. Evie was among the contestants. We cheered her on until the group rounded the corner, and then we recommenced our walk and conversation.

"What makes you think the poaching has more to do with pride than hunger or love of mischief?"

He shifted the basket to his other arm. "Only the best animals were missing. A poor man or a hoodlum would not be choosy."

"Of course, it may not be poachers after all. I've heard mention of wolf tracks on the squire's land."

"Wolves can be tamed and used for hunting."

"Taming a wolf would be rather a lot of trouble. There are many satisfactory hunting dogs around."

"True, but even a prize hunting dog couldn't rival the beauty and strength of a wolf."

"Are you suggesting someone here has a wolf?"

"Two or three, actually."

"What makes you say that?"

"Do you know you're getting to be quite a snoop? You'll end up one of the village gossips if you're not careful."

We dropped off the dishes at the pastry shop and helped Rosalie carry our dinner to Mr. Peachtree's shop for our weekly get-together.

Following the usual after-dinner chat, the gentlemen walked us home. When we reached the door, Mr. Woodsman fastened his confident gaze on me. "Good night, Miss Floraison. I will pick you up for the dance Saturday at seven o'clock sharp."

"What! I thought we agreed I wasn't going."

"We only agreed you didn't want to go. Mr. Peachtree and Miss Rosalie and I have agreed that you are going."

"I hate to disagree, but I am not going to the dance." Hands on hips, I glared at him.

His mouth curled up at the corners. "Oh, dear. This does make things difficult. The four of us would make such a nice group." He shrugged his shoulders. "I guess I could ask Miss Colter. It's of little matter to me, but I'm sure Rosalie would be much happier if you went."

Miss Colter. That flirt. I was beginning to wonder if I really didn't want to go, but now I was sure. "Let Miss Colter be the fourth. You make an attractive pair. I'm not going."

His lips twitched into a smile—a smile of challenge, not of defeat. "Good evening, Miss Floraison." He tipped his hat and left.

CHAPTER 14

"EVIE JANUS, WHATEVER is the matter?" I asked as my pupil rushed into the shop, her face the picture of worry.

"Locust's been missing two days, and I've been so afraid some horrible dog ate her. And now that I've finally found her, I can't reach her! She must be so hungry. You'll rescue her, won't you?" Her big brown eyes pleaded for my help.

"Who is Locust? And what am I to rescue her from?"

"Come on. I'll show you."

She grabbed my hand and dragged me out the door and through the town to a little grassy area near the canal bridge. A cluster of ancient mulberry trees guarded the bridge's entrance. One of the trees leaned over the water. A mournful mewing sounded from its upper branches.

"She's on the limb jutting over the water." Evie pointed out a scraggly, gray cat. "Don't worry, Locust. Miss Alexandria will save you."

I looked from her confident face to the cat. Did she really

expect me to risk breaking my neck for that ugly thing? I glanced back at Evie. Her eyes were fastened on the cat. A beloved cat was a beloved cat, I guessed.

With a sigh, I sat on the wall, pulled my feet onto it, eased up, and walked along it to the heart of the cluster of trees.

Tree climbing was such an undignified and dirty endeavor. Nonetheless, I hoisted myself from branch to branch until I gained a height of fifteen feet and a horizontal position of two feet beyond the canal wall.

"Here, kitty, kitty. Come over here." The miserable feline hissed at me and then mewed, but didn't move. "Come on. I'll get you down." I leaned out a little farther and glimpsed the sparkling blue water beneath me. It was fortunate Floraisons did not fear heights or water or falling into water from a great height. "Please come here." I beckoned her with my hand.

"Go to her, Locust. She's going to bring you down," Evie shouted.

Locust inched closer, and I grabbed her by the scruff of the neck.

"Hooray for you, Miss Alexandria! Locust and I can make it home in time for dinner."

Holding Locust to my shoulder, I lowered myself to the next branch. Three branches later the ungrateful cat began to squirm, its claws piercing my dress to bury themselves in my shoulder.

Throwing it down would be the fastest way to reunite it and Evie. Cats always landed on their feet.

"Be careful, Miss Alexandria, don't drop her."

Sighing, I stepped onto the next branch and slipped. Locust escaped. I made an unsuccessful grab at the nearest limb and landed with a thud in a reclining position on the branch where I had been standing. The blue water blinked beneath me.

"Miss Alexandria, are you all right?"

Other than a pounding heart and sore hands and backside. "Yes, Evie." The smell of wood filled my nose as I rubbed bits of bark from my hands. I grabbed a branch and pulled myself to my feet. "Where's the cat?" It had better have run down the tree.

"She's on the wall. I've got her now." Evie stroked the cat's back and scratched it behind the ears. "You naughty cat. Staying away for two days."

My lips curled into a smile at the way Evie crooned to the cat. If I managed to make it down alive then the effort would be worth reuniting the two of them. I made sure my feet were secure, leaned forward, and then jerked to a stop. The hem of my dress clung to a branch. I twisted around and pulled on the skirt, but it didn't budge.

Evie called up to me, "Are you stuck, Miss Alexandria?"

"Yes. Will you climb up on the wall and onto one of the lower limbs? You might be able to release me."

"I'm afraid of heights. I'll go see if I can find Mr. Woodsman. Miss Rosalie said he would do anything for you." She draped Locust over her shoulder and took off.

"Wait, Evie! I'm sure I can get down myself." I could just see Mr. Woodsman's blue eyes twinkling at me and hear him making some sarcastic comment. Or he might refuse to help me unless I agreed to go to the dance.

Evie didn't hear my protest and soon disappeared around a building.

I twisted and tugged at the hung fabric with renewed zeal. With a rip, it came free, and I stepped onto the next limb and continued to move down with more haste than safety. I heard footsteps and a man's voice. *Just two more limbs to the wall. I can make it.*

My foot slipped again. I grabbed a branch, but it broke under my weight, and I fell—into a pair of strong arms. My fall must have disturbed some butterflies, for they suddenly began to fly around inside my stomach.

"Are you all right, Miss Floraison?" He asked anxiously as he set me down on the canal wall.

"Yes, Mr. Woodsman. Thanks to you. I am ever in your debt it seems." I looked up into the dark eyes of Lord Devryn. The butterflies stilled. "Lord Devryn, I'm sorry. I thought it was Mr. Woodsman," I stammered.

"I'm sorry too. Should I fetch him?" He grinned impishly.

"No! It's just that Evie said she was going after him." Inhaling slowly, I counted to two, and then exhaled slowly. *A Floraison does not lose her composure.*

"I found him first. He was just around the corner." Evie pointed to Lord Devryn.

Taking another slow breath, I stood and held my hand out to him. "I am glad she found you when she did, my lord. Thank you for saving me from a very nasty landing."

He took my hand, causing me to grimace. There was probably as much bark in my hands as on the tree. "Why, Miss Floraison, your hands are raw. You must clean them at once." He tucked my arm through his. "I'll see Miss Floraison home, Evie. You'd better let your mother know you found your cat."

Evie thanked me again and ran off.

"She's your pupil, is she not?" He nodded toward Evie's departing figure and then set a course back to the pastry shop.

I smiled in answer. "You seem to know a great deal about the goings on of this village."

"Chattering landladies are a blessing on rainy days."

"Evie's a sweet girl and exceptionally fond of that cat."

"And you are a brave young woman. I don't know many women who would climb a tree to rescue a cat."

"Most women do not have little girls with big brown eyes

looking at them with complete confidence." I waved to Mrs. Sutton through her shop's window as we passed.

"I've heard the Floraisons were an exceptional family." He looked at me with what might have been admiration in his eyes. "I see that's true for all branches of it."

I smiled but made no answer. A familiar yearning threatened to overpower me. Would I ever be reunited with my family? "Have you heard anything of the Floraisons lately? I normally do not pay attention to the lives of the nobility, but I feel akin to the Duke of Henly and his family."

"That's quite natural given you have the same surname." We waited for a wagon to rumble past and then crossed the street. "I wish I could give you information, but I don't know them personally and haven't heard anything about them in years." Excitement seemed to light his eyes. "Did you know they have a collection of enchanted mirrors?"

My feet turned to lead. "A collection of enchanted mirrors?" I stuttered. Only a few enchanters knew of that.

"Yes, one of them went missing about fifteen years ago. It was quite a scandal. It was one of the more valuable mirrors. It has never been found, at least not to my knowledge."

Fifteen years ago a mirror went missing. It must have been called by me and given to the prince.

Lord Devryn's searching gaze caught my attention.

"I vaguely remember hearing about that now." I forced my feet to move.

"I wonder what could have happened to it. There is some speculation the Magic Collectors stole it, but I doubt it." He studied my face, which I hoped rather than believed was keeping quiet about my thoughts.

"I doubt it too. But what's the point of useless guesses? It's gone, and that's what's important." Were Lord Devryn and his brother enchanters? They knew too much not to be.

He examined my face once more and smiled. "That's true, but useless guesses are much more entertaining. My theory is that the mirror was taken by enchantment by some great enchanter or enchantress." He paused. "I should like to know for what purpose."

My heart skipped a few beats.

"Do your hands hurt?"

My hand bunched my dress where the wand pocket would have been if I'd had one. I smoothed the dress and let my hand fall to my side. "They sting, but not badly. Are you an experienced tree climber?"

Chuckling, he replied he was and told me a few stories of his childhood adventures. His smooth voice soon became the background to my thoughts. Was more generally known about my family than I realized? Or did he have access to little known information on enchanters? If he did, could I trust him and his brother with my situation? Or would they assume I was an evil sorceress, since I had refashioned a prince into a beast?

⊙✲⊙

Needless to say, when Saturday evening came, I was in my best dress and my hair was arranged as attractively as I could do it myself. It was a matter of principle, rather than of a desire to attract, that made me "spruce up" as they say, for the dance.

Mr. Peachtree and Mr. Woodsman arrived promptly at seven. I gave Rosalie's hair one final examination—it was a drastic improvement over her normal style—and opened the door.

"Your carriage awaits, my lady." Mr. Woodsman gave a sweeping bow and gestured toward the street.

"Really, Woodsman. It's no wonder she was reluctant to join us." Mr. Peachtree shifted his hat from his head to his hand as he walked past Mr. Woodsman into the shop. "Don't pay any attention to him, Miss Floraison. We have a simple, but functional, wagon."

Rosalie appeared, and Mr. Peachtree's eyes took on a pleased look. "You both look lovely."

He led the way outside and helped us into the wagon. He and Rosalie sat up front, and Mr. Woodsman and I sat in the back. We made a few stops to pick up more passengers, including Mr. Tinsler, who wanted to join a group instead of going alone.

The ride was bumpy and a little crowded, but I approved of the extra company. It was less awkward that way.

People were milling about when we arrived. Though I recognized patrons of Rosalie's shop, most of the guests were unknown to me.

Mr. Woodsman, being the tallest, was the first to spot a friend. He led us over to Mr. Monroe.

"Good evening, sir. I am glad you decided to join us," Mr. Woodsman said as he shook Mr. Monroe's hand.

"I don't feel as if I belong with the happy and carefree, but it's refreshing to be among them occasionally. I don't regret taking your advice," Mr. Monroe answered.

People stood around in groups and chatted until musicians called the dancers to the floor. My group continued talking. I alternated between listening to Rosalie and Mr. Peachtree's conversation and to Mr. Woodsman and Mr. Monroe's, which was more animated than I expected of one so prone to melancholy as Mr. Monroe.

My eyes drifted to the dance floor. The old men dancing with their young granddaughters was a sweet and amusing sight. The young couples danced enthusiastically, though most lacked grace. Despite the absence of lavish gowns, jewels, a full orchestra, and polished dancing, everyone, judging by their smiles and laughter, was thoroughly enjoying themselves, more so than many at the elegant balls I had attended. Still, I would have preferred a little more elegance and a splendid gown.

"May I have this dance?"

Mr. Woodsman's question startled me.

"I love a lively country dance," he continued.

My foot tapped in time with the music. Was it undignified to admit I did too? More to the point, was it improper for the daughter of a duke to dance with a woodsman? Improper? It was unheard of. But I was currently a mere shopkeeper's assistant, and there was no reason why a shopkeeper's assistant and a respectable young woodsman couldn't dance.

I curtsied in acceptance, and we joined the dancers. Mr. Peachtree and Rosalie followed suit.

As we moved about the floor, I noticed Mr. Monroe watching us with his sad, thoughtful smile.

"You hold Mr. Monroe in high regard, don't you?" I asked Mr. Woodsman.

He looked surprised and then sighed. "Yes, I bullied him into coming as well."

"If you did, I am sure it was for his own good. He seems to be enjoying himself, in his own way. But what I meant is there is something in your voice and manner that speaks of respect and admiration when you are with him or speak of him."

He twisted to look at Mr. Monroe. "He reminds me of someone I've heard stories of since childhood, someone I always wished I could have met, if that makes any sense."

"I understand what you mean. I often wished I could have met my grandmother."

"I suspect we have a good bit in common, you and I, much more than we realize."

"Such as?"

"We both love lively dances more than slow, dignified

ones." He grinned. "Don't give me that disdainful look. You do, and I'll prove it to you." With that, he swept me around the floor.

Three dances later we were laughing and trying to catch our breath at the refreshment table.

"Well, that wasn't so bad, was it?" he asked.

"No," I replied, smiling. "You're a much better dancer than I expected."

His hearty laugh gave me a strange feeling of pleasure.

"You kept up with the country ladies much better than I expected."

"A Floraison can do whatever she sets her mind to do."

"I can believe that."

"You should believe it. I have seen the daring deeds she can accomplish," said a smooth, masculine voice.

The blood rushed to my cheeks. To be seen at a country dance by a handsome lord!

I turned toward the speaker and curtsied. "Good evening, Lord Devryn. Lord Leandre."

The brothers were dressed in a simple way so as not to attract attention, but they were still remarkably handsome even without their finery.

"Forgive us for interrupting, Miss Floraison." Lord Devryn bowed. "But my brother and I couldn't spend another night alone at the inn, so we decided to accept an invitation to the dance. We know so few people here we couldn't pass by a friend." His eyes shifted to Mr. Woodsman.

"That is quite understandable, my lord. Permit me to broaden your acquaintance." I held out my hand to Mr. Woodsman, who stepped forward. "I don't believe you have ever been formally introduced. Lord Devryn, Lord Leandre, may I present Mr. Woodsman? Mr. Woodsman, may I present Lord Devryn Collins and Lord Leandre Collins?"

The gentlemen bowed. I motioned to Mr. Monroe, who stood nearby, to join us.

"How long have you been in this village, Mr. Woodsman?" Lord Leandre asked.

"I've been here a while, off and on."

"What brought you to this quaint place?"

"I found myself close by, took a liking to the village, and decided to stay for a while. What about you? What brought you two gentlemen here?"

I turned away to hide a smile. I had never met anyone so talented at evasive answers as my Woodsman. Or anyone so impertinent. Imagine asking a lord that. As if he were an equal.

Lord Leandre's eyebrows rose. "We desired to escape city life and had heard this area was especially attractive." There was amusement in his voice.

Mr. Monroe and Rosalie joined us, and I introduced them. Mr. Peachtree followed and greeted the lords.

"Yes, there are many attractive spots. Has Louis shown you High Falls?" Mr. Woodsman continued the earlier conversation.

"Ah. I see our actions are no secret. No, he hasn't. I must ask him to." Lord Leandre stepped forward to make room for a man passing by.

"He prefers to show us good hunting grounds." Lord Devryn gave an amused smile. "I dare say he saves the best ones for himself."

"I shouldn't wonder. He has a reputation to uphold." There was a hint of acerbity in Mr. Monroe's voice.

"Not that I care about the best hunting spots," Lord Leandre said. "I've never been too concerned with how many points a rack of antlers has. There is one thing, however, my brother and I would like to see, but which Louis has been unable to show us —the castle at Silvestris. Do you know how to get there?"

The horrible roar of the prince-turned-beast sounded in my

ears. They couldn't go to the castle. It might anger the beast, and there was no telling what he might do to them. Or they might fear him and try to harm him.

"Castle? What castle?" Rosalie glanced between us.

What castle? How could they not know there was a castle a couple of days ride away? They probably didn't have much interaction with it before the enchantment, but surely they would know it was there.

I looked at my companions for an answer. Mr. Woodsman was watching Mr. Monroe, who looked as pale as I felt.

Mr. Peachtree scratched his head. "I've not heard of a castle nearby, and I've been here several years longer than Miss Lightwood." He furrowed his brow. "No. No, I don't think there is one."

"Perhaps it's near another village with the same name," Mr. Woodsman suggested.

"I'm positive it's near this village." Lord Leandre studied each of our faces. "According to the entry I read, it was built three centuries ago as a country house for the royal family. Not long after, it was given to one of the king's great-nephews, a deserving young man, who because of his bravery and noble actions during battle was also given the hereditary title of prince, though he was not directly in line for the throne."

"That's interesting." Mr. Woodsman glanced at me. "A forgotten castle."

I hoped it was forgotten.

Lord Devryn promised an escape.

"Have you read any of the books Mr. Peachtree recommended, Lord Devryn?" I asked.

He stepped closer to me, frowning for a split-second before regaining his usual friendly smile. "I finished *The Man from Deaden Downs*. I can see why you suggested only reading it in a well-lit room."

After a few minutes conversation about the book, Lord Devryn and Lord Leandre excused themselves to talk to Louis, who was giving his hat and coat to the hostess. "We must talk to our guide about tomorrow's excursion, but with your permission I will find you later and claim a dance," Lord Devryn said.

"I would be honored, my lord."

"Until then." He bowed, giving me his charming boyish grin, and followed his brother.

Mr. Monroe pleaded a headache and wished us a good night.

"What an honor to be singled out by the young lords," commented one of the women standing nearby.

"Yes, curious that they always single us out." Mr. Woodsman watched Mr. Monroe depart and then turned to me. "Let's dance, shall we?"

"Yes!" Mr. Peachtree's emphatic reply startled us.

"I don't want to dance with you, Albert," Mr. Woodsman said.

"Dancing? Who said anything about dancing?" Mr. Peachtree looked confused.

"Don't mind him. He hasn't heard a thing since Lord Leandre mentioned a castle." Rosalie regarded Mr. Peachtree with a raised eyebrow.

He gave her a sheepish grin. "I'm sorry. I've been racking my brains. I had a feeling they were correct about the castle, but I couldn't remember one. It's coming back now. We never had much to do with the inhabitants, so it's little wonder we forgot about it after it was destroyed."

"Destroyed!" Mr. Woodsman quickly put his hand over his mouth.

"Burned down some years ago. We saw a dark cloud hovering over the forest where the castle was. A couple of men went to check on it, but they came back saying the woods near the castle were something from a nightmare and their horses wouldn't go into them. Something about wolves and a darkness daylight couldn't pierce." Mr. Peachtree shook his head as if the men's description was nonsense.

"That's right. I knew the lords were right, though I'd forgot about it too." A woman with a scratchy voice and frizzy salt and pepper hair shuffled closer. "It all makes sense now." She nodded at us as if we shared a secret.

"What makes sense now, Olive?" Rosalie asked.

"Why the woods near Silvestris are so dark and foul. He haunts it. I'm sure now he poisoned our roses out of spite. Everyone knows his gardens were famous for the flowers, but they probably went up in flames with him and his castle. Only roses don't come back to haunt folks." She nodded in that conspiratorial way again.

"Do castles come back to haunt folks?" Mr. Peachtree hardly blinked when Rosalie elbowed him.

"You mean the roses died the same time as the cloud appeared?" Mr. Woodsman's serious voice surprised me.

"Yes. Weren't you listening?" Olive looked askance at him.

"And now Rosalie's plants are trying to bloom." Mr. Woodsman appeared to be studying some distant point.

"They've been trying for some time. I've never seen buds take so long to form. It's been weeks, and they're just now looking like they're about to open," Rosalie said.

At length, Mr. Woodsman looked down at me. "I think it's time I went exploring."

"Exploring for what?"

"For more roses. But don't worry—I won't go until after the dance." He took my hand and led me back to the dance floor.

My feet moved in time with the music, but my mind was far away. What was happening at the castle? Was there any truth to my dreams? Was there a girl there?

"A gold piece for your thoughts." Mr. Woodsman gently squeezed my hand.

I shook my head. "My thoughts can't be bought. But what of yours? You have been as silent as I have."

"My thoughts are priceless as well. But you may have my opinion for free."

"And what is your opinion?"

"That you should thank me for inviting you to the dance."

❦

"My poor feet." Rosalie moaned when she shut the door to our little home behind us.

"I'll heat some water and get a tub. We'll soak out the soreness."

"Oh, thank you, Alexandria. I don't know what I'd do without you."

The wonderful thing about Rosalie was that when she made comments like that, she actually meant them.

"You'd get by somehow."

"Not as pleasantly."

"It wouldn't be as pleasant without you either."

An hour later, I threw out the dirty water, fastened the kitchen door, and headed for bed. My blood ran cold when I touched the doorknob to my room. Someone had been in there. My sixth sense, and the fact that the door was open a crack when we were always careful to shut doors, told me it hadn't been Rosalie. My heart pounded as it had during the most energetic of the dances.

The door swung open at my gentle pressure. No villains jumped out of the shadows. After lighting the lamp, I searched the top drawer of my chest-of-drawers. Thank goodness my meager savings hadn't been stolen. In fact, nothing seemed to have been taken. But, aside from a change of clothes and a few coins, there wasn't anything in my room to take. I had my handbag with me at the dance. It only held a couple of coins, a handkerchief, and my quill pen.

After checking every possession and every nook and cranny a second time, I blew out the lamp and crawled into bed.

Curiosity dragged me out of bed before long, and I tiptoed to Rosalie's room. Her even breathing signaled a peaceful slumber. Nothing seemed amiss downstairs. Was I imagining things? After all, what did we have that anyone would want?

CHAPTER 15

A PAN OF dishes to wash and the cheerful morning sunlight shining through the kitchen window soon drove away the dark thoughts of the night and replaced them with more pleasant ones. Mr. Peachtree had asked at the dance if he could join us for our nightly reading time. I had been wondering when something like that would happen.

I hummed as I scrubbed the pans. There was something satisfying about seeing objects come clean under my touch. Speaking of touch, I needed to teach Rosalie how to fix her hair as I had fixed it for the dance. The change in style made a dramatic improvement in her looks. Mr. Peachtree had noticed.

My hand stilled among the soap bubbles. It was true he noticed, but it hadn't changed the way he treated her. He didn't pay her any more or less attention than he normally did. It was contrary to how I grew up thinking about romance, but I honestly felt Mr. Peachtree's desire to spend more time with Rosalie had nothing whatever to do with the change.

What had Gabriella said when we berated Marcel's appearance? That he was a man of good character whose company she enjoyed? Though it pained me to admit it, neither Rosalie nor Mr. Peachtree were much by Floraison matrimonial standards. Yet, they weren't Floraisons, so they needn't adhere to our standards. Gabriella on the other hand—

"Alexandria, your hands will be as shriveled as prunes if you leave them in the water any longer."

Startled, I drew my hands out so quickly I slung water all over Rosalie. Her laughter rang like tinkling bells through the room.

"I'm sorry to startle you, my dear. I had forgotten how hard it is for a young woman to concentrate the day after a dance." She picked up a rag and began to dry the dishes.

"Is there no one in the shop?" I asked.

"No, I'll listen for the butler." She smiled at our nickname for the doorbell. It didn't present us with calling cards on a silver tray, but it announced visitors just the same. "It was a wonderful night, wasn't it? You dance so gracefully, even Lord Leandre mentioned it while you were dancing with Lord Devryn. He said you danced like a real lady."

"With a partner like Lord Devryn, one couldn't fail to dance well."

"I suppose so, though I do think you danced just as well with Mr. Woodsman."

My cheeks felt unaccountably warm. "I was rather surprised by his expertise. Of course, Mr. Peachtree isn't a bad dancer either."

Despite my hope not to dance with anyone, I danced with Mr. Woodsman, Mr. Peachtree, Mr. Tinsler, both the Lord Collins, and a couple of the village men. My Floraison pride was still nursing its bruises, but I was none the worse for what Aunt Helene would have called a "degrading and absolutely unbearable experience."

"You and Mr. Peachtree looked well together, Rosalie."

She smiled and brushed a loose wisp of hair away from her face. "It's true he's not as good of a lead as Mr. Woodsman, but I enjoy dancing with him. You know, I watched Mr. Woodsman last night. I don't think his pleasure is solely in dancing itself. Did you notice that he danced with Abby Gabbeno twice?" The admiration in her voice was unmistakable.

"I thought he danced with her to avoid Miss Colter."

There was nothing admirable in dancing with a girl lame in one leg to avoid a flirt. His desperation was somewhat humorous, in a cruel way. Remembering my experience as a hag, I couldn't find it in myself to laugh.

"That may have been part of the reason the first time, but Miss Colter was nowhere around when he asked Abby the second time."

"Oh."

"Yes, and while I was at the refreshment table, Mrs. Janus told me that after the second time Mr. Woodsman danced with Abby, Martin Hobs finally got up the nerve to ask her. Apparently, Martin and Abby had been friends in school but teasing from the other men had prevented him asking her to dance before."

"Oh." The admiration in my voice surprised me.

A bell sounded from the store.

"There's the butler. I'd better get back out front." Rosalie put down the rag, and I redirected my attention to the dishes.

Sooner than I expected, the door swung open.

"Alexandria, this young man says he has a message for you."

A boy about seven years old followed Rosalie into the kitchen and held out a note to me. I dried my hands and took it, taking care to avoid what looked like chocolate smudges. "Who gave you this?"

"He never gave his proper name, miss. He did give me some coins though." The boy smiled a brown smile.

Rosalie fingered a towel as she looked at the boy's dirty face and hands. "And you went straight to the mercantile for a chocolate bar, didn't you? Next time, deliver the message before you spend your reward."

The boy looked at the towel and dashed out the door. "Yes, miss. Good day, miss."

Rosalie chuckled as the door slammed behind him. "I would love to scrub his face clean." She picked up a plate and wiped it dry. "Can you read any of it?"

"I can't make out the signature. I haven't looked at the body of the message yet. Let's see. It says: 'Don't tell anyone you know about the castle, and especially not about the enchanted mirror. *Hide your wand.*'"

My head spun. Was this a joke? Or a warning?

A warning? *Alexandria Floraison, pull yourself together. What are you afraid of? That people will think you're a sorceress and shun you—or worse—if they find out you enchanted the prince? Really, you worry like a commoner.* But then, it was addressed to Lady Alexandria Floraison, not Miss Alexandria Floraison.

"Whatever does it mean?" Rosalie asked.

"I haven't the faintest idea. I wish I knew who sent it. Perhaps it's some kind of a joke the kids are playing on me because of the stories I've told Little Marie and Evie."

"Some are playing Magic Collectors whilst some are playing informants?"

"Perhaps."

Game or no game, I didn't need this hint to avoid mentioning the castle and mirror, and I didn't know where the wand was so I didn't need to worry about hiding it.

The next week was as dreary as the previous one had been eventful. It misted for days, and though we had a fair number of customers, they were as dull as the weather. Lord Devryn and Lord Leandre were gone, which meant Louis was also away. I didn't care much for Louis, but at least he livened things up a bit. He always brought in a group of men. Mr. Tinsler was at home with a cold. Mr. Monroe forgot to pick up the socks I mended for him, and he barely managed to smile a "thank you" when I delivered them to him. Had the weather gotten to him that much?

Even Mr. Woodsman had deserted us.

"It will just be the three of us tonight, I'm afraid," Mr. Peachtree said as he welcomed us into his store the next Sunday afternoon. "Woodsman has gone exploring. Don't know when he'll be back."

I hoped it wasn't a permanent exploration. I hadn't repaid him for the dress he bought me.

"I hope he doesn't have an accident out there in the woods. There would be no one to help him." Rosalie began to unpack our dinner. "Speaking of help, I'm worried about Mr. Monroe. He didn't come by at his usual time this week, and Alexandria said he didn't seem himself when she delivered his socks."

"Come to think of it, I haven't seen him since the dance." Concern was evident in Mr. Peachtree's voice.

Perhaps because I was a daughter without a father and he was a father without a daughter, I felt a special anxiety about Mr. Monroe's solitude. My eyes rested on Mr. Woodsman's empty chair. He would simply march over to Mr. Monroe's house and insist he rejoin society.

"Why don't we invite him to dinner?" I surprised myself by standing and turning toward the door. "He lives nearby."

Rosalie's eyes opened wide and then her smile opened wider. "That's a wonderful idea. We'll hold dinner for you."

A few minutes later I knocked on Mr. Monroe's door. The maid, Agnes, answered. His farm had done well the last few years, and being a shrewd businessman, he'd managed to increase his earnings enough to hire a maid.

"Good evening, Miss Floraison. I'm so glad someone's come. The master hasn't been himself lately. Could you try to get him to eat something?" She reached out and touched my arm as she spoke.

"Tell him I'm here, Agnes, and I'll see what I can do."

She showed me into a small sitting room and then went to find her master. I looked around as I waited. The room was comfortably furnished. The walls were decorated with still lifes. Roses were the common theme of the paintings. A collection of framed miniatures sat on a small table near the window. I couldn't resist looking at them. One was of a young Mr. Monroe standing beside a healthy and radiant Anne. Another was of a baby. The last one was of Belle—I assumed it was her—as a young woman. I picked up the portrait and moved to the window to study it more closely. Belle was just as lovely as her mother. It was little wonder the village men mourned her departure.

The door swung open, and Agnes announced Mr. Monroe.

I startled when I saw him. He looked like I felt when I thought about my family, and that wasn't good.

"Good evening, Miss Floraison. This is an unexpected pleasure. What can I do for you?" His voice didn't match the cheerfulness his words implied. Even his smile was sad.

His gaze fastened on the portrait in my hands. My reply fell on deaf ears.

He studied my face for a minute before he sighed and sank into a chair. "She's about your age, you know." He stared down at his hands.

"Belle?"

"Yes."

"This is her portrait, isn't it? She is as beautiful as they say."

"She's the image of her mother."

I decided to meddle. "Please forgive my impertinence, but I know what it is to be lonely for one's family. Why don't you travel to Belle's aunt's house and visit for a while? I'm sure your daughter is as lonely for you as you are for her."

His face contorted as if in pain. "If only it were as simple as that," he cried. "I never should have let her go, but she was so determined. Nothing short of force would have stopped her. I had to promise. It's my fault." He covered his face with his hands.

What on earth had he promised? His daughter's hand in marriage to someone not as worthy as previously thought? Surely not. Mr. Monroe doted on Belle and would never force her into a marriage. What then?

"I fear I have distressed you. You do not look well. Why do you not come to dinner with Miss Lightwood, Mr. Peachtree, and myself? I came on purpose to issue an invitation. Friendly company and a hearty meal would do you good, I'm sure."

He lifted his head to reveal such a stricken look that I wished he had left his face concealed.

"How can I enjoy the company of such excellent people as yourself and your friends while my Belle is tormented by the presence of a—" He stopped suddenly and looked out the window.

He stood, crossed the room to me, and took my hands in his and held them to his chest. "A father would rather die than see harm befall his daughter. Don't ever think you can save your father by accepting danger on his behalf. It would only sharpen a knife to cut at him for the rest of his natural life."

His eyes implored me to heed his advice. I broke his gaze

and looked down at my hands. I had already grieved my father. Who knew if we would ever meet again?

He released me and stepped away. "Forgive me, Miss Floraison. You were right in saying I am not well. I daresay I shall be myself again in a few days. Thank you for the kind invitation, but I regret that I do not feel up to joining you today."

My heart ached for the man even as my brain tried to conjure a reason for his distress.

"Perhaps another time then. I am sorry you are not well."

"Thank you, Miss Floraison. Good day."

"Good day, Mr. Monroe."

He bowed and left the room.

Agnes shook her head as she showed me to the door. "I haven't seen him so distraught since he came home alone after taking Miss Belle to her aunt," she whispered.

Rosalie and Mr. Peachtree shared my concern for Mr. Monroe. He had no close family, so we decided it was our neighborly duty to discover the cause of his distress and help in any way we could. We were to be co-conspirators, and, as such, we had to start calling one another by our first names, which meant we needed to extract Mr. Woodsman's real name from him. Despite his absence, we elected him not only a member of our little band, but the leader.

CHAPTER 16

THINGS BEGAN TO pick up over the next few days. Louis and the young lords came back early in the week, and Mr. Monroe paid us a brief visit and promised to eat dinner with us on the Sunday after next. Mr. Tinsler recovered enough from his illness to visit with us when we delivered his meals. Only Mr. Woodsman remained absent.

"The weather certainly has been fine lately, hasn't it, Miss Floraison?" Martin Hobs said as I poured him a drink. Ever since the dance he had been *happening* to come by for a pastry the same time as Abby.

"Well, look who's coming," he said right before the butler told me the "who" was now in.

But it wasn't Abby. It was my Woodsman. The bell must have startled me, for my heart beat strangely fast.

As I walked back to the counter, I nodded to Mr. Woodsman and attempted to suppress the foolish grin trying to take control of my face. We needed a softer bell. Its loud chime was unnerving me.

Setting the lemonade pitcher down, I stole a glance at the

woodsman while he greeted Martin. His beard was in desperate need of a trim, his clothes dusty, and his eyes rimmed by dark circles. He probably hadn't had a good night's sleep or a hearty meal since he left the village the day after the dance. I poured a large glass of lemonade and got out a few pastries.

He looked up from Martin and met my eye, smiling in that contagious way of his. He patted Martin on the shoulder and joined me at the counter. Leaning across it, he took one of my hands between his. He smelled of the forest, and his hands were warm and rough, in a manly sort of way. He was so unlike the many men I had met who wore powdered wigs and kid leather gloves.

He tugged at my hand, as if to make sure he had my full attention.

"When you do something," he said, "you do it thoroughly."

"What do you mean?" A tingle of anxiety sped down my spine.

"I've been to the castle." His tone told me he'd seen more than a grand edifice.

With a gasp, I pulled away, but his grip tightened around my wrist. *So that was why he had taken my hand.*

His gaze found mine and held it as securely as his hand held my mine. "Don't worry. I wouldn't give you away."

His reassuring smile slowed my racing heart, and I moved back toward the counter. He loosened his grip but didn't let go.

"How did you know?" He wasn't terrified of me? Or angry at what I had done?

"That's not important. Aren't you interested in how things are going there?"

Of course I was! "I suppose so."

"Good. I'll call for you later and tell you about it. For once in my life, I'll be a welcome sight to you."

He released me and straightened. He raised his eyebrows

and pointed to the glass of lemonade and the plate of pastries. "Are those for me?"

"What makes you think they're yours?" I didn't like the smug grin he was wearing.

"These are my favorites."

"Abby will be coming in any minute now. She likes these too."

He glanced over his shoulder and chuckled. "Martin has enough for both of them." He turned around with that familiar twinkle in his eyes and picked up the lemonade and the plate of pastries. "Would you like to share *my* pastries with me?"

"Working girls don't have time to eat with their customers."

He looked at me with wide eyes, and then a chuckle escaped him.

The butler announced Abby, and Mr. Woodsman walked off laughing as I went to greet her.

My stomach turned sailor and practiced tying itself in knots all afternoon. With Mr. Woodsman no longer there, my brain reconsidered what he told me. How did he know I had enchanted the prince and the castle? What did he plan to do with that knowledge? How long had he suspected me? Did this have anything to do with his helping me and staying around the village to keep an eye on me?

The butler announced a visitor as Rosalie and I finished packing the dinner deliveries. Mr. Woodsman joined us in the kitchen. He looked fresh and rested, and his beard was neatly trimmed.

Rosalie glanced at me and smiled. My stomach tied itself into a fancy knot.

"Good evening, Mr. Woodsman. It's kind of you to take my place delivering meals," she said.

"My pleasure, Miss Rosalie."

She placed the last dish in the basket and handed it to him.

He offered me his free arm, and I accepted it. His gentleman-like bearing and warm smile comforted me, and the knots in my stomach loosened.

Between deliveries, he asked me about my day, how long Martin and Abby had been meeting at the pastry shop, and what had happened while he was away.

The knots had all but gone, when I chanced to see a man walk by with a chocolate bar. Should I tell Mr. Woodsman about the note and the intruder? I should probably mention the intruder to someone, but whom could I trust? Rosalie, of course, but she wouldn't understand. Enchantments and missing wands were beyond her experience. What about Mr. Woodsman? He apparently knew about the spell on the castle and didn't seem perturbed by it. Lord Devryn and Lord Leandre appeared to know something about enchanters and objects of enchantment.

"Someone searched my room during the dance a couple of weeks ago," I blurted out.

He jerked to a halt and spun around to face me. "Searched? Was anything taken? What have you done about it?"

His anxiety took me aback. "I haven't done anything about it. Nothing was taken."

"*Nothing* was taken?"

"No."

He let out his breath. "Thank goodness for that."

Why was he so relieved? I didn't have anything valuable.

He lifted the cloth covering the basket, now empty, and lowered it back. "That was the last of the deliveries. Now, tell me more about your room being searched, and then I'll tell you about my trip."

The knots retied themselves.

"Miss Alexandria! Mr. Woodsman! Wait for me." Brown braids flying, Evie Janus ran up to us.

Please tell me that cat isn't up a tree again.

The gray bundle in Evie's arms squirmed and two green eyes stared me down.

Thank heavens.

Evie gave me a one-armed hug. "May Locust and I walk with you?"

I squeezed her tight. The castle would have to wait. "Of course, Evie. You and Locust are very welcome."

Mr. Woodsman looked around with a furrowed brow until he saw the cat. He shook his head and grinned. "I was about to tell Miss Floraison a story, Evie. I think you and Locust will enjoy it too." He winked at me.

Evie shifted Locust to her shoulder and focused eager eyes on Mr. Woodsman.

He cleared his throat and began.

"Once upon a time there was a brave, handsome, and exceptionally wise young man who was rather fond of a certain young woman. Now this young woman was as fair as a dove and as clever as a fox, but she was also as proud as an eagle and stubborn as a mule. So it was no surprise to the young man when he discovered she had, for reasons he would like to know, cast a spell on a prince, turning him into a beast and his beautiful castle into a hideous fortress."

He gave me a significant look, and my throat went as dry as the stones in that hideous fortress.

"Well," he continued, "the dear lady had spent her powers doing this and was left quite helpless. Only the ending of the spell and the reclaiming of the enchantment, which had to be done just right, could help her. When the young man realized this, he rushed to the castle to see it for himself. He quickly perceived that time was running out for the spell.

"'Oh no!' he cried. 'I must warn her to have her wand ready …'" Mr. Woodsman trailed off as he glanced over his shoulder.

Lord Devryn and Lord Leandre strode up beside us.

"That's a fascinating story. Please don't stop." Lord Leandre raised his hat in greeting. Lord Devryn gave me his boyish grin.

"Why, thank you, my lord." Mr. Woodsman's gaze shifted from Lord Devryn to me and then to the buildings lining the street.

I felt as if I knew his thoughts. We were walking through a poor section of the village. What were the lords doing here?

Mr. Woodsman made a show of clearing his throat. "The man told the young woman to take a nap, for she was very weak. When he visited the next day, she was still asleep. 'Why does she not wake? I must talk to her,' he said. He banged on a pot right beside her head and even threw a glass of water on her, but nothing would wake her. Then he did the only other thing he could think of. He went wading in the stream behind his grandmother's cottage and collected a bucketful of frogs. He went back to the woman's house and set the bucket beside her bed.

"'This will do the trick,' he said to himself. He picked up a slimy frog and pressed it to her cheek. Nothing happened. He chucked the frog out the window and grabbed another one. Half way through the bucket, when he pressed an unusually slimy frog with a brown spot on its head, to the woman's cheek, her eyes opened.

"'Oh, my darling prince,' she cried and kissed the frog. There was a blinding flash of light and some rather dramatic music. When the music stopped and the young man could see again, he looked for his friend but couldn't find her. However, he did see two frogs hopping off into the sunset."

The corners of Lord Devryn's mouth tilted up. "Did they live hoppily ever after?"

"Of course, I intended to mention that but forgot. Thank you for pointing that out."

"Is that the end?" Evie's eyes were as big as apples. "I've never heard a story like that." She twisted around to look at me. "I like your stories better."

Mr. Woodsman burst out laughing. "That's all the thanks I get for my efforts?"

"You have a gifted imagination, Mr. Woodsman," Lord Leandre said.

Imagination? He hit too near the truth in the first part of the story for comfort. In some areas. I was not as stubborn as a mule.

"Thank you, my lord." Mr. Woodsman bowed.

Lord Devryn petted Locust on the head. "Have you rescued any more cats lately, Miss Floraison?"

I was on the verge of replying when Mr. Woodsman spoke again.

"Speaking of imagination, it's time I imagine Miss Floraison back at Miss Lightwood's shop. Good day, gentlemen. Evie." He tipped his hat to the gentleman, bowed to Evie, and took my arm.

The lords accepted their dismissal with grace, wished us a good day, and walked on. Evie ran away after I gave Locust a farewell scratch behind the ears.

"That was rude, sending them away like that," I said when Mr. Woodsman and I were alone. "Lord Devryn and Lord Leandre are sons of a duke. You can't treat them like you would treat the other villagers."

He cocked an eyebrow but didn't turn to face me. "I'll treat them the same as I would treat anyone else. I don't like the way they have a knack for showing up when we don't expect them, particularly in out-of-the-way places, like the woods and poor side-streets." He looked over at me, the critical eyebrow still in place. "Sons of a duke don't normally pay attention to shop-keepers' assistants either."

My mouth fell open. I shut it quickly. What did he have against these men? They were noblemen and had always been polite. And I was more than a shopkeeper's assistant. They, at least, seemed to realize it.

"I see nothing wrong in their behavior. I am very pleased with Lord Devryn and Lord Leandre," I said sharply.

Irritation flashed in his eyes. "Have they mentioned enchant-ments to you?"

"Should they have?" Where was the harm in that?

There was that flash of irritation again.

"Where's your wand, Miss Floraison?"

My wand? Why did everyone assume I had a wand? "What makes you think I have a wand?"

He leaned in close and said in a low voice, "The castle is why. We need your wand."

The knots in my stomach retied themselves tighter than before. Needed my wand? Surely, Mr. Woodsman wasn't a Magic Collector. Had he searched my room? No, he had been with me at the dance. Unless he insisted I go so an accomplice could search my room.

Was that disappointment I felt? How could I be disappointed that a commoner had deceived me into thinking he was my friend? I should be angry. In fact, Mr. Woodsman would make a nice piece of kindling.

"It would be sensible of you to avoid talking to the lords," he said.

A piece of kindling next to a roaring fire.

"You've no right to tell me who I should or shouldn't talk to. I am not the helpless young lady in your absurd story."

"Calm down and listen to me."

Me calm down? That wasn't a polished edge to his voice.

"I don't wish to hear anything else." I wished I hadn't heard anything he'd said for the past half-hour. "I don't know where the wand is. I haven't seen it since I left the castle, and I have nothing else to say. If you'll excuse me, I'd like to imagine myself back to Miss Lightwood's shop alone."

He jerked to a halt, his face pale. "You don't know where it is?"

"No." I grabbed the basket from him and marched away.

As I rounded the corner into the main street, I heard him beg me to wait, but I kept walking.

Mr. Woodsman's chair was empty at dinner on Sunday. According to Mr. Peachtree, he was off exploring again.

CHAPTER 17

I WANTED TO go home. Hadn't it been long enough for my letter to arrive? Maybe my family had sent a reply.

I stole away from the shop—it was my afternoon off—and walked to the mercantile.

Mrs. Colter greeted me as I entered. She was a sensible woman, unlike her flirt of a daughter.

"Do you have a letter for me?" I asked.

"No, dear. Nothing came for you in the last delivery. Were you expecting one?"

"I was hoping. I thought there might have been enough time for my letter to have reached Florenburg and been responded to by now."

She must have noticed the disappointment in my voice. "When did you post the letter? I can ask my husband if he thinks there's been time. He's better at estimating that sort of thing than I am."

I told her the date and she hurried away to the back of the store. A few minutes later she returned with a look of embarrassment.

"I'm sorry, my dear, but your letter was never posted." She handed me several coins—the price to mail a letter to Florenburg.

"What do you mean never posted? Did I not pay enough?"

"You paid enough, but ..."

"But?" The coins fell with a clink into my handbag.

"It was just never sent anywhere." She seemed hesitant to meet my eye.

"Why not?" My glare demanded a straight answer.

"Mr. Woodsman asked my husband to intercept any letters you sent," she blurted out. "He said you were distraught over the recent loss of your family and hadn't accepted the fact they weren't alive. He didn't want you to distress the Duke of Henly with more inquiries after them, since your family comes from that area."

I grasped the counter. The nerve of that man. I'd turn him into a ... a ...

I was so mad I didn't know what I'd do to him.

Mrs. Colter's anxious look calmed me. *Floraisons did not lose their temper.* After all, she and her husband weren't to blame. I gave her a surprisingly polite "thank you" and "good day" and marched out of the store.

I'd get home even if I had to walk all the way. Mr. Woodsman's tricks weren't going to stop me, though they did hurt.

☙❧

"I'm sorry, Alexandria. I don't have any maps of Sonser for sale," Albert Peachtree said.

"None?"

"They were all bought recently." He looked at me curiously.

Oh. "Mr. Woodsman bought them, didn't he?" I wasn't sure if it came out as a question or an accusation.

Whatever it was, Albert took it with nothing more than a quirk of the eyebrow. "Yes. He said he needed them for his explorations."

Or to stop mine. I murmured my thanks and left.

My mood requiring a long and strenuous walk, I marched through the village, over the canal bridge, past green fields, and half way up the hill Mr. Woodsman and I had descended several months ago. The trees rising around me and the familiar smell of the forest worked together to soothe my soul.

When my lungs demanded a rest, I sat on a fallen log and admired the striking contrast of the dark blue canal water and the bright white walls of the half-timbered houses below.

The houses of my village.

I wrapped my arms around myself. If only when I walked out of the woods I would find the village adjoining my father's estate.

A cloud shadowed the rooftops, and I gasped. Was I trying to get home the wrong way? I hadn't gotten here solely by walking. Part of my journey had been by enchantment.

❦

My side ached and my chest burned by the time I passed underneath the weather-beaten sign for Peachtree's Bookstore. It was a long shot, but he might have what I wanted.

Albert glanced up at the sound of the bell, looked me up and down, and then smiled. "Welcome back, Alexandria. You're looking much more cheerful."

"I'm sorry for being out-of-sorts earlier."

"It's forgotten. What can I do for you?"

"Do you have a book on enchantments for sale?"

He stared at me a moment, a perplexed look on his face. "I'll be right back," he said, motioning for me to stay.

Instead of searching through the dusty bookshelves, he went through the door leading to his personal chambers above the store. He returned with a leather-bound book entitled *The Beginning and End of Enchantments: A guide to advanced spells.* "I never thought I'd sell this book. It's been sitting on a shelf for years, and now, within a few weeks, two people have wanted to purchase it."

My heart sank. Two people wanted? "Is it not for sale?"

"Mr. Woodsman asked for a book on enchantments right after the dance. He stays in my spare bedroom when he's in town, you know. I sold him this one, and he stayed up half the night reading. He finished it before his latest trip and left it in his room. I'm sure he wouldn't mind if you borrowed it." He placed the book into my hands as if to prevent my refusing.

"Are you certain he won't mind?"

"I'm certain."

His assurance and my need lessened my aversion to accepting anything else from that snake-in-the-grass Mr. Woodsman.

☙❧

My day off came to a close, and I had only read a few chapters. Over the next week I read whenever I could. Yet, what I read wasn't comforting. My parents could do nothing to undo the change in my appearance wrought by the mirror, and, until the spell on the prince ended, I wouldn't have any power.

It seemed I had a greater capability for enchantments than I suspected, but only when faced with a purpose for the power was it released—all of it. It had all gone to enchant the prince, and I couldn't get it back until the spell was broken or the prince died a natural death.

How enchantments of that type returned was still unclear to

me, but it was clear that the enchantment could be lost or transferred to someone else when the spell ended or some important deadline was reached. I took that to mean some power, probably a good bit, would be released when the rose died and the beast-like condition of the prince became final.

How would I know when it was about to end? How could the power be lost or transferred? It was my chance of going home. I didn't want to lose it. I flipped through the remaining third of the book and sighed. The author was unorganized. If I didn't read the entire book, I'd probably miss something vital.

The fragrance of freshly baked bread drifted up from the kitchen, and I replaced the book in my chest of drawers and went downstairs to help Rosalie with dinner.

Fairly soon we left for Albert's bookshop for Sunday dinner. Mr. Monroe promised his attendance. Would Mr. Woodsman be there? I rather hoped not for I was still angry with him. I didn't suspect him of being a Magic Collector any longer, though I couldn't say why. I once thought he might be the ex-servant of a nobleman. The ex-servant of an enchanter perhaps? That would explain his shrewd guesses about me. I still wanted to know what his interest in me was, and what right—what good reason—he thought he had to conspire to keep me in this village against my inclination.

I focused on that thought as Rosalie and I knocked on Albert's door. It was better I met that hairy commoner glare for smile instead of smile for smile.

But he still wasn't back from his explorations. Where could he have gone? He hadn't met with any wild boars, had he? Or wolves? Or careless hunters?

I scolded myself for my anxiety. I had other things to concern myself with. Tonight was the night Albert, Rosalie, and I were to uncover Mr. Monroe's troubles and see what we could do about them.

"Mr. Monroe will be here any minute," Albert said as he led us into the dining area, "but I'm afraid we'll have to cancel our little plot to draw out his troubles. When I mentioned our scheme to Woodsman the last time he was here, he said it was a noble purpose but that we wouldn't do any good by prying. In fact, it would be the worst thing we could do. 'Keep him company' was Woodsman's suggestion. He even made me promise."

Just like Mr. Woodsman to boss us around.

"He seemed rather surprised you were going along with it." Albert caught my eye, a question in his glance.

"I don't know why we shouldn't." It was irritating that Mr. Woodsman presumed to know my mind. Yet, was there some reason I, in particular, wouldn't want Mr. Monroe's secrets revealed?

The doorbell sounded and Albert welcomed Mr. Monroe while Rosalie and I finished laying out dinner.

"It's been a long time since I've enjoyed dinner with friends. I'm grateful for your invitation." Mr. Monroe wore a smile as he strode into the room.

☙❧

"I was hoping to see Mr. Woodsman tonight." Mr. Monroe wiped his mouth with a napkin before taking a drink.

"He's off exploring again."

A distant look in his eye, Mr. Monroe spread butter on a roll. "He's an enigmatic but likeable young man. I feel as if I know him somehow better than our short acquaintance justifies. I'd like to spend more time with him."

"I wonder why he goes exploring." Rosalie looked around at us. "Do you think he's trying to find the castle Lord Devryn and Lord Leandre mentioned? It presumably burnt, but ruins are often just as interesting as intact structures."

Mr. Monroe's smile fell, and it took him a few tugs to get it in place again.

Albert shot me a glance.

I looked down and twisted the napkin in my lap. Was it because we'd quarreled? "I don't believe it was for the castle." Not this time. "Perhaps it was to find those poachers of yours, Mr. Monroe."

He nodded slowly. "Perhaps."

"Oh, my book merchants came into town yesterday." Albert looked like a little boy who had gotten a new toy.

"How long will it take you to finish reading all the new books so you can put them out for sale?" I asked with a grin, relieved at the change of subject.

Rosalie tried to hide her laughter behind her napkin.

Albert raised an eyebrow. "I do not read each book before putting it out for sale—unless I only ordered one copy of it. You wouldn't want me to recommend a poorly written book, would you?"

A chuckle escaped Mr. Monroe. "Belle was always pleased by the books you recommended. She never gave you time to read the ones you ordered for her. She knew when the merchants would come." His smile fell again, and he looked out the window.

Rosalie and I exchanged glances. We had agreed not to meddle, but it would be horribly impolite not to inquire after Belle when he had mentioned her.

"Have you heard from Belle recently? I do hope she is meeting new people and making friends at her aunt's," Rosalie said.

He gave an odd laugh. "No. Her … aunt doesn't interact much with the world."

We had finished dinner and were passing through Albert's shop on our way out when an "oh" of sudden remembrance stopped us.

"Oh my. I almost forgot. Again." Chuckling, Albert stopped beside the front counter. "My sister made me promise I would ask, beg if necessary, for your apple tart recipe, Rosalie. She threatened to mail me a book worm to destroy my shop if I didn't send it to her in my next letter."

Rosalie's laughter brightened the room. "Well, she's too far away to be serious competition. I suppose I could divulge the secret family recipe."

"Excellent." Mr. Peachtree grinned. "If you will dictate, I shall be your scribe." He moved behind the counter and retrieved pen and paper from a drawer.

With an "I never measure, so I can only guess at the amount" Rosalie began to dictate the recipe.

Mr. Monroe wished us a good night and left.

A stack of newspapers on the end of the long counter caught my eye. The papers were probably months old, as Albert's merchants only passed through once a quarter, but that didn't stop me from gasping at the headline of the top paper.

"The Duke of Lofton's House Broken into. Guard Murdered.
Important Document Stolen."

The Duke of Lofton's house was entered sometime after nine p.m., on Saturday, the twenty-ninth of March. Several valuable pieces of jewelry were taken, but the duke, who was at a dinner party during the robbery, believes the jewelry theft was only a ruse. The real object, he asserts, was a document known as *The Enchanter's List*, a record of all known objects of enchantment, their keepers, and their locations. "I wouldn't normally mention this publicly, but it's urgent that those of you who have belongings on the list guard them more vigilantly than ever. With the decline of sorcerers, we have grown lax. The rise of the so-called Magic Collectors calls for a return to vigilance. We do not know what evil purpose they plan, but we now know to what lengths they will go to achieve it. Guard your possessions well, *and make sure the enchantment returns to you.*"

"Alexandria, you're as pale as a pear blossom. Are you all right?" Rosalie made me sit on the chair beside the counter.

Was my family all right? The Magic Collectors, for certainly they were responsible for the break-in, knew our identity and what objects we had. It wasn't exactly a secret we were enchanters, but it wasn't knowledge we spread about. What if we had something they wanted?

"Forgive me. I … uh … don't know what came over me. I'm better now." I stood and smiled, though, to my shame, my knees felt weak.

Albert glanced at the newspaper and then at me, his expression contemplative.

"Are you finished with the recipe? I'd like some fresh air," I said.

"Yes, it's time we headed home." Rosalie's eyes still held concern. She put her arm around me as if she was afraid I would topple over any second. It was embarrassing, but her touch was comforting.

Albert opened the door for us, and we three walked out into the street.

Not far from the shop, near where the merchants were set up, we spotted Lord Devryn and Lord Leandre walking on the opposite side of the street. They waved and strode over to us.

Lord Devryn tipped his hat. "We were out for our evening walk. May we join you?"

Mr. Woodsman's remark about lords not typically paying attention to shopkeepers came to mind, but I dismissed it. Lord Devryn's friendliness seemed genuine. "Of course. You are always welcome." Despite Mr. Woodsman's antipathy and their habit of showing up at unexpected moments.

"That is a comforting thing to hear." Lord Devryn took a place beside me while Lord Leandre began a conversation with Albert and Rosalie.

"I'm sorry we interrupted your story the other day," Lord Devryn said. "I didn't realize until later that Mr. Woodsman was trying to tell you something through it."

Frowning, I brushed at my skirts. "It's no matter. I'm sure he enjoyed the challenge of making up a new ending."

"He's rather a singular man. In some ways he reminds me of a friend of mine, only making up outrageous stories is just one of his eccentricities."

We discussed the oddities of our friends and acquaintances until we reached Rosalie's door, where the fragrance of gardenias greeted us.

"Sir Winfred never rides his horse on Thursday because the 'hurs' of Thursday looks rather like 'horse' but sounds more like 'hearse' ..." Lord Devryn's voice trailed off and he glanced around.

Lord Leandre caught his eye. "It's the gardenia you smell." He motioned toward the gardenia, but his hand brushed the tip of a rose bud, which after weeks of sitting, was about to bloom.

My door was ajar again that night, and the book on enchantments was missing. I really didn't need another reason not to sleep. The newspaper headline still flashed before my eyes with deadly intensity.

In place of the book was a note, which read: "What does an enchantress need with a book on enchantments?"

My heart quaked. Whoever broke into my room knew I was an enchantress. Who was it? Of course, the Magic Collectors, if I had met one, would know who I was. It was something they could sense. Now that they had *The Enchanter's List* they would also know what I might have. It was possible the mirror, the wand, and the enchantment on the prince were ascribed to me. With my wand they might be able to capture the enchantment. The chocolate-smudged note warned me to protect my wand. I didn't even know where it was. The book on enchantments hinted wands could change shape, but I would have to read the remaining third of the book to find out more.

I took my worries to bed with me. Eventually, the light of the stars outside my window faded into the lights of the castle I so often dreamed of.

The prince paced around a dimly lit room talking to someone I couldn't see. He cast a large and horrible shadow on the wall.

"Isn't it ironic?" he growled "When I was a man, women sought me because of my position, fortune, and good looks, and I scorned them because they weren't rich enough, or beautiful enough, or didn't have the right connections. Now, as a beast, I must win the heart of a woman without title or fortune." He swept a massive paw toward a small table on which stood the vase holding the wilting rose. "I must seek this village girl because she can free me from my curse."

"She is beautiful," said the other person.

"Yes, but that only adds to my shame."

"Matches are often made for what can be gained through the union."

"What has she to gain? What would induce her to marry me?"

"You are wealthy and able to give her a life of luxury."

"A life of luxury confined to a castle and the company of a beast would hardly be worth it. Not that she would ever marry for money."

"No, I don't think she would. She's a romantic."

The prince was silent for a moment. "Can you truly love someone whose affections you seek for selfish reasons?" He looked at his companion. "You seem surprised to hear me say the word. I will say it again: selfish. She has used it against me until I see the truth of it."

"Don't you enjoy her company?"

"Yes, but I also enjoy the company of a good book. What do I know of love? I'm a beast! What chance do I have for receiving it?"

"She no longer avoids you."

"There's nothing like solitude for making even the most repulsive companion bearable."

"Or perhaps to reveal what's truly important in a companion."

The prince gave a great sigh and moved to a window overlooking the castle courtyard. A girl walked around the courtyard, admiring the flowers blooming there. She had a bouquet of roses in her hand.

I woke with a start. I knew why Mr. Monroe paled at the mention of the castle.

My dreams weren't simply dreams. There was a girl in the castle, and she was Belle Monroe.

I buried my head in my thin pillow. What was I to do? Who was I to trust with my secrets?

CHAPTER 18

DISTRESSED BY THE theft of the book, Rosalie sent me off to Albert's store mid-morning to tell him about it.

"The book was the only thing taken?" Albert's concern was evident in his voice, though he walked away from me.

"Yes."

He twisted the "open" sign in the window to read "closed" and then returned to me, studying my face for a moment before speaking. "This wasn't an ordinary theft, was it?"

How did he know? "No. No, it wasn't, and I do not understand it."

"Alexandria, I know you and Woodsman aren't who you seem to be. Won't you confide in me? I will do whatever I can to help you, especially now that Woodsman is away."

I opened my mouth to speak, but nothing came out. Pride held my overburdened heart in check. Did I want to humiliate myself by confessing everything? Albert might tell Mr. Woodsman when he came back, and I wasn't sure how much I should trust him.

When I didn't respond, he patted my shoulder. "You don't have to tell me anything now, but think about it. I'll be here whenever you want to talk."

I nodded, giving him a weak smile.

He cleared his throat. "You may not be ready to tell me your secrets, but I am ready to tell you mine. I'm going to ask Rosalie to marry me."

"That's wonderful news!" In my joy for my friends, I kissed him on his pink cheek and then felt my own cheeks flush at my enthusiasm.

Far from being alarmed, he gave me a quick hug. "Promise not to tell her before I do?"

I grinned. "Promise."

"Off with you then. I have books to inventory." He shooed me away, waving toward the door with a thick book.

My grin faded as I neared the market and was engulfed by the crowd. Gone were the days when the throngs made way for me. A woman with a large basket jostled me into a group of people waiting to buy livestock.

"Watch where you're going, miss," a man called out.

The people shifted and pressed together as a farmer with a hog pushed his way through.

"Excuse me. Please let me pass." I struggled to slip through any gap I could find.

A strong pair of hands clasped my shoulders and shoved me through the crowd, his speed and closeness preventing me from turning around. "Where's the wand, enchantress?" my guide hissed in my ear. "We have the woodsman's mirror. All we need is the wand. Time is running out."

He thrust me out of the crowd, and I stumbled into a booth, thudding to a stop at a cookware-laden table. I spun around and rushed out to the street. Oscar examined a horse. Roger stood talking to a few men, who, judging by their attire, were a merchant and his hired help. No one else among the villagers was known to me or looked ... well, like a Magic Collector might look.

Forgetting about dignity, I ran back to the pastry shop, the implications of the note and the verbal warning pounding in my head. The Magic Collectors assumed I had a wand. Mr. Woodsman assumed I had a wand. Therefore, I must have a wand. It had appeared suddenly at the castle, replacing the rose brooch in my hand, and then disappeared after I enchanted the prince. Where could it be?

I clutched my handbag to my chest and dashed between two men blocking the path as they stood chatting. My fingers distinguished the hard shaft of the quill pen from among the other items in the bag. *The rose-decorated pen.* Hope flared in my heart. I might know where the wand was hiding after all.

With *The Enchanter's List*, the Magic Collectors would know I had a wand, but what made Mr. Woodsman suspect it? Since he apparently wasn't a Magic Collector—my heart felt lighter at the thought—then who was he? Where was he? And who were the Magic Collectors?

The door to the pastry shop banged shut behind me. Lord Devryn and Lord Leandre rose to their feet, empty plates sitting on the table before them. "Miss Floraison, Miss Lightwood told us of the intruder last night. If there is anything we can do, you have but to command."

Surely these men could help me. I slowed to a more elegant pace and met them at their table. "I thank you. In truth, I have reason to believe the book on enchantments was not the only belonging of Mr. Woodsman's stolen recently. I'm anxious for his safety. He's been gone two weeks." My hand on my burning chest, I panted out the last few words.

Lord Leandre took my elbow and guided me to a seat. "Louis has just returned from a hunting trip, but as soon as he gets a fresh horse, I will send him and Roger to search for your friend. Would that ease your mind?" He glanced at his brother, who nodded and then stared at the floor.

I sighed in relief. "Very much, my lord."

"Consider it done then."

"What did they steal from Mr. Woodsman? Did someone break into his room at Albert's bookshop?" Rosalie joined us at the table.

The ears of the other customers pricked in my direction.

"I don't know where the theft occurred, but Mr. Peachtree didn't mention a burglary." Lowering my voice, I touched one tender shoulder. "A man in the market said *we* already have … something of Mr. Woodsman's."

A customer called for Rosalie, and she hurried off.

"Who are *we*?" Lord Leandre whispered. "Did you recognize the man in the market?"

"The Magic Collectors, I believe. I don't know who the man in the market was."

"The Magic Collectors," he exclaimed. "Then, Mr. Woodsman is …"

I shrugged. Was he an enchanter or had he stolen—no, he wouldn't steal—been given an enchanted mirror?

"We'll see what information we can find." Lord Devryn spoke with haste. He bowed and left. Lord Leandre followed.

When they were gone, I rushed to my room and emptied the contents of my handbag onto the bed. The few coins clinked as the quill pen landed on top of them. Its soft silver feather wasn't at all ruffled. I moved to the window and held the pen's shaft in the sunlight. A faint engraving of roses circled up to the feather. Had I ever cut a new tip for the pen? Or refilled it with ink after the first dip? No. Strange I'd never noticed that before.

I was a fool. I'd had the wand with me all along!

The afternoon and evening passed quickly as I busied myself in the shop with whatever tasks I could find. I caught snippets of conversations.

"The merchants' caravan is leaving this evening."

"A heavy rain is expected in the next few days."

But my mind was never far from my hunted wand and my missing Woodsman, to whom I owed an apology.

Rosalie patted my hand the next day as we packed the dinner meals. I jumped at her touch.

"You look so worried, Alexandria. I'm sure you'll hear from the lords soon. Why don't you stay here tonight and rest, or work on the knitting requests? I can make the deliveries by myself."

I was embarrassed my anxiety was so obvious, but I didn't protest. I had a feeling Albert would accompany her anyway. She left, and I went upstairs and pulled out my bag of knitting projects and was soon lost to my thoughts, the rhythmic movement of the knitting needles a mere background to them.

A little before dark our bell-butler announced a visitor. Or an intruder. Could it be the Magic Collectors checking to see if anyone was home? Why had I not locked the door?

I tiptoed downstairs and peeked through a crack in the kitchen door. Hat in his hands, Lord Leandre glanced around the empty shop.

Scolding myself for my silly fears, I made sure my skirt was straight and free of yarn and then opened the door. "Good evening, Lord Leandre."

He stepped forward eagerly. "Good evening, Miss Floraison. I was afraid you might be out tonight."

"No, Rosalie took the meals by herself."

"I'm glad. I have some news about Mr. Woodsman." He held his hat in front of him, fingering its brim.

"Yes?" *Don't sound so excited.*

"Louis found him. He's eager to talk with you, but he doesn't want to come this far into town. 'The Magic Collectors' goons'—those were his very words—tried to waylay him. He asked me to take you to him."

"He's not injured, is he? Did he say what he wanted to tell me?"

"No, to both questions. He only asked that you bring *it* with you, in case the Magic Collectors were watching the house and decided to search for it again."

"I'm so glad he's not injured," I said, already turning toward the kitchen door. "I'll get my things and be right down." I wouldn't have left it anyway.

"You'll probably want to leave Miss Lightwood a note"—he stepped forward, raising his hand to delay me—"in case she returns before we do. Since we're in a hurry, I'll write it for you."

"But—"

"Mr. Woodsman stressed urgency."

Write it simply, or she might not be able to read it. With a nod, I ran upstairs, grabbed my shawl and handbag, and hurried back down.

Lord Leandre placed the note on the counter and led me through the doorway. He picked up a lit lantern outside the door. "It may be dark before we return."

"Where is Mr. Woodsman? Is he far?"

"He's just outside of town."

Lord Leandre set a fast pace, and we soon reached the canal, stopping in the shadows of the clump of trees at the foot of the bridge. This time there was no cat meowing for help. There was no one.

Lord Leandre raised the lantern, scattering light about the empty lane and throwing darker shadows against the unlit buildings along the canal. A lamppost standing watch over the bridge gave an eerie glow to the misty air churning in a faint breeze over the river below.

"Devryn was supposed to meet us here with the horses." Frowning, Lord Leandre looked around impatiently. "The livery stable is close by; I'll go see what's keeping him. You'd better stay here in case he shows up."

Lord Leandre walked away, leaving me alone with the wind and the shadows.

The songs of the tree frogs and the lapping of water against the canal wall grew louder and louder, as if they were closing in on me. Stepping closer to the clump of trees, I blocked those sounds and focused instead on the gentle rustling of leaves and the waving of the shadows on the ground as the wind passed among the branches.

I blinked and looked at the ground again. One shadow was too large for a branch, and it didn't bend with the wind.

My mind told my feet to run but before they could obey a hand clamped over my mouth, and an arm snaked around my waist.

CHAPTER 19

Y OU BROUGHT IT like a good little girl, didn't you?"
hissed the voice from the market. Alcohol and dog
odor assaulted my nose as the man dragged me
deeper into the shadows. I reached above my head and tried to
poke him in the eye, but he caught my wrist, twisted me around,
and violently thrust me away—into the grasp of another man. A
man with a grip of iron.

Everything went dark, not because I was unconscious, but
because those despicable brutes blindfolded me. The loss of that
sense made the bitter taste of the gag forced into my mouth
stronger and heightened the roughness of the tie against my
cheeks. What were they going to do to me?

As if in answer, one of them yanked my handbag—holding
my quill pen—off my wrist, tied my hands together, and patted
me down.

The loathsome knave. I'd turn him into a goose at Christ-
mastime and see how he liked the feel of the flames.

"Doesn't she have it?" asked the hisser. I didn't recognize the
voice, though his blend of unsavory odors was familiar.

"This is all she has. She must have disguised it as something else. They said she might have, but they'll know it when they touch it."

I knew that voice. Louis! Then the other must be Roger. They were trying to steal my wand and give it to the Magic Collectors?

I kicked them both and jerked forward, but Louis caught me and pinned me to his side.

"It's not time to leave just yet." His whisper was laced with a threat.

Roger cursed at me, and I tried to kick him.

"Shut up, Roger," Louis ordered. I doubted he even flinched when I kicked him again.

His grip grew painfully tight. I quit struggling and listened to the water beat against the stone wall as a watercraft glided up the canal.

At the poor imitation of a whippoorwill's call, Louis dragged me out of the trees and onto the smooth cobblestone of the bridge.

"Steady. Okay, you can lower her down now," a voice called from below.

My heart raced as I realized what was happening. Screaming into the gag, I thrashed about in Louis's arms, trying to break free. Roger slapped me, slamming my head into Louis's chest. Louis picked me up and leaned forward, holding me out from him.

"Happy landing." The smirk in Roger's voice was almost drowned out by the unnaturally loud lapping of the water below.

Cool air brushed against my arms where Louis's hands had been, and I plummeted through the darkness.

I crashed into someone. The man lurched forward to regain

his footing, and the boat rocked violently beneath us. I squeezed my blindfolded eyes shut until the rocking lessened and I was certain I wouldn't have to learn how to swim with bound hands.

"Okay, Sammy. You can put her down now. I've got the blanket ready." The man's voice was a raspy whisper.

Sammy laid me on a rough blanket stretching from my shoulders to my ankles. He brought the edge of the blanket over me and tucked it under my side. Then he rolled me over, and over again, until I was wrapped so tightly I couldn't move.

My head ached from where it hit the wooden boat with every turn. If I had my powers, I'd put that man in a little dinghy in a large whirlpool where he'd go round and round for the rest of his miserable life. But I didn't have any powers. Wouldn't have any powers now that I'd lost my wand.

All I could do was listen to the sweeping of the oars through the water, and cry.

❦

I assumed it was morning when I woke. The two men weren't trying to be quiet anymore, and they had put a heavy covering on me that extended beyond my feet and head.

"Is this Bradshaw's Lock?" one of them shouted.

"Yes, it is. Do you want through?" the lockmaster—I presumed—called back.

"No, we're getting out here. There's a caravan of merchants camped nearby, isn't there?"

"I saw some folks—a whole mess of them—camped a little ways down the road, but I didn't ask them their business."

The boat bumped against the shore, and the men wrapped the heavy covering more closely about me, and hefted me onto a shoulder.

"That's a mighty colorful rug, you've got there. Could you not sell it in the village?" the lockmaster asked.

"We had to get it back from someone who didn't want to pay full price for it."

The lockmaster laughed and wished us a good day.

After much walking, some cursing at the rain I was too well wrapped to feel, and one change of shoulder, we came to the merchants' camp, or so my ears told me. Men's voices and the neighing of horses filtered through my coverings.

With no warning and little ceremony, I was dropped, unwrapped, and unblindfolded. When my head stopped spinning, I saw the gaudy furnishings of a merchant's tent and, not surprisingly, the merchant I observed talking with Roger in the market place.

The merchant, a man with prematurely gray hair and a well-trimmed beard, knelt before me and examined me with his eyes as if I was some sort of exotic creature. "Yes, she's the one. Enchantress is written all over her." He touched my chin and tilted my head to the side. "But one without a wand and moving farther and farther from her spell. They say that has a curious effect on them. Do you know what it is?" He raised an eyebrow at me in question.

I shook my head. We rarely used our powers for anything beyond our own amusement and did not study them deeply.

"Pity. I don't think I'll be with you long enough to observe the effects. Of course, when the spell breaks—which should happen soon—and you're not there with the wand to receive back the enchantment, the consequences will be more ..." his eyes glowed with anticipation, "... dramatic." His gaze fell to my gag. "As it is, the only changes I'll see will be those of ill-treatment."

He called to a maid and ordered her to take care of me. He turned back to the two men who brought me. One was tall with a severe widow's peak, and the other—short, stocky, and wrinkled—appeared to be the descendant of a gnome.

"Tell my servants to finish packing quickly so we can move on. The other merchants left earlier this morning. We don't want to be too far behind them for safety reasons nor do we want to be so close they notice our ..." he sneered in my direction, "... special guest."

Widow's Peak and the gnome nodded and then left. The maid, a petite, mournful looking girl, helped me to my knees and unbound the gag. I breathed deeply of the free air.

She dipped a sponge in a bowl of cold water and wiped my tender face. My hands were still tied, so she spoon-fed me porridge. There was pity in the young girl's eyes, but she never said a word.

With a warning that I would be not-so-gently re-gagged if I called out or tried to draw attention to myself, the merchant stuffed me into one of his wagons. He unbound my wrists and retied them so that I was secured to the side of the wagon on a short leash. He left and the wagon jerked into motion.

I looked around but couldn't find so much as a partially exposed nail to rub through my bonds. In desperation, I tried the side of the wooden crate but gave up as pain pulsed through my wrists.

Time bumped along slowly, punctuated only by unpleasant questions. What would happen to me? If they really had taken an enchanted mirror from Mr. Woodsman, what had they done to him? The Magic Collectors killed a guard to get *The Enchanter's List*. Had they killed my Woodsman to get the mirror? *Please, God, no.*

The steady rain didn't stop when we halted for lunch. The gnome untied me and led me to the merchant's tent.

The merchant put down his fork and looked me over.

"There's no change, other than some bruising from the ropes, but that's of no interest to me." He looked rather disappointed.

I mustered as much dignity as I could in my bedraggled state, brushed off the servant, and stepped toward the merchant. "What is the meaning of treating me like this? I'm no criminal."

"You're an enchantress."

"We have no quarrel with the Magic Collectors."

"But we have a quarrel with you." He didn't look at me but speared a piece of meat with his fork and stuffed it into his mouth.

My stomach remembered the little porridge it had eaten a long time ago. "Is it that we have the power of enchantment you desire?"

"Perhaps." He cut another bite of meat.

My stomach threatened to humiliate me by pleading for food in a rumbling voice, adding to my ire. "You Magic Collectors are like little children who, after petting a foal, grow to envy and hate the men who tame the stallions you could never master."

The merchant jumped to his feet, his chair clattering to the ground. "There's much more to it than you think, Miss Floraison. You enchanters think you're so much better than everyone else and that your powers give you leave to do whatever you please." He stepped back to the table, his hand tightening around the stem of his glass. "Well, that's about to change."

The anger in his eyes frightened me, and I stepped back.

He gave a scornful grunt. "Why don't you stop playing the brave martyr and ask what you really want to know?"

What's going to happen to me? I pursed my lips. I wasn't going to give him the satisfaction.

He looked at me with a smug twist to his mouth. The gnome righted the chair, and the merchant resumed his seat and continued eating as I stood there silently lamenting my brash comment.

After several minutes, the merchant called to the maid and ordered her to bring me lunch. He laid his soiled napkin beside his plate.

"I see by your expression you're penitent for your foolish tongue. So, I'll tell you what you want to know." He took a sip of wine and wiped his lips. "My plan is to carry you along with me, keeping you under lock and key whenever we stop at villages, and then drop you off at some city, probably Gilden. By that time, it will be too late for you to go back and claim the ended enchantment." He gave a satisfied smile. "You'll be an enchantress with no power." He rose, donned his slicker, and strode from the tent.

My eyes followed him out into the rain. I was finally going to Gilden, and I couldn't be more miserable.

Or so I thought.

The unbinding of my wrists during lunch and the rebinding for the afternoon's journey was excruciating. It took all my self-control not to cry out, though I did allow myself a few whimpers when I was alone again.

Dinner was at dusk, and it was much the same as lunch. The merchant inspected me and then moved away to talk business with a couple of his helpers.

"I expect we'll do well in the next village. The squire's wife has always been free with her husband's money." The merchant chuckled.

"What wife isn't free with her husband's money?" said Widow's Peak.

They snickered, the gnome remarking that in some noble families the husbands were free with the wife's money. Their humor continued in the same vein for several minutes before the merchant brought the conversation back to business.

"We didn't do so well in the last village, aside from picking up this package for my brethren. Overall, though, 1771 is looking to be an exceptional year."

If I'd had anything in my mouth I would have choked. 1771! Was this some sort of joke? I had left home in 1826, and then slept for fifteen years. It couldn't be 1771.

Yet, they didn't seem to be jesting. Not about their yearly profit expectation anyway. Did they have some reason to lie? Oh, I hoped they did.

I searched back through the last few months. Villagers didn't go around saying or writing the entire date and year very often. The headline of the only newspaper I'd seen engrossed me too much for me to pay attention to the year on it. Of course, there were the "old" books Albert recommended as currently popular, and the fashion … well, that small difference could be the difference in place and social standing. Fashion in Sonser didn't change with the rest of the world because of the sense of its people and the enchantresses' requirement for skirts that could conceal wand pockets.

I fought the idea until I went to bed—on a thin mat in the bottom of a wagon shared with the female servant. In the solitude that darkness brought, I confessed what I had feared all night—I couldn't go home. I was fifty-five years in the past. The mirror I gave to the prince wasn't the one that punished me but the one that vanished seventy years before my time.

My parents weren't even born yet. I would be an old woman before I could see them and my siblings as I had left them. And where was I to go? I couldn't very well go to my grandparents and say, "I'm your granddaughter from the future. Please take me in."

My grandmother had suspected a connection between the vanished mirror and the reclusive prince—and I was it.

But that hardly meant she'd know me if she saw me.

I was lost. I had no one, except a few friends in a village I was moving farther and farther away from, and one very dear friend I'd parted with in anger and distrust, and I was afraid to know where he was.

The wind wailed through the trees, and rain fell like tears from a mourning woman all through the long night.

CHAPTER 20

T HE OTHERS ARE tired of waiting. They're moving on," Widow's Peak yelled as he dodged a puddle on his way back from the front of the caravan.

The merchant scowled. "All right." He pointed to a group of four men. "Hurry and get that wagon out of the mud. We might be able to catch up to them before the turnoff for Claveden. With all this rain, mudslides and flooded bridges are a greater danger than highwaymen."

The men struggled with the wagon as I stood with the merchant next to the nicest wagon, the one reserved for his personal possessions.

Twenty minutes later, the muddied wagon rolled onto solid ground.

The merchant handed a rope to the gnome and looked at me. "'Never trust an enchantress' is the golden rule of my people."

The gnome grasped my wrists, coiled the rough rope once around them and then paused, his attention drawn to the sound of pounding hooves.

The merchant's face paled. "Never mind her. Get the guns," he spat.

The servant dropped the rope and dashed off. I wiggled my hands free of the loose coils and glanced around, but there was nowhere to run that promised safety. The merchant hoisted himself into his wagon and jumped out a few seconds later with a pistol and began loading it.

But it was too late.

Two masked men on horseback thundered into the camp, boldly brandishing two pistols each. They made straight for the merchant. He dropped his weapon and jumped back, narrowly avoiding the hooves of the leader's horse as it reared and kicked at him.

The two horsemen calmed their mounts and backed away a few feet, herding all the servants—including the empty-handed gnome—into a tight huddle with a few waves of their pistols.

"Well, well. Did a little lamb stray from the flock?" jeered the taller of the horsemen.

"What do you want?" The merchant practically growled.

The highwayman holstered one of his pistols and rested his free hand on his horse's neck. "I was hoping you'd ask. I'd like your cashbox, which, if my brethren of the road are correct, just happens to be under the floorboard of that wagon." He tilted his head toward the merchant's personal wagon.

The merchant's face reddened. He glanced at the wagon and back at the horseman.

"They've found that's the usual place." He flourished his pistol in the direction of the wagon and then indicated his partner with a tilt of his head. "Murdering Montague will help you retrieve it."

The merchant nodded to Widow's Peak, who moved toward the wagon. The other highwayman, a broad-shouldered man, walked his horse behind the servant. They returned shortly with the box.

The tall man took it and shook it. His eyes probably gleamed with greed, but I couldn't tell behind the lowered hat and mask.

The merchant crossed his arms and glared at the thieves. "Now that you've got my money, why don't you leave?"

The highwayman shook the box again. "Ah, my favorite melody. Just listen to those coins beat against one another in perfect time." He lowered the box to his lap. "You needn't worry, good merchant. I'll leave. But not yet. Your generosity has emboldened me to ask another favor—let me see your women. A well-to-do man such as yourself would never travel without a jeweled beauty or two."

The merchant's mouth fell open. "You might as well go. I have no jeweled beauties. These are the only women traveling with me." He gestured toward the maid, who cowered behind a male servant, and me.

"What? You disappoint me. What do you carry with you?" The highwayman walked his horse a few feet closer and looked the maid and me up and down.

Of all the impertinence.

"This maiden is quite skilled with scornful looks." He pointed to me and then patted his horse's neck. "I don't think she likes you, boy."

The horse snorted and shook his mane. Light glinted off a silver streak near its ears.

That horse ... I know that horse!

He examined me again. "But she wears a yellow dress. I've always fancied a girl in a yellow dress. I think I'll take her as my jewel."

The merchant stepped forward in protest but backed away at a gesture from the highwayman's pistol.

The rogue tossed the moneybox to his partner and swept me

onto his horse. "Have a profitable day, gentlemen." He spurred his mount. "See if you can hit the lead pursuer with the moneybox, Murdering Montague," he yelled as we galloped away from the curses and cries for horses and guns.

Sitting practically in his lap, with my head against his shoulder and his cloak wrapped about me, I was perfectly comfortable for the first time in days.

❦

When the pursuers gave up, my highwayman reined in his horse to a slow walk. "We seem to have lost your friends." He cocked his head to look at me.

Next to us, Murdering Montague shrugged his broad shoulders. "And the moneybox."

My highwayman fastened his twinkling blue eyes on me. "So we went through all that danger just for you?"

I held his gaze. "It seems so."

"This will never do. What will the others of my guild think?"

"Do the others of your guild call you Mr. Highwayman? Do you change your name for each of your vocations?"

His laughter warmed my soul. He turned to his partner. "Off with the disguise, my friend. We've been found out by a clever lady." He pulled off his hat and mask with a flourish, revealing the familiar eyes and hairy face I had hoped for.

I peeked at his companion, who also doffed his disguise. "Mr. Monroe?" My jaw dropped.

Mr. Monroe's laughter boomed through the forest. "You didn't expect me, did you?" He grinned. "Not even a melancholy man could refuse an adventure to rescue a lovely woman." His face turned serious. "At least, I have helped to rescue one young maiden," he murmured.

Should I tell him Belle was comfortable at the castle?

"Alexandria, your wrists," my Woodsman cried. With a gentle touch, his finger traced the edge of the rope burn. "What did they do to you?" A fierce anger clouded his blue eyes, and it both frightened and thrilled me.

"The merchant was afraid I would escape, so he bound my hands and tied me to the inside of a wagon." I rushed through my explanation, not wanting to ignite his anger, but also not wanting to lose the feeling of protectiveness it gave.

"I'd like to horsewhip that man." He tensed. "Was that all he did?"

Heat crept up my neck. "Yes, that was all."

He relaxed a little and looked over his shoulder at the road we'd traveled. "I'd still like to thrash that man."

"There's no time for retribution now, son." Mr. Monroe's voice was firm. "We need to focus on those who put her in the hands of the merchant."

Mr. Woodsman reluctantly turned back around.

Mr. Monroe used his bandit mask to wipe his forehead. "Tell us what happened to you, Miss Floraison."

I told my story, beginning with the theft of the book. "Roger and Louis kidnapped me. I'm not surprised about Roger, but I would have thought better of Louis. He's so well-respected in the village," I concluded.

"Louis is respected for his talents and appearance, not because of his character," Mr. Monroe said. "I've watched his pride grow over the years. Of late, I've come to suspect it led him to overlook property lines in order to hunt for bigger game, but it seems to have led him to greater ills. Left unchecked, who knows where it will take him?"

With a glance at Mr. Woodsman and an unpleasant feeling that I already knew the answer, I asked the question that nagged me. "Do you think Lord Devryn and Lord Leandre had any part in my abduction? Or were they genuinely trying to help us meet?"

"They didn't send Louis and Roger to help me." My Woodsman scoffed and rubbed the side of his head. "I know you thought they were your friends, but I'm certain they're Magic Collectors. From your description, it sounds as if the merchant is too." His eyes held a compassionate light. "I'm sorry, Alexandria."

I yanked at a seam in my dress, embarrassed by my foolishness and pained by the deception. "How could I have been so blind? You even warned me against them."

He gave a slight smile. "I had a reason to distrust them that you did not."

"The last time I traveled this way, the road was buried in snow." Mr. Monroe's voice startled me.

We turned to him, but he seemed oblivious to us as he stared out through the forest.

"What was that, Mr. Monroe?" my Woodsman asked.

"What? Oh, nothing." He coughed and looked up at the sky. "We'd better pick up our pace if we want to make it to the village before tomorrow night." He nudged his horse into a trot, and Mister picked up his pace to match.

We rode or walked beside the horses the rest of the daylight hours, stopping once to eat lunch and once to retrieve a pack of supplies they'd deposited on the way to lighten the horses for the final length of the chase.

☙❧

It took a while but we managed to locate a reasonably dry spot to camp for the night. I sorted the supplies while the men went to gather wood and hunt for game.

Harboring the secret hope of finding a clean outfit, I pulled out the blankets and cooking supplies. No dress, but I did find a bar of soap. Did I have time to wash? I was alone after all. The sounds of wind in the trees and squirrels scurrying through the underbrush magnified in intensity.

Alone in the forest.

With Magic Collectors' henchmen after me.

Stifling a scream, I spun around at the sound of a man's voice.

"Everything is so blasted soggy." Mr. Woodsman slipped on the wet leaves at the forest's edge. He steadied himself and straightened one of the loose pieces of firewood in his arms. He saw me—and probably heard the frantic beating of my heart— and smiled. "If you knock against anything in the forest, the trees will cry all over you, and if you don't watch your step beside the road, the mud puddles will try to eat you." He lifted a mud-splattered boot in evidence.

No longer in danger of screaming, I dropped my hands from my mouth, scanned my boots and dress, and then groaned. It looked as if a mud puddle had chewed me up and spat me back out. Embarrassed, I turned my back to him and brushed at the stains with my handkerchief.

Mr. Woodsman whistled an old war song as he cracked the branches into evenly sized pieces and piled them together. The tune rose to a crescendo and was joined by the boom of Mr. Monroe's pistol.

I jumped.

Mr. Woodsman whistled louder. "Dinner is on the way. Get the coffee out, won't you, Alexandria?"

❦

When we finished dinner, Mr. Woodsman carried the scraps of food away from the camp so as not to attract visitors. Mr.

Monroe walked off a little ways and lit his pipe, and I scooted back from the fire and leaned against a rock. The rain clouds had drifted away, and the stars were reveling in their freedom. The night musicians were playing for them.

My Woodsman returned. He brushed a leaf from the unoccupied half of the slicker I had laid out to keep my dress from getting dirtier, and sat down beside me.

"Did the Magic Collectors really steal an enchanted mirror from you?" Out of my long list of questions, that was the first to jump from my mouth.

His shoulders tensed. "Yes."

"Are you an enchanter?"

"No, I'm not. The mirror was given to me by an enchanter. I can't tell you anymore about it."

I cocked my head and studied him. "Why are you always so secretive?"

"I can't tell you that either. I would explain everything to you if I could. I'm not evasive because I enjoy it." His voice sounded sincere, with a hint of pleading.

Annoying as it was, I admired his discretion. "I'll not ask you to break your confidence."

"Thank you for understanding." He relaxed his shoulders. "Say, don't you want to know how Mr. Monroe and I happened to come dashing to your rescue? I can tell you that."

A chuckle escaped me. I was so happy to have been rescued I forgot to consider how it had happened. "I would love to hear the tale. Poor Rosalie probably thinks I ran away to Gilden without saying goodbye."

"The thought never entered her mind. You see, someone left a note saying you ran away to marry me, and she knew that couldn't be true." His mouth curled into an amused smile.

My cheeks burned. No wonder Lord Leandre insisted on writing the note.

"Rosalie consulted Albert, and they went to search for you in the village," he continued. "They called on Mr. Monroe, and he mentioned seeing you walking toward the canal with Lord Leandre. They went to the inn and questioned the lords. Those two scoundrels claimed I asked them to arrange a meeting for us outside of town, which they did, only to have you"—he pointed a finger at me in mock accusation—"disappear at the canal when they went to get horses. Louis, who was with the lords at the inn, supposedly saw me riding into town about dark."

Chuckling, he brushed a cricket from the slicker. "It looked pretty bad for us. Three reputable citizens—two of them nobility—asserting we had run off together in the night." He paused, probably for me to insert a comment on my indignation at such an idea.

I nodded for him to finish.

"I suspect the romantic Rosalie hoped the notice of our elopement was true, but, fortunately, the unromantic-but-wise Albert thought it sounded more like a good excuse to make both of us disappear. He and Mr. Monroe set off in pursuit of *us*, but only found me, near where I told Albert I'd be exploring." His smile faded, and he gingerly touched the side of his head. "I'm thankful they came along when they did."

The anxiety I felt for him earlier returned in double strength. "They hurt you, didn't they? When they took the mirror?"

"They hit me upside the head." He hesitated. "Don't look at me like that, with those big, worried eyes. I'm all right now."

I smiled weakly and leaned toward him to get a better look at his head.

He edged away. "I don't need a nurse, so don't get any ideas."

I arched an eyebrow, and he grinned at me. A funny warm

feeling melted away my anxiety. When was the last time I had seen that grin? Oh. That last day in the village.

"I'm not being a stubborn male. It's truly nothing for you to worry about. Now, as I was saying, Mr. Monroe and Albert found me—"

"Why did you leave the village so suddenly?"

He raised his eyebrows but left his mouth open. It was a comical, but cute, expression. He closed his mouth and crossed his arms. "I went off to pout because a certain young woman was angry with me."

Self-reproach bit my soul. I looked down and tugged at a seam in my dress. "I know a certain young woman who was angry at a friend. He knew so much it frightened her and made her wonder if he wasn't really her friend after all. She knows her anger and fear were foolish."

His hand touched mine for a brief second, the comfort of the gentle squeeze lasting much longer. "I'm glad she knows her fear was foolish. Her anger, well, it was partly provoked by the friend's attitude toward two men who also seemed her friends." He cleared his throat. "Back to your rescue. Mr. Monroe and Albert told me about your disappearance. All the suspects were still in town, and you wouldn't be the first person to be smuggled out by merchants, so Mr. Monroe and I chased after the caravan while Albert went back to town just in case we'd made a mistake. We hadn't, of course. So Mr. Monroe and I donned masks—cleverly made by myself from handkerchiefs—daringly rode into the camp, and absconded with the merchant's most priceless treasure."

"You won't get into trouble for robbing the merchant, will you?"

"No. Murdering Montague took care to leave the money box where they would find it."

"'Thank you' seems insufficient after all you and Mr. Monroe have—"

"Alexandria?"

"Yes?"

"It was my pleasure."

My mouth was poised to respond, but I closed it with a smile. Perhaps the best way to express my gratitude was not to embarrass him with a profusion of words. He already had the idea.

Leaning back against the rock, he gazed up at the swaying trees and whistled along with the whippoorwills.

The peaceful feeling in the air seeped into me, and we sat there together for some minutes, until I happened to look over and see Mr. Monroe, standing a few yards away, relight his pipe. I brought my knees to my chest. What would happen to Belle Monroe and the prince? Was there anything I could do?

Mr. Woodsman touched my arm and threw me a quizzical expression. I hesitated, but only for a second. He had earned my confidence. Yet, I feared what he would think of me.

I filled my lungs with air and courage. "I once said my thoughts couldn't be bought. Now, I give them to you in friendship. Mr. Monroe's daughter didn't go to stay with an aunt. She's living at the castle. It wasn't burnt, but enchanted, and she's a prisoner, of sorts, of a beast."

My Woodsman's eyes widened. "How do you know Belle Monroe is at the castle?"

That was all he had to say? "I dream about the castle. I've seen her and the prince—the beast—in my dreams."

"You dream about the castle?"

I dropped my gaze. *Here it comes.* "I have a strong connection to the castle. You once told me, referring to it, that I did things thoroughly. You were right. I enchanted it."

"Why did you do it?" His warm hand wrapped around mine.

Perhaps he wanted to make sure I wouldn't run away without answering, but whatever the reason, his touch gave me the courage to continue.

"It was part of my punishment. My sister was being courted by a kind and admirable young man, but in my pride, I thought he wasn't suitable, wasn't worthy of marrying a Floraison. In an attempt to separate them, I forced an enchanted mirror to lie. As punishment, I was banished to wander an unfamiliar land as a hag. After a few weeks, I came to the castle. I was tired and lonely and starving when I reached it, but the prince refused to help me. My power of enchantment returned, and I cast a spell on him. I somehow felt as if it were my task."

As the words flowed, I realized it was for pride itself, not merely for misusing the mirror, that I had been punished. Shame weighed heavy on me. Mr. Monroe had lost his daughter, and my Woodsman's life had been put in danger, all because of me. "Do you wish you had never found me?"

I risked a brief glance into his face. There was no judgment there, no horror at my power, only a strange smile. "No, I don't. I'm glad I found you, Alexandria."

Something about the way he said my name made my heart do a strange flip-flop. Was it true? That despite what I had done, he was still glad to have found me, glad to be near me? Me, the plain, the poor, Miss Alexandria Floraison, the shopkeeper's assistant? I met his gaze.

His blue eyes, no longer twinkling, but steady, were focused somewhere deep in my soul—where frost was beginning to bite a flower trying to bloom.

My eyes broke from his. Did I want it to be true? Despite my situation, I was still Lady Alexandria, and if I regained the wand, I would return home. Surely it was as impossible, as undesirable, for the proud daughter of a duke to love a peasant man as for the beautiful Belle Monroe to love the Beast. Wasn't it?

A sudden howling of wolves brought us to our feet. He still held my hand, and I moved closer to him as another wolf joined its voice to the cries of its brothers. My Woodsman turned toward the sound. The coarse, common fabric of his cuff brushed against my arm. It burned me with the reminder of our differences. I stepped away.

He jerked around as his hand fell empty to his side.

I took another step away—into Mr. Monroe. He wrapped his arms around me and hugged me as if I were his daughter. "I guess we've found her fear, Woodsman. Kidnapping merchants and pistol-toting highwaymen she gives but a scornful glance, but wolves, not so easy to dismiss." He gently pushed me away, but retaining my hands, studied my face. "Or is it that you've had all three in one long and weary day?"

If only it were that simple. "In one long and weary day." I sighed and returned his hug, grateful for his fatherly affection and opportune appearance.

"I think it's time we said goodnight. Let's see to the horses and get the blankets, Woodsman." Mr. Monroe knocked the ashes from his pipe and put it in his shirt pocket. "Don't worry about the wolves tonight, my dear. We'll keep watch over you." He patted my arm and walked away toward the horses.

I glanced at Mr. Woodsman. The fire's light flickered across his furrowed brow. He turned from me and followed Mr. Monroe.

◈❧◈

I pulled the blanket over my chest and stared at the stars. They stared back at me. The events and the emotions of the last few days tumbled through my mind. Roger's hissing, wolves howling, the merchant's cold look, the chaffing of ropes around my wrists, the touch of clothing that shouted "peasant." After a while, all the different images and sounds faded into one man's voice. *We ... absconded with the merchant's most priceless treasure.* It was a bittersweet thought. Had I overreacted? Misinterpreted the kindness of a friend? Why would he love me? I was poor and plain, couldn't even bake a decent pastry.

CHAPTER 21

DAWN INTRODUCED ITSELF with a wet kiss.

"I hope this shower doesn't last long," Mr. Woodsman said as he handed me his slicker. "The streams are already at flood stage."

A comforting thought.

"There's only one bridge on our path that worries me." Mr. Monroe rummaged through the supplies for an extra slicker. "The rest should handle the flood waters. But if that one gives way, or if the steep slopes slide and block the road, we'll have to cut through the woods." He glanced at the forest.

Was that longing I saw in his eyes?

We ate a quick breakfast and started the day's journey.

"Poor Mister. He doesn't have anything to keep him dry." I patted the horse's neck. Mr. Woodsman seemed to have forgotten my odd behavior of the night before, and as I didn't want to draw attention to myself by requesting to ride with Mr. Monroe, I once again shared Mister with him.

"He doesn't mind the rain, not on summer days. He'd rather

be out than cooped up in a stable. Wouldn't you, boy?" He gave the reins a gentle shake.

Mister snorted.

"You'd rather be drying yourself next to Miss Rosalie's fire, I'm sure," Mr. Woodsman said to me.

It would be infinitely more comfortable than sitting sidesaddle in front of him. "Yes, I would. A ride in the rain is only pleasant for an hour. After that, the pitter-patter of drops against my slicker begins to annoy me." This was a perfect day for a long bath and an even longer read beside a small fire. I soon found myself yearning for Rosalie's little parlor and life as usual.

My wrists stung as they brushed against the slicker, a sudden reminder that my kidnapping had repercussions—and not all minor scratches. Would there be a return for me?

Anxiety sped my heart, and my speech. "Can I go back to Rosalie's? What if Louis or the others know I've returned? Will they try to abduct me again?" I looked up at my Woodsman and then sputtered and blinked in a most undignified manner at the unexpected face-wash.

He managed to stop at one chuckle and slipped me a dry handkerchief. "Mr. Monroe has offered to let you stay at his house for now."

I wouldn't have to leave the village! Dipping my head to avoid the rain, I peeked around Mr. Woodsman to look for my benefactor, anxious to thank him. "Where is Mr. Monroe? He's not beside us."

"He's following at a discreet distance. Which is well. We need to discuss our situation."

My chest tightened, threatening to push my heart right out.

"As you know, I had an enchanted mirror—"

Oh, that situation. My chest loosened, and my heart sank back to its normal position.

"What kind of mirror?" I bit my lip for having interrupted.

He hesitated. "A Demandez à Voir mirror."

I looked up in surprise and got rain in my face again.

He sighed. "Yes, I know they are rare, and, no, I cannot tell you how I came to have one. Back to what I was saying, I had an enchanted mirror that I must now retrieve, and you had a wand —disguised as a quill and kept in a dark handbag—that you must get back." He paused and chuckled.

"What's humorous about that?"

"When you told me you didn't know where your wand was, I asked the mirror to show it to me. I saw a vague shape shrouded by darkness and assumed you had lost it in the forest near the castle and that it was covered by leaves."

"So you went exploring to find my wand, which wasn't really missing, and ended up having your mirror stolen. And now we must recover both of them."

"Exactly. I knew you were a clever lady. With your brains, coming up with a plan to get the wand and mirror back will be a cinch." Mr. Woodsman reached around me to brush a leaf from Mister's mane. His sleeve rode up, revealing a red mark around his wrist that matched the one around mine.

The full danger of our situation hit me. I swiveled to face him, not caring about the rain. "They tied you up and left you after they took the mirror, didn't they? You could have starved there in the forest or been attacked by wolves or wild boar." My blood went cold at the thought.

His eyes widened. He cocked an eyebrow and regarded me with an odd expression. "You're getting rain in your face again, and I don't have any more dry handkerchiefs." He put his hand on the top of my head and turned me back around.

Great. I was acting like a distraught female. *Floraisons do not act like distraught females.* In an attempt to regain my composure, I took a deep breath, but I didn't hold it long enough. "The newspaper said the Magic Collectors killed a guard when they stole *The Enchanter's List*. They failed at their first attempt to get us out of the way. What will they do when they realize that?"

"They won't realize you're not with the merchant." There was an edge of determination in his voice.

"What about you? They're more likely to harm you than me."

He didn't answer.

I took another deep breath and let it out slowly. "I don't have to get my wand back."

"You're an enchantress. You must have your wand."

"It's not that important."

"You need it to get home. You're the daughter of a duke. You don't want to stay here forever."

He had a point. Home, family, beauty, wealth, influence. But was it worth risking his life? The life of a peasant for the "life" of a duke's daughter? What a horrible thought.

"I can get home without the wand." If one defined "home" as a little room above a pastry shop.

"No, you can't. Haven't you figured it out yet? You're in the past, Lady Alexandria."

"Of course, I've figured it out." I crossed my arms. Of all the impertinent men, he took the pastry.

"Then don't be troublesome."

Home. Where I wouldn't have to put up with rude, hairy peasant men. Especially ones that didn't even give their right name. My Woodsman, indeed. My Woodsman? When had it changed to *my* Woodsman? I uncrossed my arms. "I'd rather stay here than ... than you get hurt." And me never see those twinkling blue eyes again. Was that part of the fear eating at my heart?

"We've got to get the wand and mirror back, and you've got to go home." His voice was firm, decided. Heavy. It crushed what was left of my heart.

Alexandria, you're a fool. He's a good man, and a good man will take care of a woman and even risk his life for her whether or not he has a romantic interest in her.

"There's probably some young man just sitting around waiting for you to come back." His voice was cheerful.

Would Giles be there? No. He wouldn't be waiting on me. He probably disliked me, intensely. Even if he were, he'd feel like a stranger compared to my Woodsman. Mr. Woodsman, I should say. He wasn't mine, nor did he wish to be. He had made that clear. "No. No, there isn't."

The sadness in my voice must have caught his attention for I felt him look at me, but I didn't raise my face lest he see that more than rain could make it wet.

◈

The road sloped steeply downhill and crossed the river on a lengthy wooden bridge. The roar of the swollen river soon made conversation impossible, for which I was grateful. The foamy, debris-filled water hid all but the top of the bridge's support beams and splashed between the boards. The edges of a few boards were chinked from rot.

Mr. Woodsman brought Mister to a stop and dismounted. Mr. Monroe rode up beside me, handed me his reins, and joined the woodsman. They visually inspected the bridge, walked out a few feet on it, and came back to me.

"I think it's safe," Mr. Monroe yelled above the roar. "I'm going over first. Don't follow until I signal."

Mr. Woodsman frowned but didn't protest.

Mr. Monroe took back the reins, mounted, and rode onto the bridge. The horse pranced nervously as water splashed his hooves. Foam streamed up its legs. Mr. Monroe got off, stroked the horse's neck, and led it across. He beckoned us to follow.

Mr. Woodsman helped me dismount, and we stepped onto the bridge. The murky water with its clumps of leaves and branches rushed beneath us. *A Floraison is not afraid of water, even if it's moving with the power of a thousand horses.* Cold water splashed up my leg. I sucked in my breath and repeated my newest family motto.

Halfway across the bridge a movement from the other side caught my eye. Mr. Monroe waved his arms furiously and pointed upstream. I craned my neck to look around Mr. Woodsman and the horse. I gasped as a massive oak—roots, branches, and all—bobbed up out of the racing water.

Mr. Woodsman slapped Mister on the rump and sent him galloping toward Mr. Monroe and grabbed me by the arm, dragging me after the horse. Not that I needed any persuasion to move.

He shouted something, but I couldn't hear it over the roar of the water and the pounding of my heart. A horrific crack sounded as the tree trunk smashed into the bridge, tossing us into the railing. My chest hit the wooden rail, knocking the breath out of me. My feet fought the slick boards for traction. Snapping sounds ricocheted through the air, and spike-like branches popped up between the boards and threatened my legs as the force of the water sucked the tree under the bridge.

I regained my footing just as my Woodsman did. He half-pulled, half-ran with me across the bridge.

Blessed gravel greeted my feet on the other side, followed by a strong embrace from Mr. Monroe.

"I thought the tree would take the bridge and you with it," he said when he released us.

"So did I." Mr. Woodsman stepped back and leaned against a tree beside the road to catch his breath.

"Was that the bridge you were worried about?" I discreetly

patted the side of my ribcage where I'd hit the bridge railing. It responded to my touch with an unnecessary protest.

"That was the one."

It may have been the worrisome one, but we still had more bridges to cross. Couldn't we camp out for a few days until the waters receded?

Mr. Woodsman whistled to Mister, and the horse trotted over. He held out his hand to me. "That was exciting, but we'd best be on our way again."

I guessed not.

⚜

The rain ceased soon after we left the river. Grateful, I threw back my hood. High banks flanked the road, and I noticed clumps of mud and grass along the edge of the road and freshly exposed bedrock on the bank. I pointed them out to Mr. Woodsman.

"That's another danger of these wet spells," was all he said.

The bank on the left dipped into a ravine a few feet from the road. I watched the narrow shoulder and the steep rise to our right for wildflowers. I needed something to brighten my day.

A touch of pale pink halfway up the bank caught my eye. A wild rose perhaps? I leaned out and craned my neck to see it as we passed. Mister stumbled on the mud-covered gravel. My … ah … posterior slid alarmingly toward Mister's shoulder. Mr. Woodsman caught me around the waist and drew me back into my seat. I sucked in my breath, my bruised ribcage complaining at the sudden movement. I'd wanted something to brighten up my day, not liven it up.

"Whoa, boy." Mr. Woodsman pulled on the reins. "Let's dismount and walk for a while. The terrain is rough enough for Mister without two passengers."

Or before one passenger foolishly and unpleasantly became an ex-passenger. "Excellent idea."

He brought Mister to a halt and lowered me down.

I removed my slicker and laid it across Mister's saddle. I didn't need its extra warmth for the incline of the road was increasing and the curves with it.

Always a ways behind us, Mr. Monroe dismounted to walk his horse.

Sunflowers and bee balm dazzled me from the sides of the road. They were a little too bright. Wasn't there anything a tad less colorful? An orchid perhaps?

"The flowers are lovely, aren't they?" Mr. Woodsman peered over Mister at me.

"Yes." Instead of walking beside him as I did previously, I took care to stay on the other side of the horse.

"Do you feel up to walking? You've been awfully quiet."

"I am quite healthy." I put a little extra bounce in my steps.

He regarded me for a moment, his eyebrow raised in a skeptical arch. "Alexandria, take these, please." He handed me the reins and strode off.

Observant and concerned. The only thing worse than an absolutely wonderful young man was an absolutely wonderful young man with no interest in you. With a sigh, I resumed my visual hunt of the steep bank for less cheerful wildflowers. *Less cheerful wildflowers? Alexandria, show some spirit. Put that family pride to good use for once.* I squared my shoulders and raised my chin. *The Floraisons are an exceptional family in beauty, in rank, in wealth, in education, and only equally exceptional candidates may marry into it.* I nodded in agreement to Aunt Helene's motto.

Mister neighed and picked up his pace, a nervous prance in his steps. Tightening my grip on the reins, I stroked his soft neck. "Calm yourself, boy. There's nothing for you to be uneasy about."

He stopped and stomped his foreleg in disagreement.

I rubbed his muzzle. "Mr. Woodsman will be right back. Don't worry. He's not trying to send *you* away."

What kind of a comment was that? I re-straightened my shoulders. *The Floraisons are an exceptional family in beauty, in rank, in wealth, in education, and only equally exceptional—*

The smell of mint filled my nose and led my eyes up to Mr. Woodsman as he contemplated me from the other side of Mister.

He grabbed the bridle with one hand as the horse pranced. "Easy, boy."

When Mister settled down, I raised the reins above his neck. Mr. Woodsman released the bridle and reached for them, hesitating as his eyes fastened on me. Ignoring the reins, he wrapped his hand around mine, his mouth curving into a timid smile when I tried to pull away.

He crossed in front of Mister, and, easing himself between us, tugged the thin leather strips out of my hands and replaced them with the moist, hairy stems of wildflowers.

Sunflowers, daisies, goldenrod, bee balm, and mint stared up at me. Three brilliant blue spikes of lobelia posed gracefully in the center. My heart returned to its falling-off-a-horse beat. It was the bouquet Giles and I picked the day we found the moth. Was it possible …? I searched my Woodsman's eyes, but before I found an answer Mister reared and captured his attention.

"Steady, boy. What's the matter?"

A dull rumbling sent shivers up my legs like vibrations up a tuning fork.

"Woodsman! The bank. It's a landslip," Mr. Monroe shouted from behind.

I spun around. The trees, bushes, and rocks on the bank moved like melting chocolate toward the road.

A boulder crashed beside us. Mister reared and tore away

from my Woodsman's grip. He bolted up the road, and we dashed after him. A stone the size of a walnut collided with the side of my head. I stumbled, and my Woodsman caught me round the waist and pulled me up. Focusing on the strong hand holding mine instead of my throbbing head, I let him tow me.

Small rocks pelted us as we ran around the next curve and sought shelter behind the outcropping that formed the base of a rocky spine coming down the hill. The flow didn't cross the boundary but continued on its way across the road for several minutes. My head ached and black spots disturbed my vision as I waited, safe in my Woodsman's arms.

When all was still, he dashed around the curve and yelled for Mr. Monroe. After a horrible moment of quiet, Mr. Monroe shouted back. I said a prayer of thanks.

Leaning on the rock for support, I eased along it, peeked around the edge, and gasped. The earth, trees, rocks, and shrubs water had detached from their proper place blanketed the road several feet deep.

Mr. Monroe's voice carried over the debris. "I can't get across. I know a shortcut through the woods. I'll take it and meet you in the village."

"Wait, Mr. Monroe. We'll find a way for you." His voice was urgent as he searched the edge of the slide for a crossing.

"I'll see you in the village," Mr. Monroe cried.

"Mr. Monroe." My Woodsman stopped his searching at the sound of the departing horse and rider. His shoulders slumped.

"Is the road so dangerous?" I asked.

He stared out over the rubble. "The road is dangerous, but it's the woods that worry me. I'm afraid he plans to search for the castle instead of simply passing through."

"The prince wouldn't harm him. He's Belle's father."

"But Mr. Monroe might try to harm him. But there's nothing I can do about that now." He sighed and walked over to me. His hand softly brushed my hair away from the cut left by the rock. "We'll have to get you back to the village. How's your head?"

"Sore, but not too bad." I smiled and hoped it was convincing.

He studied my face for a breathless moment, smiled at whatever he saw there, and stooped to pick up the bouquet I'd dropped.

Mister neighed from somewhere up the road.

"Here we are, Mister." I took a few steps forward. Pain flared through my head, and the black spots dancing before my eyes merged into one, rather like curtains falling into place between acts.

CHAPTER 22

I N MY DREAM, my head hurt. When I awoke, my head hurt. I grimaced as a plump woman with a pleasant face pressed a cold compress to my forehead. Cool water slipped from the compress to trickle down my hairline to my neck. Scrunching my shoulders, I tried to catch the liquid on my collar.

"I'm sorry, dear." The woman wiped the rivulet with her handkerchief.

I blinked and looked at her again. Some wrinkles caught my eye. No, not a pleasant face in the handsome sense, but in some other sense. An association with her kindness, or my affection for her?

"That was quite a knock you got." Rosalie kissed my cheek. "I'm glad you're back safely."

She put her hand in mine, and I squeezed it tightly. "I wouldn't leave without saying goodbye." My voice was raspy from the long slumber.

Smiling, she moved my hand up to hold the compress. She slid her arm behind me, raised me into a sitting position, and then handed me a glass of water. Over the glass's rim I noticed the room's papered walls and elegant, though modestly priced, furniture.

"You're in Mr. Monroe's spare bedroom," Rosalie replied to my unasked question. "Albert's downstairs. He's pretty anxious about you. I'll tell him you're awake."

My heart lifted at Albert's concern and then sank. "Where's my—Mr. Woodsman?" He wasn't downstairs waiting for me?

"Albert had to send him to check on Mr. Monroe to get him to stop pacing the floor." She handed me a robe. "May I bring Albert up?"

He was concerned about me! I coughed, covering my mouth and my foolish grin with my hand, and then slipped on the soft robe. "Please do."

She went downstairs and returned a few minutes later with an agreeable looking man with a great deal of knowledge and wisdom showing in his green eyes, eyes that brightened when they met mine.

"I see you're finally awake." Albert's rich voice held a hint of teasing. He lowered himself onto a chair beside the bed and held up two fingers. "Let's see how awake you are. How many fingers am I holding up?"

"Three."

He frowned, until I smiled and held up two fingers. Smiling himself then, he picked up a candle and swung it slowly in an arc before my face. My eyes instinctively followed it.

He put the candle back in its place. "No sign of damage to the brain, except in the area dealing with mathematics." He winked and glanced between Rosalie and me. "I think she'll be right as rain after a good night's rest of natural sleep." Turning to face me, he cleared his throat. "Do you remember that matter I spoke to you about a few days ago?"

My mind shot back to our last conversation in the bookstore. "Yes, and I wish I had confided in you." I gingerly touched my tortured wrists.

"I wish you had, too, though I was referring to the other matter." He glanced at Rosalie, and she gave the happiest smile I had ever seen anyone give.

I couldn't quite match her smile, but I certainly tried. "Something tells me congratulations are in order."

⚜

Albert left as the clock struck nine, but Rosalie sat with me as I ate a late dinner in my bed.

I laid my napkin beside the empty plate. "Agnes is an excellent cook." For a servant in a small village. "Where's my dress? I'd like to get up for a while." Someone, presumably Rosalie and Agnes, had changed me into a nightgown while I was unconscious.

Rosalie's lips curved into a playful grin. "Hidden."

"What?"

"The physician wanted you to stay in bed until tomorrow morning. Knowing you would be stubborn, Agnes and I hid the dress."

I arched an eyebrow, and Rosalie broke into a full grin.

"Agnes is washing it. But you really should stay in bed."

"May I at least take a bath?"

Rosalie chuckled. "I suppose so."

The warm bath followed by a soft bed worked like a sedative. My mind slipped into darkness soon after Agnes snuffed out my candle. Once again, I dreamed of the prince-beast. He paced his room and then stopped to stare out the window overlooking the courtyard.

His confidante from the previous dream entered the room, shutting the door behind him. "You sent for me, master?"

"The rose is almost wilted—three petals remain. Are you losing hope?" The prince glanced at him and turned back to the window.

"Many of the servants are angry that Beauty has left."

"Of course they are. Their freedom is bound to mine." He hesitated. "I haven't forgotten."

"Why did you not stop her leaving?"

"Stop her? I sent her."

The confidante lifted his hands in a gesture of frustration. "Do you want to remain a beast forever? Don't you care about your servants, who have been faithful to you all these years?"

The prince spun around, fire burning in his eyes. "Of course I care! I haven't suffered in vain." The fire in his eyes dwindled. "What choice did I have? Her father was alone and injured and beyond my domain. I couldn't let him suffer or her grieve as she watched in the mirror. Sending her away was the only thing I could do—for both of them." He paced the room.

"You do love her then, and aren't courting her merely to win a release from the spell?"

The prince stopped beside a short table. His claws traced the intricate designs of the cut glass vase sitting on it. "I believe I do. It's said sacrifice is part of love, but it's cruel fate that it requires me to give up the object of my love!"

The prince fell silent, his paw closed around the vase. The servant turned to leave.

"She pledged she would return," the prince said.

The servant paused at the door. "Yes, but will it be in time?"

A petal slipped from the wilted rose and landed on the prince's paw, which trembled at the petal's silken touch.

I woke once during the night and thought I heard voices and

people running back and forth. But the noise quickly blended with the hoot of an owl, and I drifted back to sleep.

The sun scowled at me for my laziness when I woke the next morning. My dress lay across a chair, and I donned it and washed my face before going downstairs.

Rosalie met me at the foot of the staircase, her face pale and drawn. "Oh, Alexandria. What happened to our quiet life? The physician has just returned to check on Mr. Monroe."

An unpleasant sensation settled in my stomach. "How serious are his injuries? When did Mr. Woodsman bring him back?"

"He was thrown from his horse. Belle and Louis brought him back last night. Mr. Woodsman doesn't know and is still out searching for him."

She pointed to Mr. Monroe's room, and I rushed to it but stopped short at the door. A dark-haired young woman hovered around the bed as the physician examined Mr. Monroe. I recognized her from the portrait—Belle. She was as beautiful as everyone claimed. Would she ever return to the prince?

Agnes twisted to peek at the physician as she tied back the window curtains. "The master's been murmuring about wolves and castles and beasts all night. What do you suppose happened to him out there? The woods are awfully dark and spooky where Miss Belle found him." She had the eager eyes of a child listening to a ghost story.

"His horse took fright and threw him because of some wild animals. The rest is just delirium from his fever." Belle glared her servant into silence.

Agnes took extra care as she tied back the last curtain. Light filtered in, and I squinted, having been a stranger to the sun for over a day.

The physician released Mr. Monroe's wrist. "His fever certainly could have caused the kind of raving Agnes described as having occurred last night. However, your father does appear better this morning, Miss Monroe. His temperature has dropped two degrees and his pulse is stronger." He washed his hands in a basin. "Let's hope his condition continues to improve so he'll not frighten Agnes during her next watch." He paused while Agnes huffed and put her hands on her hips. "I'll check on him again this afternoon."

With a good-humored smile, he wished Belle and Agnes a good day and collected his hat and bag. I retreated to the hallway with Rosalie, and he joined us a moment later. "How are you this morning, Miss Floraison?"

"I am much better, thank you."

Despite my answer, he cupped his hand around my chin, studied my eyes, and felt the side of my head. "Hmm. Very good," he declared and released me. He tipped his hat to Rosalie, and left.

Rosalie tugged on my elbow. "Come, eat breakfast. I have to get back to the shop, but Belle said she would like to see you as soon as you've eaten."

I stole a glimpse of Mr. Monroe—my heart pained by the sight of the strong, kind man lying in a sick bed—and followed Rosalie into another room for breakfast.

There was a knock on the door as I finished eating. Belle stood at the half-open door, her knuckle resting against the wood.

Encouraged by her friendly smile, I laid my napkin aside and rose to greet her. "Miss Monroe, do come in."

She closed the door behind her and joined me beside the table. "You must be Alexandria Floraison. I'm happy to meet you." She held out her hand. "Agnes told me you, Miss Rosalie, Mr. Peachtree, and another gentleman—a Mr. Woodsman— have been good friends to my father during my absence."

There was something in her eyes that made me wonder if

she had seen us with her father in the mirror. Whether she had or not, I admired the gracious way she accepted me, a stranger, into her house, especially during this time. I shook her hand. "I owe a great deal to your father. I am honored to meet you, Miss Monroe, for I have heard nothing but praise of you."

"Please call me Belle. May I call you Alexandria? I feel as if I know you somehow." There was a blush of self-consciousness in her voice.

She had seen us. "Of course, you may."

She opened her mouth to speak but then closed it and motioned for me to resume my seat. "Please don't let me disturb your breakfast."

"I'm finished. What is it you were going to ask?"

Chuckling, she fingered her locket necklace. "My curiosity almost led me to forget my manners. We have a small garden behind the house that makes for a pleasant stroll. Would you take a walk with me? I'm anxious to hear more about what happened to my father."

"I would love to, and I will tell you all I am able." That is, without giving away the prince's secrets, or my own.

She led the way to the door. "Mr. Peachtree, who received his information from Mr. Woodsman, said you were abducted by a merchant, and my father and Mr. Woodsman posed as highwaymen to rescue you." She opened the door. "But you were separated on the way back during a landslide. Is that correct?"

"Yes. Your father is a brave man."

She smiled, and a fond look lit her eyes. "He is, and I'm proud he was able to help free you."

My wrist brushed against my skirt as I walked, and I grimaced. Belle's smile slipped into a frown, and she glanced toward my wrist as if asking permission to touch me.

I extended my arm, and she examined the rope burn.

Belle let my arm fall back to my side. She looked at her elegant gown and stroked the rich fabric. "I had forgotten the treatment of a prisoner depends on the captor and that captors vary greatly." She gave a half-smile as she studied the gold ring on her right hand. It was ornamented by the seal of a noble family. A gift from the prince? She looked up at me, the smile still in place and accompanied by a pink tint to her cheeks. "I'm sorry. We were going to the gardens, weren't we?"

"There you are, miss." Agnes scurried down the hallway. "Mr. Louis is in the parlor."

My heart pounded. Had I brought danger to this house? Was there a window low enough to jump from?

Then Agnes winked at Belle, and my heart slowed as realization came to it.

Belle groaned, and I noticed weariness in her eyes. Had she rested any since arriving? "Tell him I'll be right there." She touched my arm. "Forgive me, Alexandria. I will rejoin you as soon as I can." Pinning a loose wisp of hair into place as she went, she walked slowly down the hallway.

How could I warn her against Louis without revealing too much of my own story or that of the prince? "Belle, Louis isn't as worthy of respect as the villagers think. Don't trust him."

She spun around, her eyes wide—probably from surprise at my bluntness. Then she grinned. "I knew I'd like you."

"And Belle, please don't mention Mr. Woodsman or me to Louis."

She furrowed her brow, but nodded and then continued to the parlor.

I retreated to the breakfast room and received a good scare when Agnes burst into the room a few minutes later.

"The mistress said for me to take you to 'the confessional,'" she said.

Her mischievous expression made me wary. "The confessional?"

"Yes, it's a closet next to the parlor where you can hear everything going on just as clearly as if you were in there yourself. Naturally, whoever's in the parlor will be able to hear you too, so you must be careful."

I nodded at her sage advice and followed her to the official eavesdropping spot.

Louis was proposing to Belle. At least that was what I assumed. He systematically praised himself as a good catch, an excellent provider, the strongest and most handsome man around, the best hunter, etcetera, and etcetera. *Poor Belle*. He remarked more than once how he had *providentially* found her and Mr. Monroe in the woods and rescued them. *What had scared Mr. Monroe's horse?* I was beginning to yawn when he finally got around to mentioning Belle.

"You're the most beautiful woman in this part of Sonser, probably in the entire kingdom. When first I saw you and heard everyone praise your beauty, I decided you would be a perfect match for me and that I would marry you."

A faint sigh passed through the walls to me. "I am sorry to disappoint you again, Louis, but my absence hasn't altered my decision. I thank you for your assistance last night, and I am sure my father will thank you as well when he recovers. But the answer is no." Belle spoke with confidence. Anyone with sense would know he had been politely and finally rejected.

"No? Who've you found that you think is better than me?" There was a snarl in Louis's voice I'd not heard there before.

"I don't reject you because I've accepted anyone else." Her voice sounded closer, as if she'd moved nearer my hiding spot.

"Of course there's someone else. I'm not a fool. I see how you're dressed," Louis thundered.

"I've been living with a wealthy aunt, to whom I am

returning once my father is well," Belle said, displeasure in her voice. I crossed my arms, wishing I could infuse my infuriation with him into Belle's voice as well. "See, I cannot accept your suit. You must resign yourself to that."

"He's at the castle, isn't he?"

"I repeat. I've been staying with an aunt." Her firm tone slipped into a weary one. "I haven't slept in over twenty-four hours. I would appreciate it if you would leave so I might rest."

He moved closer. "You've refused me for the last time, Belle. You're not the only one with a fancy mirror. I know where that castle you're so fond of is. Soon I'll pay a visit to your *aunt*. When the castle's mine, you'll marry me whether you like it or not." Louis stomped to the door and out of the house.

I ran to Belle.

"The arrogant, insufferable fool," she cried when she saw me. She twisted her hands as she paced around the room. "How many times must I refuse him? I know his friends rib him about my rejection of his attentions, but it only seems to increase his determination."

"The wounded pride of the hunter can only be healed by the capture of his prey."

She nodded her agreement. "He even dared insinuate I was some sort of … and he threatened my … as if he were clever enough to find and harm him." She sank into a chair and covered her face with her hands. "Oh, Alexandria. I wish my father were well."

I pulled up a chair beside her and let her cry out her distress on my shoulder.

☙❦❧

The book toppled from my hand, and I rubbed my eyes. The clock on the mantle had long since chimed one in the morning.

I stood and stretched my back. Two hours still remained of my watch.

Looking beyond the ring of light from my candle, I considered Mr. Monroe, his chest rising and falling in shallow, even breaths in the dim firelight at the other end of the room. His breathing quickened, and he turned his head and began to murmur.

I hurried to him and laid my hand on his forehead. *Still too warm.* Humming a tune Belle taught me, I dipped a cloth in the basin of water on the nightstand and bathed his head and neck to cool him. He wrinkled his forehead, and I caught a glimpse of my Woodsman in his features. Perhaps all strong and noble men bore a certain resemblance.

My patient quieted, and I gathered the empty bowl and the candle and headed to the kitchen. With Agnes gone for the day, and Belle asleep in her room, the house felt empty, in an unnerving way. I walked on tiptoe, not wanting to disturb the silence. A draft from an open window flew down the hallway and wrestled with my candle's flame. I tucked the bowl under my arm and shielded the flame with my hand. Had Agnes not closed the windows before leaving? The sound of wind rustling through the trees outside the house floated in to me, sending a shiver up my spine. An urge to see someone, to be assured I wasn't alone, came over me. My feet changed direction, taking me to Belle's room.

My soft steps weren't the only sounds in the hallway. Was Belle awake? A floorboard squeaked beneath me, and I jumped. *Calm down, Alexandria. You're behaving a like a child who's heard too many ghost stories.*

When I reached Belle's room, it was quiet and no light shone under her door. I raised my hand to knock but decided not to disturb her slumber. I turned the doorknob slowly and pushed the door open enough to peek inside.

With a jerk, the door swung open. I stumbled into the room. The bowl clattered to the floor, and someone caught me by the arm.

"What the—how did she get here?" hissed a familiar voice.

Still gripping the candle, I swung it like a club in Roger's direction. He sidestepped it and shoved me backwards. As I fell I noticed two silhouettes against a moonlit window. One rushed toward me and the other grabbed for the first one.

I hit the floor with a bruise-worthy thud. Pain surged from my elbow. Roger jerked me up by the arm and shoved a foul-tasting gag in my mouth. I twisted around to hit him in the face, but Louis wrenched my arms behind me.

Holding both my wrists in one large hand, he pressed against my back, forcing me to bend over. Murmurs drew my attention, and my heart sank as I saw Belle, also bound and gagged, struggling to rise from the floor, where that brute Louis had probably pushed her to stop her flight.

"Hurry up with that rope, Roger. And put out that candle. Do you want to set the house ablaze?" Louis's whisper was fierce.

"I don't understand how she got here," Roger whined as he wrapped the rope around my wrists.

"It doesn't matter. She's here, and we'll have to take her with us."

My hands now bound, Louis let me up. I grabbed the edge of the table behind me for support, my head spinning from all the ups and downs. Belle's murmurs grew louder, and she looked pointedly toward the table. I glanced over my shoulder and spotted her ring. I caught her eye and she nodded.

My back and arms ached as I leaned backward and felt the table for the ring, hoping Louis and Roger were too distracted arguing over which rear window would be the best one to carry two abducted women through to notice my movements. My fingertips brushed cold metal, and I arced my back until I was able to tease the ring close enough to grab. Thinking I had a tight hold, I straightened. The ring slipped from my hand and hit the table with a thud.

Louis glared at me and snatched up the ring, shifting his glare to Belle. "I'll not let you bring any trinkets from your lover."

He flung the ring across the room and then picked up Belle, slung her across his shoulder, and marched out the door as if he carried a towel instead of a person. Roger followed suit, only he huffed and puffed as he lifted me to his shoulder and then staggered and cursed his way out of the house—through the kitchen door and out into the gardens where two horses nibbled the grass. He shifted me from his shoulder to the horse's and then yanked me back off.

"We forgot the sacks."

The horse pinned his ears back and gave Roger a look that said, "You're even an incompetent kidnapper."

Louis growled. "Hurry up then."

Roger pulled two large sacks from his saddlebags, tossed one to Louis, and shoved the other over my head. He put me back on the horse, cinched the sack below my feet, and mounted the horse behind me.

The blood rushed to my head, and my lungs burned with every clap of the horse's hooves against the road as I struggled to draw air through the tight weave of the sack. *Don't faint, Alexandria. Breathe and count. Breathe and count. One, one thousand; two, one thousand; three, one thousand ...*

I lost count and was beginning to hope for unconsciousness when we finally stopped. Roger dragged me off the horse with a complaint about my weight, carried me a little ways, and dumped me on the hard ground. He snatched off the sack, revealing a wonderful abundance of air and a not so wonderful abundance of disturbed dirt.

I blinked away a dust-induced tear and looked around. A single lamp lit a simple room. Nothing covered the rough plank walls other than a coiled rope hanging on a nail, and an empty gun rack. A crude bench and a cot stood against the far wall. Bare earth claimed the title of flooring. A hunter's shelter?

Roger took the rope from the sack and bound my feet and then took another length of rope and bound Belle's. When Roger left us, I scooted closer to Belle. She looked at me with an apology in her eyes and closed the gap. As we leaned against one another, my heart burned with indignation. She was upset by my situation, but it wasn't her fault. It was Louis's. It was the Magic Collectors'. It was … mine.

For what seemed like an age, Roger skulked in a corner drinking from a flask while Louis strode about the room with a contemplative air. Was he reconsidering his actions or formulating some other crime?

Wolves bayed close by, sending a shiver through me. How deep in the forest were we? And what was their plan for us?

Belle squirmed at the sound of the howls and pressed closer to me.

Louis gave a contemptuous grunt and scowled at us from across the room. He pulled a mirror from his jacket and smirked. It was a Demandez à Voir mirror. He held it up in Belle's direction. "Found this in your room. So, he let you keep the fancy mirror, did he? How touching. What else would he do for you? Your wealthy *aunt*? Do you think he has the guts to fight me? Winner take all. You, the castle, the fortune."

Belle straightened, her protests muffled by the gag.

"Don't waste your efforts defending him." Louis twisted the mirror in his hand as he spoke. "He's not worthy of you. I haven't even asked the mirror to show him to me. I relish the challenge of defeating this unknown opponent and taking everything from him." He grasped the mirror and held it up like a winner's trophy.

"The lords can keep the enchantment and their magic toys," Roger slurred, waving a hand at Louis, "and you can keep the castle, but don't forget I get a share of the fortune." He stuffed his flask into his pocket.

"You'll get it. Come on. Let's go get the swells and tell them we're tired of waiting. We're heading for the castle at dawn tomorrow."

With another scowl at us, Louis and Roger—and the light—left. A fierce barking started and was then quieted by a harsh command from Louis.

"I still don't think it's fair to allow those things in dog fights," Roger said.

"You call those mutts you and the others bring dogs?" Louis scoffed. "Here is strength and beauty. Look at them. They can tear your best fighting breeds apart. Why should I bring anything other than the best to the matches? Here you are, my pets." The animals snarled and snapped as they, presumably, fought over some treat Louis threw them.

A few minutes later the howling began again, and I came under the horrible conviction that we were guarded by wolves.

CHAPTER 23

THE LATE-MORNING LIGHT brought with it men's voices. I recognized Lord Devryn's along with Louis's and Roger's.

"Good heavens, man. Why did you bring those? We're not going to one of your accursed dog fights."

"They say the woods near the castle are haunted and filled with vicious creatures," Louis said. "You may be glad of their protection, Lord Devryn."

"What do you mean 'they say'?" Lord Leandre asked. "You claimed you found the castle after you got the mirror from Mr. Woodsman."

"I tracked his path from where I met him back to where the forest goes shadowy. There's an overgrown road there. It must lead to the castle."

"It had better. Come on, let's get going," Lord Leandre said. "I feel the spell may break any day now."

An idea came to me, and I scooted over to the wooden wall and threw myself against it, creating a dull thud. Belle followed my example.

"What was that?" Lord Devryn asked. "It sounds like there's something in the shack."

"Probably some wild animal. Roger, go check," Louis answered.

Roger strode into the room and gestured toward me with a knife in a way that assured me I was dispensable. I slumped to the floor.

Roger left, and Louis called to his wolves. The horses neighed nervously, and the group trotted away from the shelter.

Those inhumane brutes. We'd had no food or water all night. My stomach rumbled to second my protest. Belle laid her head on my shoulder. Perhaps this was part of Louis's plan to break her to his will—starve her like she was some stubborn dog.

About ten minutes later, I heard the clip-clop of an approaching horse. It stopped outside the shelter. Did it bear a rescuer or one of the villains? The rider cursed at the horse. It bore the villain Roger. He stomped into the shack carrying two ropes and a water canteen. He untied our gags and gave us both a drink. The two gulps I managed before he moved away hardly wetted my mouth, much less quenched my thirst.

He threw the canteen's strap over his shoulder and began to replace the gags. His breath reeked of spirits. He glowered at Belle. "Louis wants you close by in case your rich friend doesn't want to play without first seeing the prize." He scowled at me. "And you, just in case the swells start a fuss. They were adamant about you not being hurt. Can't understand why they'd make a ruckus about an ugly thing like you. But who cares? I'll be a wealthy man with the pay from them and my share of the castle's fortune. Those idiots think it's abandoned because of the spell on it, but Louis saw you," he eyed Belle again, "walking outside of it in the mirror. Louis hasn't seen your *aunt*, but I've no doubt he's nothing but a cowardly, foppish, powdered wig."

He pulled us to our feet, led us outside, and hoisted us both onto a scruffy brown mare tied to the fence. He tethered the mare to his horse. After mounting, he kicked his horse and led the way into the woods.

Our poor mare was stumbling under our weight by the time we stopped to make camp at dusk. Roger saw to the horses and then ungagged and unbound us to let us eat some crackers and drink a cupful of water.

We spent the night tied to a tree. Belle laid her head on my shoulder, and we watched Louis's campfire flicker in the distance. The wolves howled outside of it. *I hope it gives Devryn and Leandre nightmares. Maybe they'll think twice about consorting with men like Louis and Roger.*

I laid my head on Belle's. I felt like a small fish on a hook and wondered what would happen. Would my Woodsman rescue me? If the prince-turned-beast survived Louis, would he devour me, his enchantress?

❦

Roger poked us awake in the morning, fed us, and loaded us onto the mare, but didn't gag us again.

Fear squeezed my stomach tighter and tighter the farther we rode into the forest. We passed the tree that sheltered Mr. Woodsman and me from the wild boars, and not long after it I noticed a change in the forest. An ominous darkness obscured the summer greenery, and the friendly chatter of songbirds faded. The overgrown road wove its way through the forest, and Belle hung her head as we trotted down it.

Roger took a flask from his jacket and drank from it. He repeated his talk about becoming a wealthy man. The longer we rode, the more he brought forth the flask and the more his tongue moved about in his mouth.

"Why'd the merchant have to lose you?" Roger grimaced in

my direction. "Maybe they didn't want you neither. Can't say I'd want you. You and that Rosalie Lightwood. All high and mighty and ugly to boot. Rosalie can at least bake a pastry. You can't even do that."

I scoffed at the malicious drunk. But then I remembered Belle seated behind me. She was beautiful, kind, and beloved by all who knew her.

The long night and lack of proper food hung heavy on me and did nothing to dispel the gloom Roger's words brought. Maybe I was a nuisance. How many times would my Woodsman come for me? A poor, plain woman who wasn't even talented in the everyday things of life? It was fortunate I was fifty-five years in the past and unable to return to my family. They might reject me as well.

My mind settled into the shadows. The movements of the horses and the passing of time meant nothing until Roger dragged me off the mare and tossed me to the ground beside Belle, igniting a surge of pain from my previous injuries.

A prickly hedge scratched my arms as I used it to pull myself up. Above it loomed the prince's castle. A shudder passed through me at the sight of the changes I had wrought on it. The smooth, white walls were now rough and gray, and the sky blue roof a covering of black scales. The once lovely ornamental statues and waterspouts were sickening to behold—deformed creatures, animals missing eyes or limbs, and emaciated or grossly bloated figures of undeterminable origin.

I crouched down and gazed through an opening in the hedge. To one side of the castle, most likely the entrance to the gardens, was the only statue lovely to behold. Yet, it was the most horrible. A man knelt with hands raised in supplication, a look of desperate fear on his face, before a towering woman with all the beauty of dawn and all the warmth of marble.

A loud rapping drew my attention to the castle's main

entrance, not more than thirty feet away. Louis smacked the door with the butt of his revolver. "Cowering servants, tell your master he has a visitor," he bellowed.

Devryn grabbed his arm. "What do you think you're doing? If a man does live here, he's under a spell. There's no telling what he may be capable of. We're paying you to help collect things needed to capture the magic as it's released, not to fight with the enchanted."

Louis brushed him off. "Blast you and your collecting. This is a personal matter. She rejected me for him. What could he have that I don't? Strength? Skill with weapons? Good looks and the envy of every one who knows him? He couldn't have more of those than me. Wealth is the only thing he could trump me with. Well, I'll take it from him, and then we'll see if she'll not have me." He slammed his fist into the door. "Servants, fetch your master. Tell him I've come to claim Belle Monroe as my own. Will he dare to stop me?"

"You fool." Leandre grasped Louis's shoulder. "Don't do this."

Louis spun around and knocked him off the steps onto the pavement below. Devryn raced down the stairs and pulled his brother up.

Leandre gripped his elbow and grimaced. He glared at Louis and then turned to Devryn. "Let's leave before the master of the castle repays him for his insolence."

Devryn took his brother's arm and helped him limp toward the gate.

Louis was now in a fine rage, but the castle ignored him. After a few more taunts, he called to Roger, who answered. Louis jogged to our place of concealment.

"It's time to let the fish see the bait." He untied Belle's hands and then dragged her to the castle doors. "I know you're peering out of a window somewhere," he yelled. "Won't you come down to fight for your beautiful woman?"

No answer.

"Coward, perhaps this will stir your blood." Louis leaned down to kiss Belle, but she bit him. He cuffed her, sending her crashing to the stone pavement.

A roar blasted the castle walls, bushes snapped, and the prince-turned-beast leaped over the hedges, landing on the steps between Belle and Louis.

Roger yelped and ran off, leaving me alone. The wolves howled from their tethers at the gate.

Louis staggered back and stared at the prince. He gazed at the fur, the claws, the bared teeth. He slipped his revolver into his belt and laughed. The sound chilled my soul. "I thought I was on a manhunt, not a beast hunt. The lords were right. There is enchantment here."

The prince bent and offered Belle his arm. She took it, and he gently raised her to her feet and tucked her behind him. He took a threatening step toward Louis.

"Don't," Belle pleaded.

The prince stopped but glared at Louis. "You'd better leave," he growled.

"Not until I've accomplished what I came for." Louis lunged forward, grabbed Belle's wrist, and dashed down the stairs, dragging Belle with him.

Belle reached for the prince as he reached for her. His claws grazed her arm, and she screamed.

Louis stopped short of the prince's range. "Monster, you may have scarred her, marred her beauty." Louis waved his hand over the bloody streaks on Belle's arm.

"Beauty, forgive me! I truly am naught but a beast." The prince shrank back, appearing but half of his former height.

"It's not your fault. It's only a scratch." Belle clutched her bloodied arm to her, as if trying to hide it.

The prince took another step back, horror written in his face.

"Don't let her fool you. Women will say anything for wealth." Louis gestured toward the castle and then pointed at the prince. "You're a beast, an animal."

The prince stared wide-eyed at Louis and only barely shook his head. "What do you want?"

"The castle."

Whispered voices came from the castle and fueled my anxiety. The prince's servants had as much at stake as he did. Would they interfere? I hoped not, as I sensed this was a fight the prince must win or lose on his own.

The prince's gaze swept from Belle to the castle and back to Belle. She shook her head. He straightened and looked Louis in the eye. "No, the castle is as much the home of my servants as it is mine. They have suffered enough for me. I cannot give their home away, or give them such a master as you."

"A convenient excuse. You're a coward." Louis spat on the ground.

"I am a wealthy ma—I'll give you as much money as you want, just let Belle go."

"I'm not yours to sell, Louis." Belle stamped her foot. "This is a civilized land. You can't treat Beast or me this way."

"And who would you complain to?" Louis smirked. "Who would believe you? After one look at your Beast, they'd beg me to protect them from the vicious brute."

The prince took a step forward. "I'm not a brute." His gaze flew over Belle's scratches and Louis's arm clasping Belle to his side. His eyes flashed, and he held out his clawed paws. "But I could be one. It's rather an uneven fight you're hinting for."

Louis gave a smug grin. "You do have a backbone under all that fur."

"No." Belle pulled against Louis's grasp. "Beast, you can't do this, not even for me. I should never have called you Beast. That's not what you are. There's no need to fight. Louis will come to his senses and let me go. And then, when my father is well, I will come back, just as I promised I would."

Louis spun Belle around to face him. "You'd choose him over me?"

"Yes!"

His cheeks burned crimson. "Men have laughed at me—at me—because you spurned my attentions. I'll not have them mock me for being passed over for a hideous creature like that." He moved his free hand to his revolver.

My heart thundered as the hammer cocked into place. The prince stood motionless.

Louis took a step back, pulling Belle along with him. "Roger, bring my pets."

The prince stared at the barrel of the pistol pointed at Belle.

"You're right, Beast." Louis took another step back. "It wouldn't be a fair fight. Everyone knows I'm the best hunter in the land. No game escapes me. But I brought my own creatures of fur and fangs. Since you care so much about an even match, you'll have it."

The prince looked beyond Louis to the five wolves on their leather leashes pulling against Roger, hurrying him on.

I glanced at the castle as the whispered voices grew louder. A window opened, and a small metal box crashed onto the pavement at Louis's feet.

He jumped back. Keeping an eye on the prince, he eased up to the box and lifted its cracked lid with the toe of his boot.

"The deed to your estate," he exclaimed. "Your servants have decided in my favor."

Belle jerked against Louis's hold. "This is his home. He can't leave it, and I won't let you take it from him."

Louis ignored her, slipped the pistol into his belt, and

reached for the box. Belle kicked it away, and he lunged after it. She kicked him in the shins, breaking free from him as he fell. She snatched up the box and sprinted toward the gardens.

Cursing, Louis pushed himself up. He glowered at the prince, who was staring at the pack of wolves not ten feet from him.

"Let them go, Roger!" Louis dashed toward the gardens.

The prince swung around and started after him. Roger let go of the leashes, and the wolves leapt upon the beast.

A human cry rent the air, followed by the snarling and yelping of wolves.

CHAPTER 24

Tears burned my eyes, and I turned from the cries into a man's chest. Arms wrapped around me and the smell of the forest enveloped me. My heart lifted despite the pain of the prince's plight. I raised my head to look at my Woodsman. He had come for me.

He wiped a tear from my cheek. "Can't get rid of me, can you?" He took a knife from his pocket and cut the rope from my wrists. He shuddered at another cry from the prince.

"Is there nothing we can do to help him?" My heart begged for a hopeful answer, but he frowned.

"No, there isn't. It must happen."

I saw pain in his eyes before he gently pressed my head to his chest. I cried into his shirt—rough, working man's shirt though it was.

When the tears subsided, he brushed the hair from my face and handed me his handkerchief. "The spell will break soon. We need to get your wand."

I stared at him through watery eyes. He squeezed my shoulders. "Belle and the prince will look after one another—I promise. It will end well for them."

I didn't know why I should believe him, but I nodded and dabbed the remaining tears from my eyes. "But Lord Devryn and Lord Leandre have the wand and they left."

"No, they didn't. They're just inside the gate. Magic Collectors would never leave an aging spell."

I looked around and noticed it had grown unnaturally dark, like it had when I cast the enchantment on the prince and his estate.

My Woodsman glanced at the sky. "It won't be long now. We must hurry." He removed a gold ring—similar to the one Belle wore when I met her—and put it in his pocket.

He caught my puzzled gaze. "It's a traveling ring. Beast gave one to Belle. I saw it on the floor at her house. It's how she found her father. It's how I found you." He patted his pocket. "But they only work over relatively short distances and for only one person at a time."

I cocked an eyebrow. How did he know of such things?

"Yours isn't the only family with enchanted objects." He grinned, took my hand, and led me from hedge to tree to bush until we reached the gate. I spotted the brothers just inside, on the opposite side of the lane from us.

Leandre leaned against a tree while Devryn paced beside him. He grabbed his brother's arm. "I don't like this any more than you do, Dev, but we've got to see it through. You know what will happen if we go home without the enchantment."

"I haven't forgotten." Devryn jerked away from Leandre's grasp.

"Watch out. That's the arm I landed on." Leandre patted his jacket sleeve.

"Then don't use it against me." Devryn raised his eyes to the blackening sky. "Any time now, if you please."

My Woodsman slid two pistols from his belt and cocked the hammers. I nudged his arm and shook my head vigorously.

He rolled his eyes. "I don't shoot unarmed men. I just like to scare them a bit." He winked and pushed me back a few feet. "Now stay out of trouble."

With confident strides and a pistol directed toward each of the brothers, he crossed the lane. "I think this is as good of a time as any."

Leandre bolted upright and put his hands in the air.

"You!" Devryn spun to face him, his fists clenched. "Louis said you tucked tail and ran when he and Roger took the mirror from you."

"That's a trifle difficult to do when you're tied to a tree and knocked unconscious."

Devryn's eyes widened, and he uncurled his fists and raised his hands.

My Woodsman shrugged his shoulders. "What did you expect from them? If it hadn't been for the interference of friends I'd be a rather dead decoration on a tree somewhere in the forest." He used the barrel of one pistol to tilt his hat up. "And speaking of somewhere in the forest, I sent word to the magistrate to bring a posse up here. So, you might not want to stay too long after you give me back my mirror and Miss Floraison's wand."

"He's bluffing." Leandre lowered his hands. "He wouldn't shoot us."

"Not to kill." My Woodsman stepped forward.

"If Louis and Roger disobeyed our orders and treated Miss Floraison as shamefully as they did him, I wouldn't blame him." Devryn slipped his jacket off and laid it on the cobblestone lane a few feet from my Woodsman.

He tucked one of his pistols in his belt and moved toward the jacket.

"Wait." I lifted my skirts and dashed from my hiding place. My anxious heart screamed they might try to hurt my Woodsman if he came near enough.

"Alexandria, I told you to stay put." He glared at me from beneath furrowed brows.

"You told me to stay out of trouble. I'm going to pick up the jacket so you can keep both eyes on them." I pointed to the Magic Collectors, who stared at me wide-eyed. Devryn opened his mouth but then bit his lip and looked away.

Frowning, my Woodsman stepped back from the jacket and focused both eyes on the two lords.

I knelt and rummaged through the pockets of the jacket.

"What are you doing? Just take the whole thing."

"I'm not a common thief." The mirror, wrapped in paper, was easy to find in the deep inside pocket. I laid it aside. A cold fear crept over me as I searched the remaining pockets and felt the lining of the jacket. "I can't find the quill." The spell was about to break, and if the Magic Collectors had the wand and acquired the spell's power ...

My Woodsman aimed his pistol at Leandre. "All right, off with your jacket."

Tidbits from the book on enchantments jostled each other in my mind. One fought its way to the forefront. *Wands can change shape.* "Hold on." I opened Devryn's purse and ran my fingers through the coins inside.

"I thought you weren't a thief?" My Woodsman arched an eyebrow.

Relief stole through me as I held up a gaudy brooch—the one I wore as a hag—and pinned it to my dress. "I'm not."

"When I touched the wand—the quill—it transformed into that." Devryn's statement sounded like a question, but I chose not to answer it.

I drew the strings of the purse closed and stuffed it into the inside jacket pocket. Devryn caught my attention as his gaze fastened on something beyond me and his face went pale.

"Alexandria, look out," my Woodsman yelled.

A gunshot exploded over my head. My Woodsman cried out as the shot grazed his hand. His pistol fell to the ground and went off in a burst of smoke. I tumbled back still grasping the jacket.

Someone caught the back of my dress and jerked me upright. I pulled away, but my captor dragged me backwards and pinioned me to his side.

Roger.

With wide, crazed eyes, he swapped his now empty pistol with a loaded one from his belt.

My heart pounded in my chest—my Woodsman was in front of a frightened, malevolent drunk with a loaded pistol.

"Stop where you are," Roger cried. "It's all gone wrong. All of it. Louis's dead. The castle's haunted by invisible people. I hear them whispering but can't see them." He glanced around, his hand shaking almost as much as his voice. He refocused on the men. "But I didn't go through all this for nothing. I'm still claiming my fortune." He pressed me to him as if trying to squeeze the gold from me.

"Let her go, and you can have all the money we have." My Woodsman tossed his moneybag on the ground in front of Roger and raised his hands.

"Yes. Mine's in the jacket, and Leandre will give you his." Devryn nodded to his brother, and Leandre tossed his purse on the ground beside my Woodsman's.

Roger laughed hysterically. "You expect me to turn her loose for pocket change?"

I craned my neck to stare at him. If Leandre's purse was anything like Devryn's, it wasn't pocket change, not to a poor villager.

"I want the mirror, and the enchantment. It must be worth a fortune or you wouldn't want it so badly."

"Don't be daft, man. You can't handle it. You're not an enchanter or a Magic Collector." Leandre shook his head.

"Louis used the mirror to watch Belle once."

"That's different. The mirror's a mere toy," Leandre said.

I stifled a scoffing grunt. It was no toy.

Devryn nudged his brother. "The wand and the power returning to it are worth more." He gestured at the castle and grounds. "There are many well-to-do Magic Collectors who'd pay a king's ransom for that much power."

Roger shifted in Devryn's direction. "A king's ransom?"

"Yes, but you'd need the right connections." He pointed to himself and Leandre. "Which we have. You also need the wand."

"Don't you have it?"

"You do, or rather she does. It's the brooch." Devryn glanced at me but wouldn't meet my eye.

Roger eyed the brooch. "I always thought they were long and pointy."

"They change shape." Devryn inched toward us, his eyes focused on Roger.

A twig snapped under Devryn's foot, and Roger jerked back. He tightened his grip on the pistol and waved it toward the three men. "Don't come any closer. You, Woodsman, move over by them."

My Woodsman, who was much closer to us than when Devryn started talking, strode over to the two lords. The hard set of his jaw worried me. *Please don't do anything rash and get yourself hurt.*

"You should take the wand from her before the enchantment ends. She'll get the power if she has it. Enchantresses are danger-ous." Devryn's voice had a certain silver-tongued feel to it.

Roger nearly broke a vertebra as he shoved the pistol into my back. I bit my lip to keep from crying out. "Give me the brooch."

Ohhh. I'd like to turn him into a mangy cur and put him in one of his own dogfights. "I can't move my arms."

He loosened his hold, and I wiggled my arms free. I slid the pin from its catch and slipped the brooch from my dress.

"Wait." The pistol barrel skittered down my spine.

My hand stilled.

"What's happening?" Roger asked.

I followed his gaze to the sky. Outside the gate it was light. Inside, dark clouds began to swirl. The sound of a woman weeping came from the castle gardens.

Sorrow cloaked my heart and found expression in a whisper. "The prince is dead."

The pistol slipped away from me.

"No. The beast is dead." My Woodsman leapt forward, grabbed my wrist, and pulled me to him.

The brooch and jacket fell from my grasp. Roger cursed and lunged after them.

Brilliant colors shot through the sky and attacked the darkness of the clouds and the castle.

"It's happening. The spell is breaking," Leandre cried. "Isn't it magnificent? We've got to have it." He spun in circles and gazed up at the sky.

"I've got it." Roger thrust the brooch into the air.

Color had all but destroyed the darkness and was playing off the white walls of the castle.

"Yes, Roger." Devryn's voice quivered. "The enchantment. The fortune it will bring. It's all yours. Just don't drop the wand."

My Woodsman let go of me. "Don't listen to him, Roger. The

enchantment could kill you when it returns to the wand. Give it to Alexandria."

Roger swung his pistol between my Woodsman and Devryn as if unsure who was lying.

A blast of color hit the wand. With a piercing scream, Roger threw it down at the edge of the lane and collapsed.

Devryn and I sprang toward the brooch. Leandre blocked my Woodsman with a fist to his stomach.

I slipped on the fallen jacket and crashed to the cobblestone. Pain shot from my knee, and my eyes squeezed shut in response. I forced them open. Where was the wand?

Devryn knelt a foot from me with the brooch in his hand. Another burst of light hit it. He jerked back and dropped it.

I lurched forward. My hand knocked against it as it fell, and it flew into the hedge beyond the lane.

I scrambled across the grass alongside Devryn. A jolt of pain took my breath away as I fell to my knees and searched under the holly with my hands.

"Let me find it, Alexandria. Please." Devryn knelt beside me.

"No, it's mine." Dirt burrowed under my fingernails, and the holly's spiny leaves stung my arms.

"I was sent to get the enchantment. I can't go home without it. Please give it to me freely."

"No." My fingers skimmed the narrow branches diverging from the holly's base. At a split, my fingers touched cold metal. They glided over it, trying to see it, to make sure.

"Alexandria."

The imploring tone drew my attention.

"It doesn't have to matter which of us finds it." The dark brown eyes in the handsome face were intent on me. "Come with me when we leave." He paused, the pleading in his voice matching that in his eyes. "I know you're under a spell. At times, I can see you as you truly are—the most beautiful woman I've ever seen. With the power of this enchantment, I can free you from the plain façade you're cursed to wear and put you back among the nobility where you belong."

Something leapt within me at the thought of being beautiful again. *He's a Magic Collector. Don't listen to him.* "I can free myself once I have the wand."

"No, you can't. You can't unlock the power while you're still under a spell."

Even if I had the wand I couldn't go home? "You're lying." My fingers identified the brooch. My hand closed around it.

He pulled my arm from the hedge. "Listen to me. I'm sorry about the kidnapping. I'm even sorry Louis bumped Woodsman on the head. But you'll never regain what you lost. No end was put on your curse, was there?"

A retort died cold in my throat. My mind replayed the conversation in the mirror. I felt the strange flatness and heard the voices in the dark. One talked of mercy, of my fate being linked to another's, but never of an end to my punishment.

My fingers tingled as they rubbed the brooch hidden in my fist. *Grow warm. A wand should grow warm at an enchantress's touch.* Cold, sharp metal laughed at my fingers.

"Magic Collectors have a certain power over spells." His brown eyes tempted me. "I couldn't break a spell this strong or send you home, but I could restore your beauty and give you a title. Lady Alexandria. How does that sound?"

Familiar. No more waiting on tables or scrubbing dishes or avoiding mirrors. No peasants telling me I was worthless.

I studied his face. Devryn was handsome, intelligent, titled, pleasant company. His eyes spoke of affection for me. He had everything a Floraison woman was brought up to believe made a suitable husband. And he had freely offered his money and tried to distract Roger to protect me.

My fingers loosened their hold. The pin of the brooch pricked my palm.

Had I learned nothing? "I appreciate your offer, but I'm staying."

"But you've nothing to keep you here."

"I have friends. People I care for, and who care for me."

"Who? The shopkeeper?"

"Yes, Rosalie. And Albert and Mr. Monroe and ... my Woodsman." A smile broke through my defenses at the memory of my Woodsman holding me in his arms while I cried on his shoulder.

"You can't stay for him." Devryn's eyes took on that hard look again. His slack grip on my arm grew firm. "He's a commoner, plain and rude. You don't love him."

"He's kind and virtuous. That's more important than appearance or title. And I do love him." *I love him*. My heart thrilled at the thought.

Heat flared across my palm.

"I don't want to be a villain, Alexandria. I'm not as bad as you think. Give me a chance to prove myself."

The wand pulsed in my hand as if awaiting my command. I studied Devryn's face. He had a good heart, but like mine, like the prince's, it needed refining, the impurities burned out.

I jerked my arm from his grasp, twisting the brooch in my fingers until the free pin faced forward.

He reached for me, and I brought my hand back and raked the pin across his palm, leaving a bloody line. *Burn. Serve ever as a reminder of his impurities until he's gone through the fire and come out as gold.* Heat from the wand flowed through me.

Devryn cried out and clutched his hand.

I scrambled up, my heart trembling at the horrorstruck look in Devryn's eyes as he bent double in pain. "I'm sorry. I—you'll understand in time," I cried.

He stilled, wiped the blood on his pants, and staggered up. "I guess I was wrong. There was an end put on the spell." He held his hand open and stiff, the cut an unnatural, fiery red, as he looked at me. "You are as beautiful as I thought you."

I glanced down and gasped. My dress was the same lavish gown I had worn when I enchanted the prince. My skin was like the purest marble, and I held a long and pointy, traditional wand. My punishment was over. I had my power of enchantment. My knee didn't even hurt.

I spun around. My Woodsman and Leandre paused in their grappling and stared at me. I glowered at Leandre. "Let him go."

They released their hold on one another and straightened up like scolded schoolboys.

A chorus of cheers rang out from the castle garden, and my heart leapt for joy. Belle and the prince had looked after one another.

My Woodsman strode to me and slipped his arm around my waist. My cheeks burned. Had he heard Devryn's question and my answer?

I looked from brother to brother. I couldn't quite read their faces. Failure, fear, maybe a little relief? "Get out of here. Please. Before the posse comes."

Surprise flickered across their faces, and they knelt to pick up their belongings. Leandre pocketed his coin purse, nodded a thank you, and walked through the gate. Devryn slung his jacket over his arm. His hand hovered near the mirror. He looked up, his eyes lingering on me. He grabbed the mirror, put it in my hands, and followed his brother.

When the sound of hooves pounding the cobblestone faded, my Woodsman stepped away from me. An awkward silence hung between us. It was broken by a moan from Roger.

"Leave him to the posse." My Woodsman glanced from

Roger to me and then ran his fingers through his hair, studying me out of the corner of his eye.

I tucked the mirror under my arm. My hands danced up and down the wand in time with my racing heart. "We should probably return to the village. Rosalie and Albert, undoubtedly, are worried about us." *I can spare a little more time before I think about going home.*

He gave his hair a final rub and straightened. "You can't go looking like that." He gestured at my face and gown. "They wouldn't know you. I'd be happy to say goodbye for you—I know how you don't like farewells. I have some business to take care of in the village anyway."

My hands stilled.

"I'll take the mirror back now." He tugged it from under my arm. "Thank you." He smiled at me, a mock consoling smile. "Oh, now, Alexandria. Don't look so glum. I always meant to see you safely on your way home. Why, with the wand, you can be there in a jiffy. And I can go back to the carefree life of an ordinary woodsman."

I gaped at him. Surely the man who rescued me countless times, who wheedled me into dancing with him, who put up with my ill humors, who let me cry on his shoulder, wasn't sending me away like this?

He turned the mirror over in his hands and bent his neck to examine its design, but that didn't hide the smug smile playing on his lips.

I cocked an eyebrow. Surely the man who knew I belonged to the future, who knew of the prince's spell, who gave me a familiar bouquet, and who had the same striking blue eyes as Giles, wouldn't send me away like this?

Unless …

Putting on my sweetest smile, I held out my hand. "You've been so very kind, Mr. Woodsman. I only wish you could accompany me all the way home. I'm sure … Lord Cedric would love to express his appreciation for your assistance personally."

His head snapped up. "Who?"

"Lord Cedric. I probably shouldn't have mentioned it. Our engagement hasn't been officially announced yet, but I'm sure you won't say a word about it."

His mouth fell open, and his eyebrows disappeared into his shaggy bangs.

A star-crossed lover's sigh escaped me. "I can't wait to see those lovely brown eyes again."

His blue eyes flashed.

"Or that silky, clean-cut blond hair." I cast a sideways glance at him and sighed again. "Lady Alexandria Dancer. How does that sound?" Ignoring his scowl, I smoothed my skirt, encouraged by the presence of the wand pocket, and met his gaze. "Well, I know you dislike thanks as much as I dislike goodbyes, so I'll just go. Enjoy your life as a carefree woodsman." I waved goodbye and raised my wand. "Home, please."

CHAPTER 25

Roses everywhere. They trailed up trees and over arbors. They shot color from bushes lining the path, and their aroma sweetened the air.

I was home, and it was my birthday, for all the roses were in bloom.

Dawn had banished the night, but I lingered at a garden bench. In person, I was as I had been when I left my family. I had no worries of rejection on that account, but would they forgive my pride and deceit? I could but ask.

I ran through the gardens and into the house. "Papa, Mama, Gabriella, Eva!"

The few servants hustling around in the early morning light cried out when they saw me. Between their cries and mine, the whole house knew of my return. I dashed up the stairs where four beloved figures still clothed in their dressing gowns met me with hugs and tears.

The voices of those gathered for my birthday celebration faded as Gabriella and I slipped away down the sunken garden walk.

"You really do forgive me?" I forced myself to look Gabriella in the eye.

"Of course I do." She threw her arms around my neck and hugged me. "We were taught to admire virtue, but only in those who also possessed extraordinary beauty, wealth, and talents. When you tried to separate me from Marcel, you were acting on our mistaken notions of worth. I can't blame you for that." She shook her finger at me. "Now, I don't want to hear any more about it."

She tucked her arm through mine, and we continued walking. My heart relished the sweet taste of forgiveness.

The swish of our skirts and the feel of the cobblestone pavement beneath my feet reminded me of the many walks we had taken down that path, but it felt almost like a new place to me. Perhaps because I had changed so much.

Gabriella glanced around at the trees and the roses and squeezed my arm. "It's hard to believe you were a prisoner of that horrid mirror for two days. It must have been dreadful."

Laughter bubbled within me. I had gone back seventy years, wandered for weeks, slept for fifteen years, spent several months in a quaint village, and yet only two days had passed, and it was now my twenty-first birthday. How old was I really?

Gabriella looked at me strangely, and I chuckled.

"I wasn't in the mirror for more than a few moments, but I spent months and months far away in our own world."

Her wide eyes elicited another chuckle from me, and I patted her hand. "I'll tell you all about it later." Different memories flashed through my mind. "And it wasn't all dreadful."

She opened her mouth as if to question me, but closed it as I tugged her forward. We strolled along in silence.

A bridge arched over the path, and the roses dangling from it fluttered in the wind. One of the stems was missing a rose. Where was the man who had picked it for me? The smile I had worn all morning slipped. Had I been wrong? I had greeted all the guests but had not seen Giles.

Voices drifted to us from around a bend in the path. I gave an exaggerated sigh. "They've caught up with us at last."

Gabriella laughed. "It's time we returned anyway. I'm surprised Mama and Papa let you out of their sight this long."

"Very true. I shouldn't trifle with their generosity. Back to the party we go."

We picked up our pace as we neared the corner. The path split just around it. One branch wound deeper into the gardens and the other out to the lawn where the refreshment tents were set up and most of the guests mingled.

The approaching voices resolved into two familiar ones: Marcel's and Giles's. They rounded the corner, and the four of us came to a sudden halt, each of us staring at the others.

My cheeks burned under Giles's intent look. Perhaps they would cool if I focused on Marcel instead. He hadn't changed since last I saw him, except he wore a traveling ring. A pink color graced his cheeks as he looked at me.

"Marcel!" Gabriella's face brightened enough to compete with the sun.

I wasn't sure if he offered her his arm or if she took his, but they were soon standing side by side, grinning at each other in a ridiculous way.

My heart fluttered. I wouldn't care how ridiculous I looked if my Woodsman—I meant Giles—would look at me like that.

The sweethearts remembered they were in company and turned to me. There seemed to be something of unease or uncertainty in Marcel's expression when his eyes rested on me.

My cheeks now burned from a different cause. With a

humble heart, I met his gaze and extended my hand. "I'm truly glad to see you back at Henly Manor, Marcel."

He hesitated, but then took my hand. His mouth spread into a goofy grin, but it was a nice grin nonetheless, one of a forgiving man. I'd take him as a brother-in-law.

"Ahem." Giles cleared his throat.

"Oh, hello, Prince Giles." Gabriella giggled. "I'm very glad to see you too."

"I'm delighted to see you again, Lady Gabriella."

I allowed my eyes to turn to him. Tall, dark hair, blue eyes. He was the same handsome Giles I remembered. But there wasn't a hint of whiskers on his face. Oh dear.

He gave me a formal bow and took my hand. My heart thundered. He, too, wore a traveling ring.

"Lady Alexandria, I wish you the most joyous of birthdays." He stepped closer and raised my hand to his lips, his eyes scolding me. "Lord Cedric is your cousin, and he's engaged to a Lady Florence Milford," he muttered.

I bit back a grin. I still had my Woodsman.

And he still had my hand.

He glanced over at Gabriella and Marcel. "Do excuse us a moment." And then he winked at Marcel.

Marcel winked back, Gabriella giggled, and my cheeks surely turned as red as an enchanted rose.

Marcel bowed, and then he and Gabriella strolled down the path, quickly disappearing around the corner. Giles gently squeezed my hand, and I mustered my courage to face him, trying to think of something to say.

But with a deft twist of his wrist, Giles tugged me forward, throwing me off balance, and I stumbled into him. He caught me by the arms, a mischievous grin playing on his lips and lighting his eyes. He cocked his head as he righted me, pulling me to him. "Why, Lady Alexandria, an engaged woman like you throwing herself at a man. I am surprised."

My breath caught, and I pushed against his hold. "But I didn't, and you know I'm not engaged," I stammered. But my efforts were vain.

He smiled down at me. Beneath the mischievousness, and beneath the confidence of his gaze, was an intensity that made my heart stutter, my mouth go dry. He slipped his arms about my waist and rested his cheek against my forehead.

The warmth of his touch, as well as the firmness of his arms around my waist—tight enough to be possessive and yet gentle enough to be protective—reminded me of all the times that he'd watched over me, that he'd come back for me. All the times he'd scolded and encouraged me, urging me to be the person he knew I could be.

Tenderness and gratitude welled up in my chest, and I relaxed against him, letting him drape my arms around his neck.

He rubbed his cheek—with a faint, reassuring prickle of stubble—against my forehead and then raised his head, drawing my gaze up to his face.

"Oh, but you are engaged," he whispered. "To me." Then he kissed me like a man kisses the woman he intends to marry. And I responded, trying to tell him in a language that needed no words how much I loved him, had loved him, and would always love him.

At last, he drew back. Tugging my arms from around his neck, he kissed each hand. His lips curved into a mock frown. "And I don't want to hear any arguments about it."

"About what?" My mind was still in a daze of bliss. The most wonderful man in the world loved me. Me. The snobbish, anything-but-flawless woman who couldn't even bake a decent pastry.

"Our engagement."

"Oh!" My thoughts snapped back to attention, somewhat, and I grinned at him. "Well, I was rather hoping to marry a woodsman, but I suppose a prince would do."

Laughing, he pulled me to his side, and we strolled down the lane toward the party. He tilted his head to look at me, his eyes twinkling. "Did I ever tell you about my grandfather Prince Gérard? How some busybody enchantress turned him into a beast until a handsome and clever woodsman talked some sense into her?"

EPILOGUE

O NE WOULD THINK you were getting married, as many congratulatory messages as you've received." Giles eyed the letter on the salver, a frown on his face that didn't match the twinkle in his eyes.

I slid the letter off the silver tray and then thanked and dismissed the servant. "I can't imagine why anyone would think that."

"Nor I." Giles gave me a sideways glance and then broke into a smile. "Well, perhaps I can."

A thrill shot through me. *Just two more weeks.* Something told me I had a silly grin on my face. I coughed and made an effort to control my facial muscles. "Good. I was hoping I wouldn't need to remind you. Now, what were you saying before the servant came in?"

"Aren't you going to open the letter?"

"It can wait."

"But it's too thick for a mere congratulations."

I weighed it in my hand. It was heavier than I expected. Slipping a fingernail under the seal, I broke it and unfolded the letter.

"What is it? I see that furrowed brow." Giles leaned forward in his chair.

"It's signed Devryn Ashby, the Duke of Maram." I held the last page of the letter out to him. "Why would he write to me? I don't know him."

Giles glanced over the page. "Nor do I, but judging by the thickness of the missive, I'd say we're in a fair way of solving the mystery. He couldn't write that much and not explain why he was writing."

I smoothed the crease of the first page and began to read.

Lady Alexandria,

I have desired to say many things to you should we ever meet again—some things more pleasant than others, as you can no doubt imagine. Forgive the liberty I take in writing to you— and if the name Lord Devryn Collins means nothing to you, then burn this letter. But if you are the Miss Alexandria Floraison I remember so vividly, I beg you to hear me out. Fifty- five years have passed since our parting, yet I still bear a scar from your wand. You said I should go through the fire, and I have. Whether or not I have come out as gold, I leave for you to decide. I hope you shall find it so when I tell you all that has befallen me …

Coming Summer 2020

Even a Curse Must Have an End

Belinda Lambton knows a curse when she sees one. She also knows the wisdom of agreeing with a powerful enchantress. So when she gets mixed up with a cursed Beast and his enchantress, she finds herself tasked with the role of Curse Breaker. That's not an easy position, for Beast has reasons of his own to keep his curse. There's also someone determined to break it by whatever means possible and claim Beast for herself, and she doesn't take competition well.

With wit, clean romance, and a touch of danger, *Midnight for a Curse* is a retelling of the beloved Beauty and the Beast tale.

FROM CROWNS TO CURSES TO SPACE CAPSULES, A
COLLECTION OF FAIRY TALE RETELLINGS

Experience six of the world's most beloved stories in a whole new
light! From historical to futuristic, these retellings will take you to an
enchanted forest, a cursed castle, and far beyond. Uncover secrets of a
forbidden basement, a hypnotic gift, and a mysterious doll. Fall in love
with a lifelong friend or brand-new crush. Venture to unknown lands
on a quest to save a prince, a kingdom, or maybe even a planet. With
moments of humor, suspense, romance, and adventure, *Encircled* has
something to offer every fan of fairy tales, both classic and reimagined.

Free short story

Janawyn Stahl is convinced there's a connection between her godfather's suspiciously talkative automaton named Theo and his lost nephew, but can she protect Theo from the evil Mouse King long enough to find out? This short story retelling of "The Nutcracker and the Mouse King" is available for free when you sign up for my newsletter.

ACKNOWLEDGMENTS

Where do I start? So many people have helped and encouraged me throughout my writing journey—a journey I never even dreamed I'd take. Writing is the surprise of my life, and I thank God for it, and for the joy and new relationships it has brought.

Speaking of relationships … Family—I love you. Thanks for loving me and for passing on those writer genes. Rocío Rueda—dearest friend, you opened my mind to the impossible—that an ordinary person like me could actually write a book. I love you! Lucy Thompson and Susan Donetti—you're the best critique partners and friends a girl could have! To all of you who have read and critiqued my book—I can't tell you how much your comments have improved it or how much your encouragement has meant to me. A special thanks to Gretchen Engel, Amy Cattapan, Kathleen Freeman, Kate Endres, and Fay Lamb of American Christian Fiction Writers; Sammie Barstow; Dianna Dollar; and Leesa Barnes, Melissa Bonds, Kathy Ernest, Jannie Robertson, Joyce O'Bryant, and Katie Cook of Forest Lake Baptist Church. To my editor April Gardner—thanks for giving my book the polish it needed to shine like a magic mirror.

A big thanks as well to my Bible study group for their support, encouragement, and prayers, and to all the agents, editors, authors, and others whose books and blog posts have informed and encouraged me.

Dear reader, you may add your name here ___________________, for I value you beyond measure for giving Alexandria your listening ear (or rather your reading eye) as she tells her tale of pride and beastliness, of beauty and love.

ABOUT THE AUTHOR

E.J. Kitchens loves tales of romance, adventure, and happily-ever-afters and strives to write such tales herself. When she's not thinking about dashing heroes or how awesome bacteria are —she is a microbiologist after all—she's enjoying the beautiful outdoors or talking about classic books and black-and-white movies. She is a member of Realm Makers and lives in Alabama. She is the author of THE MAGIC COLLECTORS series and several short stories.

To learn more about E.J. Kitchens and her books visit her website and sign up for her newsletter:
www.ElizabethJaneKitchens.com

Thank you for reading (and reviewing)!

Adventure and Romance Are Only a Page Away
E. J. Kitchens